I0726357

A Wager Worth Making

Also by
Rebecca Connolly

An Arrangement of Sorts
Married to the Marquess
Secrets of a Spinster
The Dangers of Doing Good
The Burdens of a Bachelor
A Bride Worth Taking

Coming Soon
A Gerrard Family Christmas

More romance from
Phase Publishing

by
Emily Daniels
Lucia's Lament

by
Laura Beers
Saving Shadow

by
Grace Donovan
Saint's Ride

A Wager Worth Making

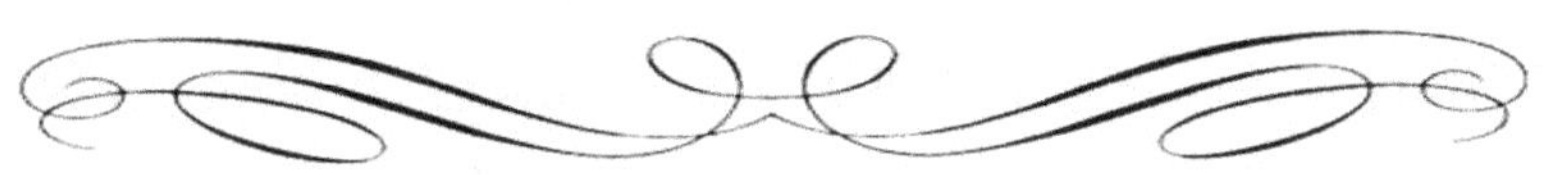

Rebecca Connolly

Phase Publishing, LLC
Seattle

If you purchased this book without a cover, you should be aware that this book is stolen property. It was reported as "unsold and destroyed" to the publisher, and neither the author nor the publisher has received any payment for this "stripped" book.

Text copyright © 2017 by Rebecca Connolly
Cover art copyright © 2017 by Rebecca Connolly

Cover art by Tugboat Design
http://www.tugboatdesign.net

All rights reserved. Published by Phase Publishing, LLC. No part of this book may be reproduced or transmitted in any form, or by any means, electronic or mechanical, including photocopying or recording or by any information storage and retrieval system, without written permission from the publisher.

Phase Publishing, LLC first paperback edition
October 2017

ISBN 978-1-943048-39-7
Library of Congress Control Number 2017955321
Cataloging-in-Publication Data on file.

Acknowledgements

For cheesecake, who has never let me down, will never let me down, and continues to be a constant source of support and delight in my life. We may disagree about calories, but never each other. And to Hannah. Because this is her favorite one, and she deserves it in so many ways. You can be Lady B if you want, I promise!

Thanks go out to the Phase family for their epic awesomeness, to Deborah Bradseth for being the artist of my life, and to Whitney for making my writing look better than it is.
Thanks to the Street Rats for keeping me in line when I need it and giving me all the good ideas.
Thanks to the family for putting up with my nerdy ways and ridiculous excitement over fictional characters. Love you, weirdos!
And to my Musketeers, I love you more than carbs. Seriously. I think. Pretty sure. Well, most carbs. Sort of.

Chapter One
London, 1823

$\mathcal{L}$ucas James Riverton Sinclair, Viscount Blackmoor, did not murder his wife.

And if anybody ever asked him directly, he would have said so. But as everyone who was anyone knew better than to directly approach a suspected murderer and question him on the said suspected murder, the discussions stayed firmly behind his back.

Within his earshot, but behind his back.

He'd learned to get over such things, having long since given up on ever being well favored in Society, but it hardly improved his mood or gave him encouragement. Particularly this evening, when he'd finally decided on a course of action that would change his life in a rather terrifying way.

If he were so fortunate.

He groaned and fought the urge to tug at his rather splendidly tied cravat, which suddenly seemed to be choking him. Ballrooms had made him chafe for years, but something about this one nearly gave him an apoplexy. His doubts and his reservations made his task impossible to comprehend, but he was determined to do it. Though the irony of so plebeian a beginning as the first ball of the Season was not lost on him and left him faintly nauseated.

Still, it was the only way to begin.

He could hardly call upon her without first showing some sort of inclination towards her person in a semi-public setting, not with his reputation and manner. They never moved in the same circles outside of Societal functions, and he was not one of those fops who could just call upon a young woman without any sort of preface.

No, if he were to do this, he would do it properly.

Though there could hardly be anything proper about it.

Imagine the Viscount Blackmoor having finally decided upon marrying again. There were less improper thoughts in the darker corners of London, and from lower characters than he. But one's reputation can hardly be blamed for everything in life, and he took no pains to correct the misapprehensions of his character. Most of the time, it quite suited his reserve and desires for privacy.

It was, however, a marked hindrance to his attaining a second wife.

There was hardly a queue of eligible females eager for a wealthy, titled, well-educated, and respectable man suspected of murder.

But he wanted no queue.

He only wanted one female in particular.

And she had just entered the room.

She could not have been more different from him. Where he was dark, she was fair. Where he was reserved and aloof, she was open and artless. Every one of his frowns could be counted against one of her smiles.

Where he was gloom, she was sunshine.

It made no sense for him to want her, all things considered, and he had spent a considerable amount of effort to argue against it.

But something about her made it impossible to fight.

They barely knew each other, even by Society's standards. They had been introduced years ago, after he'd returned to London following Celia's death, before the rumors had made any headway, but she had been a young miss with bright eyes and grand ideals, as she should have been. And he had been opposed to women and silliness of any kind, so he had paid no mind.

Or tried not to, at any rate. For some inexplicable reason, he had always been mindful of her when they attended the same functions. He knew when she entered a room, and would find his gaze drawn to her repeatedly over the course of the night. She fascinated him, piqued his deeply hidden curiosity, and attracted his attention in ways he'd never experienced.

He'd not approached her since their first meeting, but as the years passed, he'd found himself growing more and more interested, particularly when she continually went without suitors or courting of any kind. She never wanted for attention at balls or parties, and received her due praise from many at the musicales she had graced, but never once had he heard of any man pursuing her. He understood his own lack of pursuit, having sworn off marriage and female companionship for the rest of his life, but what in God's name was wrong with the rest of the men?

If he was correct in his estimation, this would be her fifth Season. A fifth Season typically set a woman firmly on the shelf, and the idea that she would be such a one irked him. There was no reason on earth why it should be so.

While not as beautiful as her sister, or some other females currently fluttering about this overcrowded and over-decorated ballroom, she was still more than attractive in her own right, and had a captivating quality about her. From his years of observations, some events more observant than others, he had never seen a single person of either sex leave her presence with anything less than a glow.

It was inconceivable that she should still be available.

He had never considered going back on his private vow. Lord knew he had enough of marriage to last three lifetimes, and he had never been tempted by anyone or anything to change his mind.

But last year, when his friend Kit Gerrard had married a woman he'd long hated and resented, and Lucas himself had not thought well of, things had changed. If Kit could marry someone he did not even like, surely Lucas could think about it, despite his past. Then the miraculous had occurred, and Kit had become happily married, in love with his wife, and the woman herself had become someone worthy of Lucas's begrudging admiration.

He'd considered matrimony again from then on, against his will, and Kit had tried to sway him from it, though never knowing the identity of the only woman he'd consider. Lucas had asked him why Kit had married his wife, knowing the vague details of their twisted past, and his words had struck him more forcefully than anything in recent memory.

I just couldn't let anyone else have her.

Lucas had contemplated those words, and his feelings on the

subject, for nearly a full year. And as the opening event of the Season had loomed closer and closer, he'd made his decision.

He would marry again.

And he would marry her.

Provided, of course, that she was willing and agreeable. Which would be more than half of the battle. Observing someone from afar and making judgments and assumptions of their character was one thing, as he knew only too well. It was entirely plausible to consider the notion that this ray of sunshine might well be a terrifying inferno when outside of the careful eyes of the public.

He doubted that was the case here, but one must be careful.

After all, Celia had been a favorite of everyone he knew. And the hell she had brought to his life had been more poignant for its surprise.

Surely it would not be so with her. He had even gone so far as to make discreet inquiries, and nothing had given him reason to doubt.

So marriage was to be the outcome, provided she matched up to the idea his years of observation had planted within him.

Faintly, his heart thumped unsteadily with the eager hope that she would.

He cleared his throat and fought the urge to tug at his cravat again. A passing woman glanced at him, her too-thin brows raised in mocking assessment, and he frankly met her gaze, daring her to speak her obvious thoughts. He nearly smirked at the startled flush that raced into her cheeks and neck, and turned back to his unnoticed observations.

"You shouldn't do that," drawled a slightly amused, mostly bored sounding voice.

He turned to scowl at the forgettable, if handsome, face of Lord Marlowe, one of his oldest and yet most absent friends. "Do what?" he asked the simply dressed man with a striking stature.

Marlowe half-yawned, which would have scandalized every matron in the Almack's ballroom if they bothered to look at him. "Oh, taunt them so with your directness. You'll only encourage the rumors."

Lucas snorted and shook his head. "Says the man who no one

remembers."

A faint smirk appeared for three quarters of a second on his friend's face. "It has its uses. I have more freedom than anyone else in the peerage."

"And what a crowning achievement that is."

Lucas turned to watch his quarry, laughing and chatting with her usual friends. She threw her head back on a jubilant laugh, and he was struck for the moment at the sight. No Society miss in her right mind would laugh with such inhibition, and even her friends seemed startled by it. But they made no effort to restrain her, or to hide their own amusement, and considering their identities, that was a surprise.

It seemed that everyone forgot themselves in her presence.

How he would love to forget himself for a while.

He doubted very much he could ever love her the way a girl with sensibilities wanted to be loved, but he felt more for her than he had about anyone in years, and had the sudden idea that he did not quite know what he would do if she refused him.

Perhaps he might never be able to love, but he could provide for her very well, give her a title, and she would always have his respect and highest regard. Surely that was enough in today's world.

What was he even thinking about love for? It made no difference if he could love her. Marriages were made for far more practical purposes, and not on a whim of fancy. It would be an agreeable match, if she could overlook his reputation.

"You look rather determined," Marlowe mused sleepily. "What are you doing?"

"No time to talk to you, Marlowe," he replied as he straightened and set aside his glass. "I am on a mission."

That drew surprised chuckle. "A mission? Dear me, how exciting. Can I help?"

Lucas exhaled and looked over at him with a raised brow. "If I am right, and I usually am, you have more than enough missions of your own to deal with."

The flash of surprise on his friend's face almost made him smile, and though it was gone in an instant, the bewilderment never left his dark eyes.

"They approached me before you, Marlowe," he muttered very

low. "Before I was infamous. Play your part, vanish into thin air, and save the world. I have a far different task before me."

With a slight bow, he turned away and slowly made his way around the perimeter of the room, eyes fixed on his target, banishing the lingering doubts on this mad venture.

He was decided, and he was determined. Mad or not, he would try for her.

And he prayed like hell it would be worth it.

"Perhaps this will be your Season."

"Yes, you mustn't give up hope. Look at us."

Gemma Templeton did look, rather frankly, at both of her friends and raised a derisive brow. "Really. You, my dear Mrs. Gerrard, married a man you could not stand because you needed to be saved, and you, Mrs. Granger, were sold off like a prized cow at market to a man who ignores you." She shrugged a shoulder, sending her blond curls dancing. "Forgive me if I hope for nothing at all, looking at the pair of you."

Lily rolled her eyes and shook her head at Marianne. "And everyone thinks she is such a cheery person."

Marianne scoffed, blue eyes twinkling, and took Lily's hand in her own. "Leave them to their delusions. An unattached woman with married friends must have her little quirks, Lily. And in the case of our dear Gemma, she is the most outspoken, unpredictable, reckless sort of spinster to ever grace Almack's."

Gemma gasped in outrage as Lily giggled behind her hand, but she soon turned it into a smile. "I suppose I deserve that, having just insulted your marriages."

"Oh, you were certainly right about mine," Marianne scoffed, waving a gloved hand. "Though you must admit, it is not my case now." She looked passed Gemma for a moment, and her smile grew warm and tender, quirking at the edges.

"No, indeed," Gemma drawled, knowing without having to look that Marianne's husband had appeared and met her eyes. "You and your husband are lovesick fools, and I can barely stand to visit anymore for fear it might be contagious."

"No fear of that on my part," Lily murmured, nervously moving a ringlet behind her ear.

That sobered the group. Lily, for all her radiant beauty and charm, had the misfortune of being an heiress and had been snatched up for her fortune by the one man whom she loved beyond reason. Her father had arranged the match with Mr. Granger, whose vast fortune had been almost entirely diminished by a wild speculation. On the brink of ruin, he had gone to the Ardens and the match had been set without Lily's consent. They had married quietly at the end of last Season, and it was a little known fact that Thomas Granger had absolutely nothing to do with his wife, and the love she once had for him was dying before his unseeing eyes.

"At least Granger lets you do as you please," Gemma said with a warm smile. "You can be here for the whole Season and play with us. And now Rosalind does not have to stay with your Aunt Augusta for her Season."

Lily smiled at that. "True, and she is ever so grateful. And you know, it could be worse. Thomas is very well thought of by everyone, so it is not as though I suffer overly much."

But just enough.

The words were unspoken, but certainly felt by all.

Poor Lily did not deserve the torment of her life. Gemma looked over at Marianne, whose eyes were also ablaze, but she only shook her head slightly. They had both done everything in their power to prevent the match, but to no avail. And it did not help that Granger was one of everybody's favorite nobodies. Gemma would spit on his boots if she did not think half of London would spit back.

"Oh, lord, is Rosalind dancing with Darlington?" Lily suddenly asked, her pains apparently forgotten.

They turned to look and all winced. "Please don't tell me she encourages him," Marianne groaned, a hand instinctively going to her stomach, where the very faintest swell could be seen if one looked hard enough.

"No, she doesn't," Lily assured them both. "She doesn't know enough to encourage or discourage anyone. I rather hoped she might take up with Captain Riverton, but I hear he is spoken for."

That caught their attention and they swung back to her with rapid inquiries, for the dashing naval captain was an enviable match, particularly since his brother the viscount had married last year.

"No, no, no," Lily laughed, raising her hands in surrender at last. "Not an engagement, for heaven's sake. Merely spoken for. Cressida Bowles, I believe."

"That cow?" Marianne cried, looking aghast. "She does not get to claim anything, I'll see to it myself. No man with any regard of mine will have to endure her. Let's give her Darlington."

Gemma and Lily snickered and watched the dancing with amusement, as the cow in question attempted a quadrille with young Mr. Hawker, and Darlington ruined Rosalind's dance with his airs. They would be well suited indeed.

"Can we make a match for people we don't like?" Lily asked Marianne curiously.

"We can try."

"Why is it that people must be so disagreeable at an event like this?" Gemma sighed aloud, watching Mr. Hawker with sympathy. "I take great pleasure in bringing amusement and enjoyment to those in my company, particularly in the dance."

"That is because you have a gift," Lily replied, patting her hand.

"I do," Gemma agreed sagely, making the others laugh. She turned fully to them and raised her chin. "I can make any man smile, I guarantee it."

Marianne widened her eyes in surprise. "Any man?"

She nodded once. "Any. I will dance with any man and make him smile."

Lily looked suspiciously coy. "Five shillings says you cannot."

Gemma snorted and shook her head. "Ten, and I can."

"Even the Viscount Blackmoor?" Marianne asked, tilting her head and offering a very small smile.

"What, that old bear?" Gemma laughed and waved her gloved hand dismissively. "I could make him smile and laugh in the same dance. He does not frighten nor intimidate me. He may be hard and dark and scowling on the outside, but inside he is just as warm and soft as anybody else. Perhaps even more so."

"Good evening, Miss Templeton."

She froze at the low, slightly rasping voice of the viscount himself standing directly behind her. Her friends tried not to laugh, each clamping down on their lips hard. She closed her eyes for a moment, then turned and gave a little curtsey. "My lord."

His stark features were softened in the bright splendor of the candlelight, and his frighteningly blue eyes shone as he looked at her. "Would you care to dance the next with me, Miss Templeton?"

She heard Marianne give a bit of a choking laugh, but paid her no mind. She swallowed hard and offered a shaky smile. "With pleasure."

He inclined his head, and held out a hand for her, which she took, and found him to be surprisingly warm. Who would have thought that the viscount was a real, warm-blooded male and not the statue of ice he was presumed to be?

As he led her into the next dance, she was further surprised to find him a most capable dancer. Not precisely light of foot, but quite graceful and elegant, despite the astonished and fearful gazes of the other dancers. Did they expect him to begin murdering them all in the middle of the dance? It would hardly be appropriate. Murders were more convenient in dark alleys and abandoned houses, certainly not at Almack's.

Blackmoor did not smile at all as they danced and said very little, which was to be expected, as he rarely said anything at all. He answered her every question with short answers, but she never got the impression that he was intentionally being rude or off-putting. They were simple questions, which only required simple answers, which he freely gave.

His eyes were fixed on her the entire time, regardless of what she or the other dancers did, and instead of finding it disconcerting, she found it almost entertaining. What did he see that rendered such intensity? It might be better to focus on the conversation at hand, rather than the eyes of her partner, as such answers could be dangerous.

He did not usually attend Almack's, she reminded him, and he agreed. What rendered this year different, she had asked, and he had replied an interest in not being predictable. He was a better dancer than she had imagined, she had complimented, and he had responded by asking what sort of dancer should he have been. The only question he had asked of her had been if she truly thought he was old, and she had smiled and replied that anyone older than her could easily be considered old in her view without the slightest bit of offense attached, and he had conceded her point, seeming nonplussed.

As the dance began to draw to a close, she caught sight of Lily and Marianne, now joined by Kit Gerrard and his curious gaze, though all were smiling. She cocked her head at Blackmoor as he led her down the row of partners in the final movement. "Could you perhaps smile, my lord?"

He looked down at her in surprise, one dark brow raised. "I beg your pardon?"

She smiled as they took their places at the end of the lines. "I have a wager with my friends, you see. I told them I can make any man I dance with smile. Ten shillings."

"I see," he murmured as they bowed to each other.

She raised her eyes and took the hand he held out. "You would not wish to make me a liar, would you, sir?"

He shook his head slowly. "No, nor to make you lose ten shillings. But you see, Miss Templeton, I have a reputation to maintain." He leaned closer and whispered, "I do not smile."

Her smile grew as he pulled back.

He shook his head. "Fetching as you are, tempting though it is, not even you will ruin my reputation."

His low voice, and the dark amusement she felt in it, sent a ripple through her. Somehow managing to find her voice, her tongue, and her wit, by the grace of God, Gemma responded, "Then I think you owe me ten shillings to pay my friends. Each."

His hand tightened around her for a heartbeat. "Bill me."

She huffed slightly as he led her back. "My lord, I do believe that may get to be a rather lengthy bill. I am quite determined, and I do not think my friends will take an IOU."

He turned to face her as the next dance began, his pale eyes somehow more intense than before. "I will be happy to pay the balance of the bill to you some other time. I couldn't care less what your friends think." He bowed over her hand, and then swept away, taking some of her breath with him.

She pursed her lips in thought as she watched him go, barely mindful of her friends now gathering around her. That was the most disconcerting man on the planet, she was sure of it, and yet she was intrigued. She gnawed on her lip as he made his way through the crush as easily as if they parted for him alone, and never looked back.

Then he reached the doors and he turned, his eyes instantly colliding with hers. Her teeth froze on her lip and her head tilted of its own accord as she took him in. He held her gaze for a number of heartbeats, and she could have sworn he almost smiled as he left the room at last.

There was something about him that gave her pause, but not for any fear or apprehension. She knew his reputation and his manner and had seen him around London for years, had certainly been curious about him, but never had she expected the sort of wit he had shown during the dance, nor that he, with all his reserve and coldness, would banter with her, short though it had been.

She was determined now. She *would* make him smile, despite his reputation.

And just let him attempt to withstand her efforts. She never lost.

She turned to her friends with a mischievous energy coursing through her.

"You did not succeed, Gemma," Lily said with a bright smile.

"Yet, Lily," she pointed out. "Raise it to a pound. I will make him smile before the Season is out."

Marianne's lips pursed, knowing Gemma's finances were hardly extravagant. "A whole pound just to make one man smile?"

She looked at her sharply. "Ask me again and it will be two. Besides," she added softly, glancing back at the door where Blackmoor had just exited, "I have a very strong suspicion it will be worth it."

Chapter Two

"What the hell are you doing?"

Lucas looked up from his breakfast to find Kit Gerrard standing boldly in the doorway of his dining room, arms folded, stance defensive.

"Eating," he said simply, gesturing to his plate.

Kit blinked once. "You know what I mean."

"Do I?"

His friend's eyes narrowed. "What are you doing with Gemma Templeton?"

Lucas slowly raised a brow. "Are you come to protect the innocent woman from the murderous villain? Here to ask after my intentions?"

Kit exhaled irritably. "Blackmoor, you know perfectly well that I trust you and your judgment. I would leave my wife alone with you in a darkened room without batting an eyelash."

"That is because your wife would eat me alive."

Kit's composure broke for a smile and he shrugged. "True, but you would be perfectly mannered. I'm not afraid of your intentions for Gemma. I just want to know what they are. For your sake, I have to ask what you are doing."

Lucas sat back and set his fork aside, measuring his old friend with a steady gaze. They had not been particularly close until recent years, but their friendship was longstanding. "Ideally, I will marry her."

It was fortunate he knew of Kit's skill with composure and reserve, for the untrained observer would have found the reaction lacking. But the sudden grip on the chair, wide eyes, and lack of breathing spoke volumes of his friend's surprise.

"Marry?" Kit finally said on a faltering gasp.

Lucas nodded slowly, his mouth in a firm line.

"You swore you would never marry again."

Lucas allowed himself a small, mirthless smile. "I told you last year I was considering marriage."

"Yes, and with all the haste of considering new drapes," Kit shot back. He shook his head and ran a hand through his hair. "What is this?"

Lucas sighed and gestured to a chair. "Sit down."

Kit hesitated, eyes surveying his friend with wariness. Then he exhaled and took the indicated chair. "All right, go ahead."

Pushing the remains of his breakfast aside, Lucas turned to face him more directly. "I meant what I had told you last year. I was considering marriage. Rolling it around in my head, testing the taste of it on my tongue, that sort of thing. Then a few months ago I was at my estate and riding my new stallion across the grounds when a neighbor fired a rifle without warning, and the blasted thing threw me over a jump and I quite literally saw my life flash before my eyes. I…" He shook his head as an echo of the cold fear hit his chest again. "I could easily have broken my neck."

He made a face, agonizing memories of that day, and the subsequent days, flitting through his mind. He wouldn't tell Kit what had happened, the extent of his injuries, or the torment of the experience. And how it had changed him.

"It was too close," he continued, "and it shook me greatly. I lay there, trying to catch my breath, hoping I hadn't broken anything, and wondering what I had done with my life. I had spent years being miserable and alone, and that was no way to live." He shook his head and shrugged. "So when I recovered, I determined I wouldn't wait any longer. Marriage was suddenly important, and trying to be something more was important. And then I further received notice of my cousin's increasingly ruinous behavior, and I absolutely could not let him inherit what I've worked so hard for. He is stupid and vain and would drain the estate for his own needs. My tenants would suffer greatly."

He looked over to find Kit wearing a pensive expression. "So… You are looking to marry because you're facing your own mortality?"

Lucas rubbed his forehead and heaved a sigh. "I suppose." It was far, far more complicated than that, but it was enough.

"And aiming to sire an heir to prevent your cousin from inheriting."

"Yes."

Kit frowned and cocked his head. "Are those really the proper reasons to make such a hasty decision? Marriage is quite a significant step, and you're being rather sudden about it."

"Says the man who married a woman to save her reputation, and with only two days' notice."

Kit was neither amused nor impressed by the attempt at needling. "This isn't something to take lightly, no matter what your reasons."

Lucas raised a brow. "Do you remember my first marriage? I've learned my lesson. I was hardly going to marry the first girl I came across. This will take time and careful consideration, a determination of compatibility… Never mind what my end goal is, I am going to do this properly."

"And Gemma?" Kit asked, looking mildly satisfied. "Where does she fit into this?"

"She is the one who triggered the idea in the first place. Years ago, if I am being honest. And…" Lucas hesitated for a moment and lowered his eyes. "It was always going to be Gemma," he admitted with a raw honesty that was unlike him.

There was no response from his friend and Lucas reluctantly submitted to his curiosity and looked up.

Kit wore a bemused smile and his brow was creased. "Are you in love with Gemma Templeton?"

Lucas snorted and rolled his eyes, finding comfort in derision. "Please, I hardly know her well enough to claim anything of the sort, which is why I intend to court her. I simply think that she would suit my tastes and needs."

"I could draw up a list of several women who would do that for you. What makes Gemma so special?"

That nearly made him laugh. What made her special? He sat back in his chair and raised a superior brow. "If you don't know, there is no point in discussing it."

Kit suddenly grinned, as he was becoming more and more prone to do under his wife's influence. "Fair enough. Do I need to give you a warning? She is a dear friend of my wife…"

"Save your breath," he muttered, shaking his head. "I'll not harm her in any way, shape, or form. Besides, she still needs to accept me. There is plenty working against me, and there's no accounting for taste."

Kit rose and clapped him on the shoulder. "Best of luck to you, Blackmoor. Marianne will be delighted to hear this." He chuckled as he started from the room.

Lucas nearly sprang to his feet. "She can't tell Gemma," he barked, suddenly panicked. "I can't… That is…"

Kit turned and gave him an indulgent smile. "Believe it or not, my wife can be trusted. She likes you, Blackmoor, and she's been speculating all night. Why do you think I'm here?"

"Because you worry about me?" Lucas suggested, relaxing just a little.

Kit laughed once. "Because Marianne was beside herself and I would not know a moment of rest until I had something to tell her." He nodded and turned from the room. "But I do worry about you."

Lucas twisted his lips in a half grimace. He didn't mean to worry his friends, but neither was he going to consult with them before making decisions regarding his life. His reserve had always suited him before, and it would suit him still.

His reasons were true, and he could not explain the urgency behind them any more than that. Not without delving into a dark part of his history that he would rather leave in the past. He much preferred moving forward and attempting to be alive again.

He *did* need to marry, and he *did* need to produce an heir. He was not about to let Thornacre go over to Lewis, who was without question the biggest waste of space that had ever come into any family of decency. In both size and habit. That prospect alone was enough to terrify a man with an entail, but when he added in the rest…

He returned to his seat and winced at the sudden twinge of pain, the most annoying evidence of how close he had come. He never looked at the scars, and he didn't need to.

He was a man with nothing but scars, and most were not visible.

He was no candidate for any sort of husband, but there was no question in his mind anymore. He would do the one duty he had yet to fulfill, and he would do it his way.

And if Gemma Templeton would have him, he would take her.

But he couldn't deny that the idea of a second marriage made him a trifle anxious.

The woman was different, quite drastically so, but he was the same.

What if the problem lay with him?

"I heard you had an interesting dance partner last night."

"Oh, yes she did," her mother crowed, sitting near the fire with a gleeful glint in her eyes.

Gemma rolled her eyes and yanked a stray thread on her secondhand gown. Her brother-in-law was a wonderful man, but he took his relationship with her far too seriously. Even Caroline was not this overbearing. And *she* never took Gemma away from practicing her music.

"Oh, you mean Mr. Palmer?" she asked innocently as she tightened the strings on her violin. "Yes, I was quite surprised to be asked. You know he only dances with those in their first Seasons."

Despite her mother's chuckling, Spencer was not amused. Being a father of three children, he had learned how to perfect a scolding look.

Fortunately, Gemma was immune.

"That is not what I mean," he told her as he sat back in his chair and drew his leg up. "You danced with Lord Blackmoor."

Gemma matched his pose in the most lady-like way possible, setting the instrument aside. "I did," she confirmed, lifting her chin.

"Why?"

"Because he asked."

"You know what they say about him."

She snorted and rolled her eyes again. "Yes, and I also know what *they* say about us."

Spencer stiffened and his eyes turned hard. "You know that's not the same thing."

"Oh no?" she asked, tilting her head. She glanced across the room at her mother, then leaned forward and hissed, "How much truth is there in the general estimation of our financial straits, Spencer?"

"Well, I…"

"Because it's far worse, and you know it," she overrode, stealing another look at her mother, who was too focused on her embroidery to hear anything. "But what the lovely members of Society don't pity is our troubles. They are inclined to find fault with Papa for apparently mismanaging the grand fortune we supposedly had in our past, and ruining my chances at a good match, and how we must have done something positively horrid to end up this way."

"Gem…"

"It's not enough to be poor, we must be poor and criminal." She shook her head and looked away. "It makes no difference what they say about him or me or anyone. *They* know absolutely nothing."

Spencer was silent for a long moment, then he sighed. "I concede to your point. My brother and his friends think well of him, so I suppose I must reserve judgment."

"Please do," she muttered dryly.

Really, sometimes her brother-in-law was too superior for his own good. Becoming a member of Parliament had washed away any insecurities he'd had about being a second son, and he took the duties of exerting his influence over her whenever he could.

She'd never wanted an elder brother, and the charm of having one wore off on occasion.

"I only wanted to ask after the dance," Spencer murmured, tugging at his ear. "I didn't mean to attack him. Or you."

"He danced very well," her mother chimed in, perking up at the word 'dance'. "Rather catlike, and graceful for a man so tall."

Gemma deflated a little and folded her hands. "You came all the way over here to ask me about one dance with one mysterious viscount?"

He flashed a grin. "He doesn't dance, and it's a bit illicit, all things considered. I wanted to see if he'd made any sort of indication as to why."

Gemma threw up her hands and rose. "You think that just because a man dances with me once, he must suddenly want my hand in marriage?"

"Blackmoor won't marry."

"Oh, so one dance ruins me," she scoffed, marching past him. "How silly of me, to not have a care with my reputation!"

"Gemma, stop!"

She screeched and whirled to face him. "No, you stop, Spencer. I get enough of the marriage and reputation lectures from my parents, who seem to think that five Seasons isn't quite enough to throw away ideas of a match of affection *and* fortune. It falls to me to save us all, but they refuse to entertain the idea of me marrying for comfort alone. And not that any of you care to notice, but no one is lining up for even that. So forgive me if I will dance with whomever I want, regardless of what anyone thinks."

Spencer stood gaping openmouthed in shock and she felt her cheeks flame as she exited the room with far more composure than she'd managed the entire interview.

But her rage was sincere, and she fled the house rather than face anyone else. Truth be told, she worried far too often about their financial situation. Someone had to, and as her parents spent all of their energies putting up the front of being fairly well-to-do on a pitiful income, they were no help. They'd always had little enough to live on by Society's standards, but recent years had only made things worse. Spencer and Caroline did what they could, but they were not able to relieve the extent of their problems.

And Gemma… sweet, little, apparently never grew up Gemma… was the only one who could see the truth.

If she didn't marry soon, there would be no more London, no more balls, no more outings. Oh, she could visit her sister and continue on as she had been, but she could not infringe upon their family life forever. She would have to retrench with her parents, and live in a less expensive place and far beneath their current manner of living. They had already cut back so much to try to live more within their means, but outward appearances were more important than inward security, it seemed.

More than once, Gemma had begged her father to just arrange a marriage with a respectable and wealthy man for her hand, as she had the sort of temperament that could get along with anyone. She had long since given up romantic notions, and she could very easily be an honorable and respectful wife to a sensible gentleman.

Her father, however, was determined that Gemma would fall in love and would not consent to any other match.

Well, he would have to deal with a spinster daughter, then, and there was no proper way to make ends meet there.

Her mother was aging far sooner than Gemma would have liked, and was only growing ridiculous. She thought it delightful that Gemma had danced with Blackmoor, and after a thorough interrogation last night in which Gemma revealed nothing, was determined it would end in a shocking match that would make her infamous in Society. Gemma feared the day, should it occur, that Blackmoor set foot in her house. Her parents might never let him leave.

Poor man. Whatever his past or his sins, no one deserved that.

She fidgeted with the ribbons of her bonnet, which she had neglected to tie when she'd left the house. She had no patience for such things, and this bonnet was her oldest, and most tatty. She had others, but she was determined to wear each out to its fullest, thus saving her the trouble of needing to buy more. She had the funds herself, as she had been saving her pin money for years, and only occasionally dipped into it for her own amusement.

Her whimsical wager with Lily and Marianne seemed fairly stupid now, but she doubted they would expect her to actually pay. But then, she could afford to pay them a pound each, should she be successful.

She shook her head and sighed. Somehow, she'd make do. She'd done so for years, and the idea of ruination had lost the terrifying effect it once had.

She looked up at the road before her and was startled to find Lord Blackmoor headed in her direction, his eyes on her, his expression one of mild surprise.

"My lord Blackmoor," she said faintly, finding him far more

imposing by the light of day.

He bowed to her. "Miss Templeton." He gave her a carefully assessing look. "Are you out alone?"

She nodded and shrugged a shoulder. "I fled the house before a chaperone could be found. A bit impudent, I know."

His lips twitched. "Why do I have the impression that you are always a bit impudent?"

She grinned and playfully curtseyed. "I'm sure I haven't the faintest idea, my lord."

His pale eyes intensified for a moment as he looked at her, then they flicked somewhere beyond her. "May I escort you back home? Or did you have somewhere else to go?"

Gemma chewed her lip for a moment, her smile still in play. "You may escort me, sir," she told him, "but I'd rather not go home just yet."

Shockingly, he asked no questions and merely held his arm out for her, which she took, and he slowly led her in the direction of Hyde Park. It was still rather early in the day, and hardly anybody was about, but given her agitation, she was not sure she actually would have cared.

Blackmoor was resolutely silent for a time, then inclined his head to say, "I was just on my way to your house to call on you."

She immediately shook her head. "Oh, you had better not do that. I had to answer a great many questions about our illicit dance last night."

He reared back, stunned. "Illicit?"

"Their words, not mine."

His brow furrowed slightly. "Your mother disapproves?"

Gemma scoffed loudly. "My mother had nothing to do with it. My brother-in-law, on the other hand…"

"Mr. Hammond?"

"Indeed. Troublesome wretch." She shook her head, still glowering at his behavior.

"I imagine he's only protective," Blackmoor said in a surprisingly sympathetic tone.

She had to allow that and made a face. "You imagine right, but if he thinks one dance could ruin a girl, he's got straw for brains, and

I should never have let my sister fling punch on him."

"She did what?" he exclaimed on a startled cough.

She glanced up at him. "Did you miss that? Yes, I suppose you must, as you were in Hampshire, I think." She gave him the loose details of how Caroline and Spencer had met, and how Gemma had been there to assist in the master plan.

True to his reserve, Blackmoor had no reaction or expression, but his eyes were far less composed. Despite what his face showed, his eyes were quite a different matter. He was amused by the story, and not at all scornful.

Perhaps the stodgy and reclusive viscount was not quite so dreary after all.

What a shocking thought.

"Do you know, my lord, I think we should be friends," Gemma said suddenly.

He glanced down at her with one thick brow raised. "Do you?" he asked, his voice wry. "Why is that?"

"You are not naturally talkative, and I can talk about anything for an exceptionally long time. You do not smile; I do. You are reserved and well behaved, I am open and rather impudent."

"Seems to me we are opposites," he mused in an unreadable tone. "What makes you think we can be friends?"

She quirked a smile at him. "Because of what we share, my lord. An overabundance of wit."

"I've never been accused of having an overabundance of anything," he informed her. "Except, perhaps, mystery."

"All the more reason to be friends with me," she replied with a light laugh. "There is no mystery about me."

"Oh, I wouldn't say that, Miss Templeton." He met her eyes and shook his head slowly. "Not in the least."

Suddenly, it was rather difficult to swallow, and she could not feel her face. But she managed to overcome herself with a brief shiver and said, "So we might be friends?"

He considered the idea for a long moment, his eyes still on her. "For now," he finally said.

They meandered about Hyde Park a little longer, conversing lightly on several topics. Well, Gemma conversed, and Blackmoor responded when necessary. He asked her a few simple questions about herself, but nothing particularly revealing or insightful. Despite never feeling uncomfortable in the presence of any man, there was a remarkable difference in comfort with him.

Comfort was there in abundance.

It made no sense, as he probably ought to have made her uncomfortable, given his rumored past and his hard appearance. But she had no such discomfort, never once had a twinge of nerves or anxiety, and found herself perfectly at ease. Even his short answers and brusque manner did not put her off. She sensed that was simply his way, and it had nothing to do with her.

In fact, if his eyes were any indication, he was quite interested in her. He focused on her with a rapt sort of intensity that skittered her heart, listened to every word she said with patience and attentiveness, and seemed as fascinated by her as she was by him. She was not anything special or particular, as she had learned over the years, and yet he seemed to see something worth attention.

Friends for now indeed.

He led her home afterwards, sparing her the awkwardness of having to explain his presence to anyone by letting her proceed the last block herself. He remained in his place and watched her go, as if concerned she would be attacked in the final unaccompanied stretch. She offered him a smile and a jaunty wave when she reached her door, and he straightened up a bit, touched his hat, and made no other response but a quirk of a brow.

What would it take to make him smile?

Gemma grinned at his retreating back and wrung her fingers. Her new mysterious friend had agreed to meet her again tomorrow, should the weather be favorable, on the Serpentine Bridge in Hyde Park, but only if she brought a chaperone as escort.

She wouldn't mind doing so, but she had no chaperone to spare. He would have to get over that.

Shaking her head, she reentered the house and tugged off her bonnet.

"Where have you been, Gemma?" her mother asked as she suddenly appeared from the drawing room.

"Just a walk, Mama," she replied airily. "The morning is quite delightful."

"Spencer was very distressed, I do hope you will apologize for your harshness."

"Of course, Mama," she assured her, having no intention of doing any such thing.

Her mother hummed and adjusted her askew lace cap. "He must mind his manners about dear Lord Blackmoor. We mustn't scare the man off before his suit is official."

Her mother turned away and headed to parts of the house elsewhere, allowing Gemma to throw her hands up in the air. One relative fearing the worst of her associating with him, and another encouraging and anticipating the most drastic of opposites.

Imagine what either would say if they knew she had just spent a full hour alone in his company.

Chapter Three

"Why is it you don't dance?"

"I am not very good at it."

"Oh, nonsense, you dance very well."

Lucas restrained a snort and looked at the extraordinary woman walking beside him, her golden hair almost hidden beneath her rather shabby bonnet. She was not looking at him for the moment, but he knew what her expression would be. Content, clear, and with a light of amusement in her eyes and a hint of a smile on her full lips.

She was not flattering him with her words. She was simply stating the truth according to her, as she always did.

Nearly a week of these meetings between them, and it was still as refreshing. She saw him as a person. Not the viscount, not a murderer, not even man of great standing or fortune. He was simply a man to her, and he had not been something so simple in quite a long time, if ever.

"You're drifting away," Gemma said, breaking into his thoughts and turning her head to look up at him.

He returned her look. "Nothing of the sort. I am where I have always been."

She nearly rolled her eyes, which was a common occurrence for her. "You're miles away, Blackmoor. Is the idea of dancing that unpleasant?"

He nearly smiled, which was becoming a common occurrence for him. "Not under the right circumstances."

That earned him a quirk of her fine brows. "Which are?"

"Someone who does not mind a partner with stinted

conversation and barely passable footwork, all while wearing a completely vacant expression. Most women find that to be interminable suffering."

Gemma laughed and linked her arm through his. "It is not *that* bad. I've danced with you, and didn't suffer a jot."

"Yes, well, you're peculiar."

"And proud of it."

And she was, he could tell. He had seen it for himself. She had no desire to be an oddity, but she made no attempts to conform if it did not suit her. Gemma simply was who she was and she was not going to apologize for that.

The impulse struck him that now was the time to ask the question he had been waiting on. Now he knew her better and she knew him, he could proceed with far more confidence. He was absolutely certain that she was perfect for his ends, more than he'd ever thought from afar. And if she hadn't shied away from him yet, there was certainly hope.

"Would your parents mind if I courted you?" he asked without preamble.

To Gemma's credit, she only glanced up at him with mild surprise. Then her mouth curved into a mischievous smile. "I think my parents would weep over your boots in gratitude if they knew."

His eyes widened and he coughed. "That I asked?"

She shrugged. "That anyone did."

"Ridiculous." He shook his head, knowing that, despite what she claimed about her parents and their eccentricities, that could not be true. Gemma was a delightful woman, and very pretty, and the idea that nobody had asked to court her was impossible. He'd never seen someone pay her any marked attention before, but he could not pretend that he had been overly observant for all of her Seasons. Surely the men of London could not be so stupid.

And the further suggestion that anyone would be grateful for his suit at all, let alone to that extent, was even more inconceivable.

She leveled him with a rather impressive look. "Try it and see."

Her tone was so serious, so without inflection or amusement that he actually felt a little chilled from it. He wet his lips and looked at the path ahead. "… weep, did you say?" he finally managed, sounding far more unsure than he'd intended.

She made a noise of confirmation and nodded. "With much wailing and overflowing compliments."

"Are your parents prone to such dramatics?" Not that it would put him off of his course entirely, but it might give him pause.

"Not usually. But they would make an exception here."

"Hmm," he murmured, frowning. That would be a hindrance to his courtship. He meant to court her, and eventually wed her, but overly emotional or excitable parents would be quite an inconvenience.

Gemma laughed and adjusted her hold on him. "Perhaps keep it a secret, my lord."

He glanced down at her. "But we will be unescorted."

"Ideally, yes," she replied, her eyes twinkling.

He felt the urge to smile, but resisted it. "What of fear of being compromised?"

She looked away with a pensive expression. "I daresay my mother has been praying I would be compromised for a few years now."

He shook his head and closed his eyes. He would think that by now he would be used to her outspoken ways and extraordinary ideas, but she managed to continually surprise him.

"Are you going to smile?" she asked suddenly. "You owe me money if you do."

He opened his eyes and glanced down at her, amused yet again. "How much is it again?"

She grinned up at him, her bonnet sliding back a little, revealing wildly free strands of hair near her ears. "We raised the price due to the difficulty. One pound."

"A pound for a smile?" he asked in disbelief. It was a ridiculous thought, and he could not see why she bothered.

She lifted a shoulder in a dainty shrug. "Ten shillings, if it makes you feel better."

It didn't, but he would play along. He couldn't resist. "Ten it is." He lifted his chin and gave her a calculating look. "What about a laugh?"

Gemma pursed her lips in thought. "A single laugh? Fifteen

shillings. Any more and it will be an additional crown."

"Exorbitant."

"It's your own fault," she told him, looking disapproving. "If you were jovial, it wouldn't be so expensive."

He cocked his head and studied her with interest. "But you like a challenge."

She wrinkled up her nose as she grinned. "I revel in them."

He gestured to a nearby bench and she took the offered seat, looking up at him expectantly. He stood before her, hands on his hips, and asked, "And what if I outright grin?"

She reared back with a faint gasp, her eyes wide. "Can you do that?"

Impertinent thing. "How much?" he asked firmly.

She opened her mouth, closed it, then narrowed her eyes. "Two pounds."

"Done."

Her mouth twisted. "Are you teasing me?"

He rocked back on his heels. "Is there a price in the wager for that?" he asked.

"Half a crown," was her lightning-quick response.

"Then no," he replied with a firm shake of his head.

She bit her lip as she grinned. "Liar."

"Perhaps."

She laughed loudly and clamped a hand over her mouth as she looked around for any that might see them. By necessity, they had been meeting in the mornings, and had not seen anyone of significance as yet, which he was grateful for. He would rather not broadcast his interest until it became necessary, as some sort of fervor would undoubtedly stir when the news broke.

But heaven help him, he loved it when she laughed.

He sat beside her on the bench, keeping a proper distance, but draping an arm across the back and turning to view her better. He tapped a finger against his mouth and narrowed his eyes as he looked at her.

"What?" she asked warily, leaning away.

"What if I make you smile?" he posed, enjoying the curious play of emotions on her face. She would make a miserable actress, and he doubted she could lie with any success.

She waved her hand at once. "Oh, there is no wager for that."

"Why not?"

She gave him a dubious look. "I smile all the time. You would leave me destitute."

He inclined his head to concede her point. "What shall I wager for, then?"

Her face took on a speculative expression and she suddenly matched his pose, watching him closely. "What can you offer?"

He gave that some thought, looking away and taking more time than he needed. Only when she tapped her foot restlessly did he turn back, the temptation to smile stronger than ever. "If I take you by surprise, I get a boon."

"Financial?"

He snorted. "No, I am hardly so mercenary."

"And I am?" she challenged, folding her arms.

He gave her a look. "You are practically a pirate."

She grinned briefly, then returned to her serious persona. "Very astute. Will your boons be negotiable?"

"Within reason."

"Your reason or mine?"

He made a noise of amusement, hoping there wasn't a charge for that. "Both, I should hope."

Gemma tapped her chin, then nodded. "Done. Let us strike hands on it."

He took her outstretched hand, removed her glove, and pressed a warm kiss to her knuckles instead of shaking. She gasped softly, and he looked up, quirking a brow. "Does that count as a surprise?"

She blinked her wide eyes and struggled for a swallow. "Mildly," she replied, clearing her throat.

"Then I am owed a boon," he murmured.

"Name your price."

He almost smiled. She ought not to be so carelessly bold. "Call me Lucas."

Her brow furrowed slightly. "When?"

"Now."

"Why?"

"Because your voice is fairly musical and I want to hear it."

"It's not proper."

She was concerned about propriety *now*? He gave her a hard look, stroking the hand he still held lightly to temper it. "This is not a negotiation."

She bit her lip, her eyes wandering down to her hand in his grasp. Then she exhaled, met his eyes, and said, "Lucas."

A faint warmth burst somewhere in his chest, but he managed to tamp it back. "Yes?"

She quirked her head and smiled in confusion. "You told me to call you Lucas."

"I did."

"And I did."

He shook his head slowly, keeping her eyes trained on his. "No, you merely said it. I wanted you to call *me* Lucas, not just say it."

Her smile grew and her bright eyes crinkled in the corners. "You're very particular, aren't you?"

He shrugged a shoulder. "Everything is in the details, my dear." He squeezed her hand and waited patiently.

She shook her head, still smiling. "Very well. Lucas, will this courtship of yours extend to taking me out in public? Perhaps to the theater?"

He jerked and nearly clenched her hand. "You're agreeing to it?"

She laughed and looked pointedly at their hands. "Would I allow this if I wasn't?"

"Knowing you, I couldn't be sure," he managed, his throat feeling rather dry.

She adjusted a strand of hair away from her face and grinned. "Yes, I am agreeing to your courtship. If you take me to the theater."

He hated the theater. But he would take her every night if he thought it would put him in a favorable light. "Of course. Anything else?"

"Dance with me."

"I can do that."

"And smile."

"No."

She hissed in disappointment, but smiled at him, which did

strange things to his stomach. "Then walk with me in the mornings. I like doing this."

He opened his mouth, then closed it and stroked her hand again. "So do I," he admitted, a bit startled by how deeply he meant it.

A slow, catlike smile spread across her lips. "Why, Lord Blackmoor, you are growing quite sentimental."

He gave her a mock glower and slowly released her hand. "You didn't call me Lucas."

She shook her head. "You told me to call you that name then, not forevermore. You will have to earn it again."

"Are you daring me to surprise you, Miss Templeton?" he asked in a low, dangerous tone.

He didn't miss the shiver, but was surprised by the expression she countered with. "On the contrary, my lord. I am encouraging you to."

What the devil had possessed her to throw something like that into his face?

While she and Blackmoor… Lucas, as she'd begun calling him in her head since this morning… had become friends, she had let herself slip into her habit of banter and taunting, always rising to a challenge when she ought to be demure. It was a usual thing to do with her friends, but she'd forgotten with whom she was dealing. The spark of interest that had flared in his eyes ought to have been warning enough, but when he'd said nothing in response and eventually changed the subject, she knew she was in danger.

Not real danger, she thought with a smirk as she watched him across the hall, mimicking a suit of armor against the wall. He was so tall and imposing, yet neither of those things were what made him the terrifying man he was. It was the energy and intensity that radiated from him, exuding power and demanding respect. It was undoubtedly why he was still admitted in Society despite the rumors.

No one dared forbid him.

But he was so much more than his cold exterior. She wouldn't necessarily call him warm, but he was… warming. Softening. Just a little. Perhaps just enough.

Not to anyone else, however. He must hate public settings of any kind, and it seemed the theater was far worse than a ball, given the stony expression he bore. Yet he had come to escort her, had not murmured one word of complaint, and aside from sitting too close and watching her more than the play, he was perfectly behaved.

How that would disappoint her mother. She had such hopes.

His head turned and his icy gaze suddenly collided with hers. His expression did not change, and yet something did. His chest moved on slow, deep inhales, his brow seemed less tense, and his eyes were suddenly the furthest thing from cold. Lucas was not a man who required movement or distraction, and his undivided attention was overwhelming in its potency.

He was a striking man, too hard and angular of features to be considered handsome by usual standards, but that seemed inconsequential at the moment. She could barely recall what constituted attractiveness anymore, and especially not when he looked at her like that. He might have had the coloring of the dark Irish, but the impressive and inexplicable pull of him knew no nationality.

No one should have that kind of power.

And if she could breathe or feel her knees, she would have told him that.

"Dear me, Gemma… Is Blackmoor having you for breakfast, lunch, or dinner? Or perhaps all three?"

Gemma blushed and turned on her heel to face the painfully beautiful and elegant Marianne Gerrard, whose blue eyes glinted with the same brilliance as the jewels at her throat. Her husband was not far behind, his possessive gaze fixed on his wife, and the gentlemen who looked upon her.

Gemma met her friend's inquiring gaze with a lift of her chin. "Who's to say I am not having him?"

Marianne grinned broadly, despite her previous rules of moderation in expression. "Very good. Now, tell me what is really going on there. Blackmoor is still staring as if the back of you is as fascinating as the front."

Gemma was tempted to look over her shoulder to verify her

words, but she didn't need to. She could feel his gaze on her, and the hair on the back of her neck stood on end.

"We are friends," Gemma said simply, folding her hands before her.

Marianne stared at her. "Friends."

Gemma nodded once, and prayed for a vacant expression.

Her friend stared at her for so long, she had to look away.

"I know what he wants, Gemma," Marianne murmured after a moment. "Do you?"

Gemma jerked her gaze up. "You do?"

Marianne pressed her lips into a thin line and waited.

Gemma glowered, knowing how stubborn Marianne could be. She looked around and heaved a small sigh. "Don't tell anyone," Gemma muttered, her cheeks flaming, "but he is courting me."

A small, satisfied smile appeared on Marianne's lips. "Is he indeed?" She cast a glance over Gemma's shoulder and slowly smiled in a curious way.

"Don't do that," Gemma scolded quickly, tempted to grab her friend's arm. "Don't antagonize him."

"I do no such thing," Marianne replied, bringing her gaze back to her. "I am only teasing him a little. I like him immensely, which would shock anyone if it were spread about. He has a droll wit, and a curious aplomb about him that is really quite endearing, once you get past his implacable façade. I am very much in favor of his suit. What do your parents think?"

She ignored the twinge of guilt and wrinkled her nose up. "They don't exactly know."

Marianne reared back. "They don't *exactly* know?"

Gemma winced and smoothed her gloves against the pale green of her gown. When he had seen her this evening, Lucas had complimented her with few words, but deep feeling, that she had felt down through her fingers and toes. She'd never felt like an ugly duckling in her life, but her sister was the pretty one, and always had been. Gemma had merely been good enough.

Until tonight.

She cleared her throat, realizing the delay she had caused with her reminiscing. "They know that he is bringing me here tonight.

They know we have become acquainted…" She chewed her lip. "I didn't want to give them hope. I know it seems ridiculous, considering it's him, but…"

How did she explain that he was different? That she was afraid her family wouldn't approve, despite her mother's ridiculous claims?

Marianne smiled softly and took her hands. "I understand, and I will not make mischief or trouble. I won't even ask. Now, let's talk about this dress. It is ravishing on you, is it new?"

Gemma sighed, relieved at the change in topic. Despite her friendship with Marianne, she was not ready to discuss Lucas yet. She was not even sure what she felt for or about him yet, how could she possibly tell anyone else?

"It is new to me," she allowed, dimpling as she held her skirt out a little more. "Though I believe it was Kate's first. Forgive me, I mean Lady Whitlock."

Marianne scowled at that. "She's told you to call her Kate so many times, I can't believe you keep doing that. Either way, the dress suits your coloring far more than hers, and it puts your figure on very fine display indeed. Now come, walk with me. Let's see how far Blackmoor's gaze will follow you."

Gemma resisted, pulling back. "You said you would not antagonize him."

Marianne looked surprised. "And we will not. But you do want to make him smile, don't you? And if this comedy won't strike his fancy, then perhaps you will."

"Are you throwing me at him, Marianne?" she asked with no small amount of suspicion as she let her friend lead her.

Marianne grinned and pulled her close. "I don't need to throw you anywhere. You only go where you want to, and I only mean to help. The more we can properly put you on display, we should. Discreetly, of course. But courtship is a long process, when done properly, so you must build up your stamina. And I must teach you how to flirt."

Gemma rolled her eyes heavenward as Marianne continued to rattle away and was caught by Lucas, whose lips quirked as if he would smile. She raised a brow at him and he sobered at once, but his eyes contained a mirth that she ought to have charged him for.

If he continued to stare so, people would begin to talk, and none of it would be good. They were ruthless about him behind his back, and she'd never paid it any mind before. It had been fairly standard gossip for years, despite its horror. Their quiet courtship would be noticed eventually, and what would she do then?

She shook her head at herself and forced her thoughts away from there. She'd had barely twelve hours of courtship and already she was overthinking it. There was no reason why anything need change between them simply because a name was put on it.

The rest of the evening would sort itself out, as would the following days, and this courtship… her very first!… would proceed however it would. She did not anticipate nor expect anything, and could not when life had given her no reason to. But she could not deny that having a man look at her thusly was a rather heady thing.

Even if he didn't smile about it.

Chapter Four

$\mathcal{G}$emma tapped her foot absently beneath the almost too-long skirts of yet another secondhand dress, this one from Mary Harris. She was too tall for Gemma to fit it perfectly, but in all other respects, it was admirable. A bit tight, considering Gemma's fuller figure, but her corset aided her there. And she had been repeatedly assured by her sister that it was hardly noticeable.

But Caroline had always been overly kind where Gemma's looks were concerned, and standing here against a wall like a potted plant told Gemma exactly what everyone else thought of her. The ball at Ashcombe was always a crush every Season, yet here she was, without even a chair.

Some wallflower she was. The wallflowers were always given chairs, and yet…

Only Eliza Mortimer had managed one, and she hadn't danced in three years.

Of course, it was practically a safety hazard to dance with her, as she was almost completely blind without her spectacles.

Gemma was a very safe dancer, graceful and light of foot. And there were plenty of gentlemen milling about, yet none spared her a look.

She groaned and fidgeted, wishing her friends would appear so that she might not feel so ridiculous in this particular corner with the old women and spinsters. She wasn't opposed to the people in general, for some of them were more amusing than the popular set. But she wasn't supposed to be over here, ignored and barely receiving glances from those who generally found her amusing.

It was far too unsettling. Was this her future? Should she become accustomed to feeling awkward and out of place? To being forgotten? The thought made her palms itch and ears burn, and a faint feeling of panic echoing glimpses of her past started swirling in her stomach.

She shook her head and forced herself to calm. This was no sign of what awaited her. It said nothing about her at all, really. Once her friends arrived, all would be set to rights.

And Lucas had also promised to attend, but had given her no indication of when. She was assured to dance at least one dance tonight, if he kept his word. She only prayed it would not be the last one of the evening. That would test her patience and resolve too far.

She waved to Mary Harris, who had just caught sight of her, but made no move to go near her. She and Mary had been paired together several times for musical events, Mary being a skilled vocalist and her voice lending itself to Gemma's violin quite nicely. They'd become friends over the years, but hardly close. She was more intimate with Mary's friends, Lady Whitlock and Lady Beverton; Lady Whitlock for her musicality and Lady Beverton for her marriage to Spencer's brother.

Several other people crossed her path who had invited her places, shared jokes and conversation with, and some had even been childhood friends of hers. Others she had come to know through her many Seasons and endless parading about London. All told, Gemma knew very many people in attendance this evening and could call several acquaintances, or even friends.

Yet here she stood.

Alone.

And that said a great deal.

Oh, she was not so silly as to think anyone thought ill of her. She was rather well liked and she was proud of that fact, but very rarely was she included in the smaller, more intimate events in Society. She was forgotten quite often, and was not particularly close with anyone, except Lily and Marianne, and that had only occurred recently.

She had wondered about it for years and years, lingering thoughts of some significant faults or errors in her ways flowing in and out on a semi-regular basis. But no one had ever criticized her behavior, for all they might notice her attire or comment on their lack of funds. She simply was not the sort of woman that anyone found the need to truly confide in or seek out, unless one wanted a laugh or a lark.

In the eyes of all of London, it seemed, she was still Caroline Templeton's little sister, no more than ten years of age, despite all of the evidence to the contrary.

She ought not to feel sorry for herself. But given her circumstances, she rather needed something to change.

And she had never been very good at changing herself.

Nor had she any desire to.

But she had to admit that she was tired of being the second thought and never the first.

She barely restrained a sigh as she watched her sister glide across the dance floor with Spencer, unintentionally drawing attention to herself with the sheer brilliance of her natural grace and beauty. She was the sort of beauty that drew surprised gasps whenever she went anywhere, as if people had forgotten what she looked like. Worst of all, she was as wonderful in person as everybody wanted her to be.

Conniving as a fox, possessed of a surprisingly sharp wit, and intolerant of superiority, but rather wonderful.

She was not moving about in Society as much as she used to, given that she was rather occupied with her three children, and even Gemma didn't see her often. Her two hoyden daughters were to blame for that. But this evening, Caroline had come to collect her for the ball and had a great deal to say on the subject of Lord Blackmoor.

She'd apparently heard rumors, spoken with her husband, and felt it her duty to inform Gemma that rashness was unwise, and Lord Blackmoor's reputation would do her no favors. And then, true to form, she'd come down off of her high horse and asked for as many details as Gemma would give, and found herself disappointed that she would not satisfy her. She had no desire to make more of this than there already was, and considering she did not have Society's ear, she didn't know how much that even was.

Caroline had assured her that there was hardly a whisper about them, but, she had said, no one ever paid attention to Gemma like this, and as such, she, as her sister, needed to make a fuss about it.

Despite her attempts at levity, Gemma had sensed Caroline's

true concern, and it oddly rankled her even now. Why was nobody able to see Lucas with honest eyes? Would everybody believe what they heard without taking the man as he was?

She did not know everything about him. In fact, she knew very little about him. But even she could tell that there was more to him than met the eye, and that he was not as cruel as he was made out to be.

The only thing Caroline had said to her credit on the subject was that Gemma was sensible and smart, and Caroline would trust her judgment.

Gemma hid a smile now as she watched Caroline dance. Would she really do such if she knew where Gemma's mind was headed? Or that she was actually courting Blackmoor? And rather enjoying doing so?

In the three days since the theater, things between them had only gotten better. He had come around to the house and officially met her parents, which had delighted her mother, and Gemma had been relieved to find her in a composed mood that morning. She had been the version of her mother that Gemma had known in her youth; spritely and bright and witty, with no sign of ridiculousness or oddity. Her father had been vague and barely invested, but polite all the same.

Lucas had not said much about the interview, only that he liked her parents and had no idea what Gemma had been going on about.

She'd given him an earful on *that* subject, and pointed out that he had not exactly told them the nature of their relationship, to which he had replied, rather pointedly, that neither had she.

Well, she could not reply properly to that.

As the days went on, Lucas took her from weak at the knees to laughing merrily to deeply contemplative, and it was the most invigorating sort of fun to be with him. She never quite knew what to expect, but every outing was delightful, even if they only walked the park. And oddly enough, he seemed to enjoy being with her as well. She was so used to people tiring of her that it was disconcerting.

What did he see that kept him coming back?

Something in his eyes, some raw intensity, concerned her a little. There was a depth there that she found intimidating and exhilarating all at once, and it was almost as if he could see through her, perhaps to her very soul.

Did he look at anyone else that way?

He could not. There would be no escaping him if anyone knew it.

Then why…?

"Oh, look, the Ashcombes are letting murderers enter these hallowed halls."

Gemma's head snapped around to glare at the back of the beady-eyed, ruffle strewn, beak nosed older woman seated not far from her, swathed in a pea soup colored and textured gown of ridiculous size.

There was no mistaking that voice, as if rocks had lodged themselves in her throat to protest being subjected to her digestion.

Lady Greversham.

Her brows narrowed and she faintly wished Caroline was nearby. She hated Lady Greversham with a fervor that was unequaled by any, though the entire world thought ill of the crone, and Caroline had acted with surprising mischief where the lady was concerned.

She looked where Lady Greversham and her associates were staring and found Lucas at their focal point, conversing softly with two other gentlemen she could not identify.

"Why let such a man come anywhere?" another woman hissed.

Lady Greversham tossed her head and several things jangled and fluttered. "No proof. Lady Blackmoor died under such suspicious circumstances, and few actually believe her husband had nothing to do with it. Intelligent beings know better. She never liked him, you know, and was treated very poorly."

One of the women sniffled. "Such a loss to everyone," she moaned loudly. "Beautiful and charismatic and so delicate in structure…"

"That brute of a man," someone spat. "Dirty, filthy, traitorous, barbaric…"

"He will never be invited to anything that I host," Lady Greversham boasted in a carrying voice. "*I* will not taint myself with such associations."

"Whoops!"

Gemma toppled over as her heeled slippers caught on the very delicate lace of Lady Greversham's massive skirts and ripped, shredded, and otherwise destroyed the fabric as she attempted to catch herself on the chair of one of the others. Unfortunately, her glass of ratafia, so recently filled, was therefore emptied on several of them. A nearby gentleman caught Gemma before she could hit the floor, his focus not on her, but on her victims.

Screeches and gasps and scrapes of chairs resounded, and Gemma bit back a grunt of satisfaction as she found herself righted by her rescuer. However, her face held none of that emotion.

"Oh, I'm so sorry!" she cried, wringing her slightly yellowed gloves together. "I am ever so clumsy, I should never have had that second glass!"

Lady Greversham glared at her, her face mottling amidst the wrinkles, and she shook her ruined skirt for emphasis.

"You fat cow," she hissed malevolently. "You bumbling, unattractive, underprivileged, undeserving waste of breath, how *dare* you…"

"My dance, I believe, Miss Templeton," her rescuer suddenly said, steering her away with brisk ferocity.

"I am so very sorry," she whimpered loudly over her shoulder at the women, whom no one seemed keen on aiding in their efforts.

The tall gentleman currently holding her arm suddenly coughed a laugh as they continued to walk. "I pray your distress is imagined and not in sincerity, for that was one of the best moments of my life."

Gemma grinned up at the stranger, a truly gloriously handsome fellow, and wondered at his frankness. "Thank you, sir. I was quite proud of it."

"Not an accident?"

Still smiling, she shook her head. "Even I am not that fortunate. Every step was calculated and exacted with precision."

He laughed and stifled it with a perfectly white glove.

Gemma glanced behind her and looked appropriately horrified, embarrassed, and ashamed, which earned her nothing but the scorching return looks as the ladies quit the ballroom.

She sighed and returned her attention to her new partner. "I suppose I will never be invited back."

"I think you would be surprised."

She raised a brow at him. "By the duke and duchess? Hardly."

"The marquess and marchioness have a surprising amount of pull there," he assured her as he led her around another small group. "And nobody likes Lady Greversham. Not even His Grace."

She doubted that, knowing what she did of the duke, but one could never tell. After all, he was right about the Whitlocks having pull in such matters, and Lady Whitlock would never let her be barred from an event to which she was tied in any way.

She glanced over at the dance floor, which they were not approaching, but skirting around.

"Are you not going to dance with me?" she asked in a mulish tone. Despite his praise of her actions, even he would not stand up with her?

He chuckled softly. "I would, but as we have not been introduced, it is not proper."

"You know me, so all that is left is to introduce yourself," she pointed out.

He gave her a look. "Not today, princess."

She barked a laugh at his endearment and was about to ask on it when she caught sight of something a bit more intriguing.

Lucas stood only feet from where he had been before, but no one was near him now, and it was clear he was their destination. He stared at the two of them with a searing intensity that gave him a personal perimeter of shocking dimension, and people were going out of their way to avoid him.

"You see now why," the man next to her muttered. "The moment I touched you, that happened. So, for my sake and yours, I'll remain anonymous and vanish quickly."

Gemma swallowed with difficulty. "That seems prudent."

The rest of the ballroom, and all of its excessive numbers, seemed to have no idea what had just happened or what was currently happening, and aside from curious looks, no one spared them a thought.

Lucas was glorious in his eveningwear, the paleness of his eyes a brilliant contrast to the dark of his clothing and hair. His features were hard angles and taut, while his body was coiled with a peculiar tension, despite his apparent casual stance. For once, he looked like the dangerous man everyone thought he was.

And yet Gemma knew nothing of fear. Anticipation, excitement, and the curious sensation of wanting to smile, but no fear.

Then, miraculously, she did smile.

"No one smiles for him," the man next to her murmured in a hushed voice when they reached Lucas.

"She does," Lucas told him in a low rumble. He took her hand and spared a brief glance for the man beside her. "Marlowe."

"Blackmoor," he replied with a brief nod.

She had no idea who Marlowe was or if that was supposed to be significant, but she gave him a brief curtsey. "Thank you for the rescue."

He smiled at her. "Thank you for the entertainment. Now if you will both excuse me, I must vanish." He bowed and seemed to do just that.

Gemma watched him go and shook her head. "Who in the world is that?"

"No one of real consequence," Lucas said as he led her out to the dance floor. "You'll forget about him in a few minutes."

"Will I?"

"Everyone does. He's used to it."

"Seems rude."

"It's not."

She choked back a laugh as they began to dance, and even his constant reminders that she was ruining his reputation could not make her less gleeful.

At the moment, not even Lady Greversham would have managed to do that.

Lucas couldn't believe what was happening to him. And to Gemma! She'd just caused a surprising scene that would horrify a great many people for years, and could ruin her reputation completely. Yet she was dancing with him with all of the energy and enthusiasm of a first Season miss.

And he had been prepared to be the overprotective hero,

seething with righteous indignation and the temptation for less-than-righteous impulses. But she'd needed none of that. She needed no protector, defender, or, from the looks of it, any sort of escape at all. She'd had things quite in hand.

It did not lessen his feelings, not one inkling. He still wanted to rage and storm and terrorize the entire room, and such intensity of emotions, brought on by her, surrounding her, wrapped up in everything that she was, confused him immensely.

And now he was dancing with her, despite his urge to become unhinged, and the tension within him was ebbing away under Gemma's influence.

It was the most bewildering thing.

"What was that all about?" he asked her as he passed her again.

She gave him a strange look. "What?"

Had she really forgotten already? "Your impressive display."

She beamed with pride. "Did you like it?"

His grudging admiration knew no bounds for her audacity, but he was hardly going to tell her that here and now. "What was it?"

She tossed her head and snorted, despite being in public. "Oh, they were going on about you, and it was shameful, especially considering they're all terrified of you. And I was really getting bored, and any opportunity to make life difficult for Lady Grev…"

He took her hand tightly, squeezing harder than was called for in the dance. "Me?" he bit out, silencing her.

She raised a surprised brow. "Yes… Why?"

"What did they say?" he demanded, wanting to whisk her out of the room instead of turn away and follow the pattern of the dance.

Gemma watched him with a hint of a furrow between her brows as she passed the other ladies. When she was back to him once more, she took his hand and held it just as tightly as he had hers. "They spoke of your wife," she murmured softly.

He nearly swore. It was one thing for them to focus on him an his rumors, but if they were actually talking about Celia… The very last thing he needed was for the world to be reminded of her at this time.

And for Gemma to hear it.

He felt her hold on him flex again and he looked at her, the brilliance of her eyes illuminated in their concern. She asked no question, but he could see them swirling about in those endless depths.

He shook his head slightly. "I will not talk about my wife."

"All right," she said simply, inclining her head.

He fought for a swallow and met her eyes as clearly as he could, holding his breath. "All you need to know is I didn't kill her."

She smiled up at him as they parted for the dance. "I know."

If he had been less careful, he would have stumbled. As it was, he still gaped. "You do?"

Her smile grew and a slight dimple appeared. "Of course."

"How?" he blurted, forgoing any sort of restraint or composure.

Now she laughed and set her arm on his for the next movement. "Oh now, really, Blackmoor, the idea of you killing anybody is ridiculous."

He stared at her in awe, grateful that, for the moment, he did not have to move. "No one else seems to think so," he managed, a dubious tone creeping into his words.

Gemma smiled with ease. "Well, you aren't talking with anyone else. Just me."

And suddenly, that was more than enough for him. He inhaled, noting how easy it seemed to be, and released it just as freely. "So I am," he marveled.

Her eyes narrowed suspiciously. "Are you smiling?"

Instantly he wanted to, but he kept his face emotionless. "No."

"But you want to."

He took her hand and led her into the final movements, pulling her closer than was called for. "Yes, I do."

And he wasn't sure he'd ever meant words more.

Chapter Five

"Whom do you like in the room back there?"

Lucas raised a brow as he and Gemma slowly walked the gardens just off of the terrace, having opted to escape the crush of the ballroom for a respite in the cool night air. "Whom do I like?" he repeated with a hint of amusement.

She nodded with a smile, her eyes only slightly dimmed in the faint light of the house. "Surely you like *some* of the guests, despite the harpies spreading ridiculous rumors. Tiresome wretches; gargoyles the lot of them."

His chest tightened at her suggestion. "You can't say those things."

She scoffed and tossed her precariously pinned hair. "I can if I want. It's terrible how they trample over your name and your life so freely. I'd have defended you properly if we weren't being secretive." She wrinkled up her nose. "Though I'll admit that I like that we are being secretive. Not because of any rumors or silly things about you, mind, but because it gives us privacy. Even so, it is maddening under these particular circumstances."

"It wouldn't do any good," he murmured, taking her hand and squeezing it with the gratitude he could not verbalize. "They would not accept anything as proof. It would only enflame things. You will get used to it, as I have."

"I doubt that." She made a strange growling noise and glared at the windows of the ballroom. "Ruining her dress seems a paltry excuse for retribution."

"Gemma, enough," Lucas said with a sudden smile she did not

see. He composed his features before she looked back at him, and tilted his head fondly. "You've done more than enough. Far more than you should have, I think."

Her lips quirked dangerously and she peered up at him with narrowed eyes. "Call me Gemma again."

Realizing what he had done, he straightened and shook his head. "No, no, I shouldn't have said it the first time. You must forget it."

"I won't," she said with a shake of her head.

"You must."

"No."

He exhaled harshly and looked back towards the house. She made him forget himself, and there was too much at stake for him to do that. There was too much in his past, too much uncertainty before him, and he was much more unsettled by this whole affair than he'd meant to be. He had to find the strength he'd always had, the composure, the reserve…

"Lucas…"

The soft sound of his name brought his head slowly around. His breath caught in his chest as he took in the sight of her, as if he had never truly seen her before. Her features were softened in the dim light of the evening, yet nothing about her was subdued from its usual brightness. She had this unearthly, mystical way about her, and he found himself wanting to confess everything to her then and there. She was breathtaking in her beauty, charming in her ways, and captivating in all that she was.

He had half a mind to propose here and now.

"What?" he managed to ask instead.

She smiled a little and she took his arm, forcing him to walk again. "Nothing. I simply wanted to say your name again. I like the way it feels."

He nearly groaned and closed his eyes momentarily. "You wanted to know whom I like in the ballroom, yes?" he eventually said, having recovered his usual somber tone.

"Yes, please," she replied as if they'd had no interruption whatsoever.

Fighting his way through the muddle of his thoughts, he tried to recall the identities of people in the ballroom, let alone the scant number he liked. "Whitlock is a great man, I think well of him. Beverton I know better, and like very much."

"Everybody likes Nathan," Gemma said with a roll of her eyes, "but go on."

"Your brother-in-law."

She snorted. "You don't know Spencer, don't pretend you like him for my sake."

He resisted the urge to laugh and nodded obediently. "Marlowe."

She looked up at him in surprise. "Really?"

"One of my oldest friends." He would not go into details, for Rafe's benefit as well as his own.

"You didn't act like it."

Lucas exhaled as he looked at her. "We are both reserved men. He is inclined to heroism and intervening, and I was feeling rather protective. He understands."

Gemma bit her lip on a soft laugh. "I hope he does. Otherwise your friendship would seem rather strange."

"It *is* strange," he assured her as he led her around a hedge, the torches along the garden lit and blazing in the darkness. "That is the way we prefer it."

"Men are bizarre creatures," she muttered, shaking her head, but smiling. "Who else?"

He sighed and craned his neck. "I don't know, I am not inclined to scan a room and take stock of the people whose society I enjoy."

"One more name," she insisted, seeming to enjoy his distress.

He was embarrassed at how long it took him to think of people he had seen that he could list. He respected a great many men, but hardly any of them had been in attendance. They might have been in the room presently, but at the time…

"Bennett Stanford," he said at last, remembering the young man's face being somewhere in the vicinity before he'd witnessed Gemma's incident.

Her brow furrowed and she paused a step. "Who?"

"You don't know him?"

She shook her head and frowned. "That is disconcerting. I know everyone. Or most everyone, at least. Who is he?"

"The younger brother of a schoolmate of mine. You know Lord

Oliver?"

"By sight and reputation only," she replied with a shake of her head. "We've never been formally introduced."

That was not surprising, Oliver had always been rather single-minded. He was polite, gentlemanly, but a bit obtuse if one were being critical. "Stanford is the youngest brother. Just returned to London for the Season. He lives near me, and we fence on occasion."

Gemma smiled and gave him a frank look. "You fence?"

He sniffed an almost laugh. "I do all sorts of things that other men do, my dear. Prattling on about myself is just not one of them."

"No, I suppose not." She sighed and looked around at their surroundings. "I shall have to acquaint myself with Mr. Stanford. If he has your good opinion, I daresay he deserves mine."

Lucas turned slightly to give her a disbelieving look. She was willing to take his word on a man with only the barest information? She could not possibly trust him so much this early on, it was impossible, even for her.

"I don't know him well enough to give him my good opinion," he explained, leading her towards a bench. "I simply know I can tolerate him. He is young. A puppy, really. Headstrong and impulsive, head in the clouds…"

"Are you trying to talk me out of thinking well of him or just warning me?" Gemma asked, laughing as she took a seat on the bench.

He opened his mouth to reply, and then closed it on a hum. "I don't know, actually," he finally admitted.

That made her grin and she tilted her head in acknowledgement. "Well, whichever it is, as I take your word for it, I shall have to make a firm study of him. And to those who know him well, particularly the women. You can never know the measure of a man until you know how he kisses."

Lucas, having just taken a seat next to her, reared back suddenly. "Excuse me?"

Gemma shrugged one shoulder, not looking at all ashamed. "It's true."

"Says who?"

"Everyone."

He shook his head, not sure if he were bewildered, amused, or shocked. Or all three. "I've never heard that."

She hummed a light laugh. "Well, you wouldn't, would you?"

He twisted his mouth a little, watching her with interest. A lady would never speak of such things to a gentleman, and yet she had done so. There was no hint of flirtation or attitude of seduction about her. She simply was as she was, and spoke her mind.

And he was enchanted by it.

"And how many men have you tested this theory on?" he asked politely, keeping his tone and expression mildly interested.

She sniffed and shook her head. "A lady never kisses and tells." She narrowed her eyes suddenly. "Why?"

He let one shoulder rise in a hint of a shrug. "I merely want to know what I am up against."

Her eyes widened and she stilled. "Wait, so you're going to…?"

Lucas nearly smiled and raised a taunting brow at her. "When you throw out a challenge like that, do you think I'm going to let it lie?"

She swallowed harshly. "To be perfectly frank, I have no idea what you might do," she murmured, her voice hoarse.

A satisfied smirk briefly appeared as he leaned closer. "And that is precisely why I am going to do this…"

Keeping his hands entirely to himself, he closed the distance between them and very gently pressed his lips to hers. She did not move, but she did not resist him. On the contrary, she seemed, impossibly, to lean into him and his kiss. He felt her hands fidget in her lap, her pulse quicken, her breathing deepen, and he pulled back before anything could ignite in himself.

Though he was honest enough to admit that it already had.

"Did I surprise you?" he rasped, her breath panting across his cheeks.

"Yes," she whispered, her hands fluttering to his chest, her eyes still closed.

Abruptly, he had difficulty swallowing. "You owe me," he reminded her, as an odd cloud of delirium seemed to settle on his mind.

"Name your price."

He smiled. "Kiss me again."

She sighed and gripped his coat. "As you wish."

She pulled on him and he acquiesced, bringing his lips back to hers with more fervor, taking her chin in hand and tilting her face ever so slightly. Gently he wrapped his free arm around her and pressed her closer, not that she needed him too. All her natural energy and passion was suddenly focused and centered on their connection, and her lips molded far too easily to his. Too soft, too yielding, too perfect a blend of innocence and sensuality and heady delight, and he was very much in danger of losing himself entirely to her.

He hadn't meant to start this, he'd only meant...

He hadn't the faintest idea what he'd meant by it, but it was absolutely the most brilliant thing he'd ever done in his entire life.

He forced himself to break away again and was embarrassed at how such a simple kiss could leave him so shaken.

Thankfully, Gemma wasn't paying any attention to him at the moment. She had a hand at her throat, eyes wide and unfocused as they looked down at the ground.

Lucas took a moment to ensure he was as composed as possible, then cleared his throat. "How did I measure up?"

Gemma's gaze shot to his and focused with such intensity that he found himself leaning back. "I don't know," she said faintly. "Despite the boldness in the words I said, and that ridiculous statement, I've... never been kissed before."

His brows shot up and it took much of his control to keep from gaping openly. "I was... That is, I am the first?"

Her hand tightened on her throat and she nodded.

The flare of satisfaction that hit his gut was both primal and potent, and he was far too pleased for his own comfort. He reached out and pried her fingers from her throat, then raised her hand to his lips. "That pleases me," he told her, growling.

"Does it?" she asked, her voice somehow small as her cheeks flushed.

Unable to help himself, he leaned forward and seized her lips for a brief, but tender kiss. "Yes," he said, cupping her cheek. "Yes, it does."

"That is almost a smile," she murmured, reaching up to touch the corner of his mouth.

Well. So it was. He allowed it to remain and only shrugged. "Whoops."

She smiled and cocked her head. "Ten shillings."

"Almost a smile is not an actual smile. I will not be billed on an almost."

She chuckled and allowed him to pull her to her feet. She looked towards the ballroom and wrinkled her nose. "Do we have to go back in?"

He gave her a strange look. "You'd rather stay out here with me?"

"Yes," she said simply, as if it should be obvious.

He shook his head, wondering when the delusion would fall from her eyes, and looped her arm through his. "Come on."

She grumbled, but did so, and by the time they had reentered the ballroom, she was her usual bright and cheery self, even if she was standing too close to him.

He scanned the room and caught sight of Mrs. Gerrard and Mrs. Granger nearby, both of whom saw them at once, and watched with interest.

"See?" he murmured softly, indicating with his head. "Your friends are here now."

She followed his gaze and smiled faintly at the sight. "So they are." She looked up at him and her smile grew. "But you are my friend, too, Blackmoor."

He matched her expression. "No, I'm not, Gemma. Not really, and not entirely. But if you are a good girl and behave yourself the rest of the evening, I just may dance with you again."

She frowned and shook her head. "Don't put yourself out or anything. I know how you detest it, and if we aren't even friends, in your opinion…" She trailed off and let the unspoken hang between them.

"Not at all," he told her. "It would be a pleasure to dance with you again." He leaned closer and whispered, "And I think you know exactly why we are not friends… That point should be fairly obvious by now."

Before she could retort anything, he bowed and left the room, nodding once to the inquiring lift of Marianne Gerrard's brow as he passed them. She smiled a little devious smile in response, and he almost returned it.

What in the world was coming over him?

Three hours of violin practicing could not set Gemma's mind at rest. Nor had a full night of sleep.

Well, half of one, anyway. Sleep had been hard to come by.

But the extensive practicing should have done it. That usually cured everything that ailed her. She forgot her financial straits, forgot her family problems, her lack of suitors, loneliness, even melancholy. Her violin was all the aid she ever needed.

Yet it had failed her.

It could not wipe out the memory of Lucas's kisses, nor the confusion that currently thrived within her.

She set the instrument aside and sank into a chair, rubbing at her temples. Lucas was going to drive her insane. His kind attentions during their times together surprised her, his dry wit was making her laugh more and more, and his inability to show emotion of any sort was maddening. Yet he was becoming more and more important to her with every passing day. Every almost-smile was treasured up and saved in her mind, and she yearned to see what his true smile looked like.

She was learning, however, that his eyes were not as unaffected as his expressions. They could thunder with anger, beam with smiles, and cloud with thought while his face remained implacable all the while. Eyes were supposed to be windows to the soul, and the world within his was transfixing.

Marianne and Lily had interrogated her extensively last night, but she had kept everything vague and simple. She had nothing to confide, but she had plenty she wished to hide. She was not ready for admitting anything.

But oh, the pleasure of his kisses!

She had not known it, but once his lips had touched hers, she found that she had been waiting for him to kiss her for ages. Perhaps from their first dance; it was hard to say. Whatever his reserve in all other respects, he was not so when he kissed. There, he had emotion and energy and spirit that his demeanor never showed. She knew full well he had been gentle and restrained when he kissed her, for her sake, and she was touched by the thought. It had, however, sparked her imagination into a frenzy about what it could become.

She flushed and pressed the back of her hand to her cheek, then rose to walk the room.

She paused at the window overlooking the garden, folding her arms across her. The gardens were in a sorry state, and the windows were filthy, but there was nothing to be done about it. They had not the staff for proper maintenance anymore, and barely the staff for appearances. There was one upstairs maid, who was charged with the dress and hair of both Gemma and her mother; the housekeeper, Mrs. Todd, who managed to remain optimistic and efficient despite their situation; two footmen, who also served as valet and kitchen aids; and the butler, Rosings, who somehow managed, along with Mrs. Todd, to keep all public rooms spotless. Their coachman was Rosings's brother and was paid as needed, so they walked more often than not. Or others came to fetch them.

Gemma had told too many lies about broken carriages and lame horses for her taste.

She glanced down at her dress, her most comfortable, and most worn. It was frayed beyond repair and the bodice was too loose from too many battles with her natural figure and those times when corsets had been used. It gaped quite precariously when she bent over, and the lace at the edges was so discolored and ragged it hardly deserved to still be considered lace. The comfort and movement it allowed her was perfect for extended rehearsals, but she could never wear it outside of the house or to receive anyone. Not even her friends.

She sighed and rubbed at her arms. Would she ever be free of the worries of money?

The sound of footsteps caused her to turn and she smiled fondly as her father entered. He did not see her immediately, which was typical, as he was usually preoccupied with something or other. And the newssheet in his hand was still freshly pressed, so he had yet to read it.

Halfway to the worn chair by the fire, he saw her and stopped in his tracks. "Oh, I forgot all about you," he said warmly.

Gemma's smile became tight as the words reverberated within her. Those exact words, fifteen years ago, had changed her.

She shook off the beginnings of reminiscence and clasped her hands before her. "Are you coming in here to read, Papa?"

He looked down at the newssheet in his hand, then back at her. "Yes, I was, but I don't mean to disturb you." He indicated her violin where it sat. "You must practice, you know."

She barely avoided rolling her eyes. "Yes, Papa, I already have."

He winked and no doubt would have patted her cheek if she had been close enough. "Clever girl. But a bit more won't hurt, will it? You never know when some young man might hear you play and fall in love with you."

Now Gemma *did* roll her eyes. "Papa…"

"Don't give me that tone, Mouse," he scolded gently, coming to take a hand. "I've seen men swept off their feet for less. You've quite a lot to offer, you know, and your violin is a beautiful extension. I know you've had no success yet, but you mustn't let yourself go."

Gemma made a disbelieving noise at him. "All I have to offer, Papa, is my person."

"And what a person it is!" He stepped back to examine her proudly, then frowned. "That gown. I hope you aren't wearing anything this shabby in public, Gemma."

"Of course not," she replied at once with a faint snort. "I only wear it at home."

He nodded firmly. "Good. No young man would consider you looking like that."

Gemma bit the inside of her cheek, resisting the urge to remind her father that no man was considering her at all.

Then again…

"Is Blackmoor coming around today?" her father asked suddenly, his eyes narrowed in assessment, pronouncing the lines on his face more starkly.

Panicked, Gemma swallowed and attempted to untangle her fingers. "I don't know," she managed, her voice squeaking a little.

"We haven't… That is, we did not arrange anything."

"Your mother said he danced with you again last night."

"He did," she said carefully. "Once or twice, I can't recall exactly."

Her father shrugged as if it meant very little. "I am glad to see him pay attention to you, Mouse. Perhaps it will bring about suitors, eh?" He winked again and started to exit the room.

Gemma frowned at the sight of his retreating threadbare coat. "Papa?"

He stopped and turned back, his silvering hair somehow subdued despite the morning light.

"Aren't you going to read?" she asked, gesturing to the fire.

He raised a furry brow. "No, Mouse, not in here. You have more to practice, remember?" He waved his hand absently in the direction of the violin. "Lady Raeburn's musicale is in a few weeks. You will want to be especially prepared for that." He smiled at her in his warmest, most loving manner. "This is your Season, Gem. I can feel it."

Gemma watched him go, and only released a sigh when he was gone.

It was always the same with them. Marriage, men falling in love, her appearance being perfect, finding ways to impress… No one ever mentioned her pittance of a dowry or speculated on any reason why she'd never had suitors. No one seemed to see their lives for what they truly were.

Just her.

Grinding her teeth, she stomped over to her violin and immediately began the most vibrant and agitated piece she could think of, her pleasant ponderings on Lucas and his kisses long gone.

For now.

Chapter Six

"Thank you so much for rescuing me," Gemma sighed pleasantly as she looped her arm through his and tipped her face back in the afternoon sun.

Lucas quirked a brow. "What was so horrifying that warranted a simple walk being a rescue?"

She gave him a very derisive look. "My mother has it in her mind that the ball last week was a horrible moment in fashion for me, and is of a mind to amend such an egregious error. In her opinion, had I been more appropriately dressed, it would not have been such a failure."

"I danced with you twice and she declares it a failure?" He wasn't sure why, but he was offended by that.

Gemma laughed without humor, which was an odd sound to his ears. "You, she declared, obviously have good taste, but may have taken pity on me for the lack of interest surrounding me."

He frowned and steered her around a puddle. "I don't take pity on anyone. Least of all you."

"I know that," Gemma said, rolling her eyes. "It's one of my favorite things about you."

He barked a hard laugh. "How's that? It's a flaw to everyone else."

"You laughed. Fifteen shillings."

"Miss Templeton."

"Gemma."

"Tell me."

She glowered a little, then shook her head. "You don't pretend," she explained. "Not ever. I've seen you save a random female in distress at a ball, but there was no pity about it. In your mind, it was justice. I don't know any particulars, but I feel quite certain you have other such moments outside of ballrooms."

"Don't make me out to be a hero," he murmured, tipping his hat to a passing gentleman, who returned it with surprise.

"I'd never," she vowed, but he didn't believe her.

He made a soft noise of discontent, then steered her down a lesser travelled path. "And does your mother indicate how she wishes to mend the apparent error of your fashion, which I find no fault in?"

Gemma tilted her head to look up at him with a brilliant smile that caught him somewhere in the middle of his chest. "Why, Lord Blackmoor, are you unintentionally complimenting me?"

"I never do anything unintentionally, Miss Templeton," he informed her with a light sniff, his mouth quirking.

She bit her full lower lip briefly and shook her head. "Mother was tossing my dresses out of my bureau and having the maid take notes on what we needed from the modiste to mend my ways." She sighed and looked away. "Wretched business, and she will not listen."

"What, buying more dresses?" he asked, surprised at the dark tone she had suddenly taken. What woman did not enjoy such things?

Gemma hesitated, which surprised him more, as she was always so forthright. "Surely you have noticed, sir, the state of the clothing I wear."

He had noticed, but what was a little wear and tear and fading? It need not indicate anything of significance. He merely thought her frugal, which was wisdom in the world they lived in.

Without waiting for his response, she went on. "My family has never been one of large fortune, I trust you know this. I am not sure how anyone could avoid the topic, as it is all anyone speaks of with my family. The fact of the matter is, Blackmoor, that over the years, it has only gotten worse. To be blunt, there is no money. None at all. My parents cannot see it clearly, but there is very little to tempt a man with regards to dowry or standing when it comes to me. We cannot afford new clothing, a proper carriage, or the rent for our house."

Her voice broke a little and Lucas found himself pulling her closer to him so their bodies would brush.

"You may not notice when you come, but we have hardly any servants at all," she continued, her voice stronger. "And only the public rooms are kept in good condition because heaven forbid that anyone know that we cannot manage the rest of the house. The only reason we can remain in it is because Spencer covers what we cannot."

"As bad as that?" he murmured, wondering what it was costing her to admit all of this. He knew her parents were sensible people, but misguided where Gemma was concerned. He would never have guessed things were as bad as Gemma was saying, but he also knew that she was not one to exaggerate or give in to dramatics.

She nodded once. "Every bit. We've needed to retrench for two years or so, but they refuse. After this Season, I'm insisting upon it." She groaned and shook her head. "I cannot believe I'm telling you this."

"I won't tell a soul."

She glanced up at him with a raised brow. "I know that. That is not what concerns me."

He cocked his head and regarded her curiously. "What, then?"

Her cheeks flushed and she lowered her eyes. "I'm telling you that I am destitute, and the only member of my family that seems aware of it. You will either think me desperate and a fortune hunter, or you will find me ridiculous and far too honest. What sort of girl discusses such a thing with a man courting her?"

Lucas stopped and turned her to face him, then put two fingers under her chin, lifting her gaze to his. "Listen to me, Miss Gemma Templeton," he said firmly, keeping his tone low and gentle. "Nothing, I repeat, nothing you have told me affects my regard for you in any way. You are far too honest, but I have never seen a reason to find fault in that. On the contrary, I am glad to know that you trust me with such information."

A faint smile graced her lips and some of the tension left her. "I don't think anyone else would consider my blabbering anything deserving trust."

He tapped the underside of her chin playfully. "They don't know you as I do."

"That's true," she mused, her smile growing. "No one does."

The depth to that admission was not lost on him, and a possessive thrill rushed through him. He dropped his hand, but kept his expression amused. "That is because most everybody else is an idiot."

Gemma burst out laughing and took his arm once more, leaning into him as they resumed walking. "Not true!"

"Mostly true."

"You can't say that."

"I can and I will."

She shook her head and sighed. "You are being kind to me for speaking on an inappropriate topic, and you really shouldn't. I am quite ashamed of myself, and so should you be."

He doubted he would ever be ashamed of her in his entire life, but he could hardly correct her, for it *was* an inappropriate topic. That did not mean, however, that he regretted it.

"Well," he said slowly, letting her set the pace, "since you brought up inappropriate topics…"

She snickered and nudged him a little. "Yes?"

"Why is it so shocking for someone to court you?" He gave her a serious look, despite the playful tone. "I've tossed it over and over, Gemma, and it makes no sense."

She dimpled a bit and her fingers played on the fabric of his coat. "I've never really known the answer to that. I do the best that I can, but I've never been the sort of girl that attracted attention in that way."

"No one seeks your company after you play?" he asked, pretending this was all very innocent, but truly wanting to know. "You are furiously talented, and I do not say that lightly."

"You're going to forget to be stodgy and solemn if you keep complimenting me so freely," she returned with a warning look.

"Humor me."

She pursed her lips in thought. "You know, I don't think they do. Not the young men, at any rate. Perhaps it is a lack of appreciation for the violin. Girls who play the pianoforte are always sought after. I tried that, but was dreadful, and I took to the violin with ease and fervor."

"I like it," he told her. "I find it far more evocative than the pianoforte, unless one is very skilled there. It was always a pleasure to hear you play."

"Thank you." She looked up at him with narrowed eyes. "You never approached me either, you know."

He winced and looked away. "I know. Forgive me."

"Forgiven," she said at once.

"What about dancing?" he asked, changing the subject before she could ask him why. "You dance frequently enough, despite your mother's opinion at the last ball. And I can see they enjoy it, so what is it? Do you threaten them afterwards?"

Gemma snorted and covered her mouth.

"Are they dancing with you against their will and forced to enjoy it?" he continued, pretending at seriousness. "It is on pain of death, isn't it? I have danced with you three times now, and I never thought it should terrify me. Was I wrong?"

Her laughter grew and her eyes squeezed shut on the contained mirth.

"I thought I was a terrifying creature in Society," he mused, shaking his head, "and yet it seems even I am outmatched by you, Miss Templeton. I'm feeling rather free at the moment, I may even smile."

"Oh, stop," she gasped, laughing and putting a hand to her chest. "Stop, I cannot breathe for laughing."

He almost smiled at her delight, but barely kept it in check. "Yes, it is a ridiculous assertion, is it not?"

She wiped at her eyes and beamed at him. "The most preposterous."

He led her to a bench and she sat. "Why then, Gemma?"

She shrugged without care or concern, which astonished him. "As I said, I've never quite figured it out. I've compared myself to several other females, better and worse than I in various aspects, and none of them had the trouble. Perhaps it is the combination of all that is me that renders it impossible to do so." Her eyes fixed on him with sudden focus. "Save for you."

"Well, I have never been very good at doing what is popular in Society," he sighed, taking a seat next to her.

"I can see that," she chuckled. "You would never have started this venture if you had known it simply isn't done."

Lucas stared at her for a moment, more tempted to smile than he'd been in some time, and without a sensible reason. She could laugh about her situation, despite the obvious pain of it. She spoke of herself with lightness, in an offhand manner that he'd never known any woman to, but without real derision. She saw good in him, confided in him, when nearly everyone else thought him a viper of sorts.

She made him want to be happy.

And suddenly, he did not know what he was waiting for.

He straightened up and gave Gemma a serious look. "I suspect, Miss Templeton, that you prefer frankness."

She smirked and matched his pose. "You would be correct, sir," she replied, very properly, playfully somber.

He nodded once. "Then I mean to inform you of my intentions."

Gemma folded her hands primly in her lap, trying not to smile. "I think that would be wise."

He hesitated for only a moment, then lifted his chin a hair. "I mean to make you my wife."

Gemma's eyes widened and her lips parted in shock. Eventually she closed her mouth and swallowed. "That… was very frank."

"Have I surprised you?" he asked, fighting the urge to wince. Most ladies would have presumed such a thing, having been in a courtship, but Gemma was not like other ladies, and she had no reason to suspect that her first proper courtship would lead to this. And yet she could hardly have been without suspicion.

"Quite," she replied mildly.

"Apologies."

She waved that off as she wet her lips. "And when did you mean to bring this about?"

"As soon as you might be agreeable to it," he replied as simply as he could.

She nodded slowly, then cleared her throat. "Then we had best be about it."

Now it was he whose mouth dropped in shock and he found himself giving a cough of surprise. "I beg your pardon?"

A small smile appeared on her face. "Have I taken *you* by

surprise? Don't answer that, I can see that I have." She reached for a hand and squeezed it. "If you mean to marry me, I mean to accept."

An odd sort of euphoria settled on him. "You're serious?"

She nodded, still smiling. "I take it you didn't expect that response."

He shook his head, and found himself smiling back. "You might say that."

Gemma's eyes and smile widened as she looked at him. "Are you smiling, Blackmoor?"

He shrugged helplessly. "I might be."

"That's ten shillings," she told him with a smirk.

He shook his head. "I shall add it to my bill," he murmured as he leaned forward to kiss that enchanting smile of hers.

An hour later, Gemma bid Lucas farewell as he returned her to her home, promising he would return that evening to speak with her father. He'd offered to do so now, but Gemma thought her father would need some warning before that happened.

After all, in his mind, she'd have gone from perfectly unattached to engaged in one outing, and there was nothing compromising about it at all.

She entered the house in a bit of a daze.

Engaged. She, Gemma Elizabeth Templeton, was engaged. Had the world completely turned upside down?

Of course, she had wondered why a man like Lucas would court her, particularly when he had never courted anyone since she had become aware of him. But then, his first marriage had ended badly, so it was no wonder he remained a secluded widower.

If she were to be perfectly honest with herself, she would admit that she hadn't thought of how the courtship would end. She had been so delighted by it, and by him, that she dreaded considering it. But she had known it would end some way or another, and marriage had not been what she expected.

Why would he want to marry her? It had been on the tip of her tongue to ask him, but he had been so delighted by her acceptance… he had smiled!… that she could not bear to dampen it. He claimed he was no hero, but after her speech to him today, which she was still mortified about, she wondered if he might be marrying her to save her.

That would be equally as mortifying.

Even if that were the case, would it change anything?

She shook her head to herself. No, it would not change her mind. She would marry Lucas, not only because it was her only chance, but because she wanted to.

Didn't she?

"What in the world are you doing to Blackmoor, Gemma?"

She whirled in surprise to see her brother-in-law coming from one of the drawing rooms at the front of the house. She glanced around and realized she'd leaned against the door while being lost in thought. She frowned and folded her arms. "What are you talking about?"

Spencer raised a brow and jerked his thumb in the direction Lucas had gone. "The man is practically giddy. I almost didn't recognize him."

The disapproval and suspicion in his voice rankled her and she lifted her chin to meet his expression head on. "I haven't done anything. Other than accept his proposal."

Spencer gaped, his dark eyes going wide. "His WHAT?"

Gemma scoffed. "Oh, really, Spencer, why did you think he was coming around and taking me on carriage rides and escorting me about? Did you suppose I was advising him on cravat fashions?"

"You accepted?" Spencer sputtered.

"Yes."

"Without consulting your father?"

She shrugged one shoulder and shifted her weight. "Why should I? He doesn't want to marry Papa, he wants to marry me."

Spencer made an inarticulate noise. "That is much to his credit, but Gem!" He stepped forward and looked as if he was going to take her arms, as if she were a child. Again. "Why?"

Something within her started to burn and she gritted her teeth. "Why?" she snapped, surprising him. "Because he, unlike anyone else, sees me as a woman. And this woman rather likes that look in his eyes. If you'll excuse me, Mama will want to plan my trousseau."

She turned on her heel and strode towards her mother's sitting room, and Spencer, after a moment, followed.

Her father exited the room just as they were about to enter.

"Papa!" Gemma cried, grabbing his arm as he moved to go past her.

He looked at her hand on his arm, then up at her in surprise. "Yes, Gemma?"

She swallowed, suddenly nervous. "I have something to tell you."

Spencer snorted, but said nothing.

Her father sighed and an errant patch of hair on top of his head danced with the motion. "Tell me, then. I have a meeting with my solicitor soon."

That was not going to go well, and would put him in a dismal mood. And she was about to give him something else that could make things worse.

Well, there was nothing for it.

She folded her hands together before her very primly. "I am engaged to Lord Blackmoor, Papa."

"What?" her mother cried from within the sitting room.

Her father made no response and only raised a brow. "Really?" he asked with only a hint of a curious note.

She nodded once. "Yes, Papa. I know it must come as a shock, as you were unaware of our relationship…"

"Oh, I knew he was courting you, Gem," her father interrupted with a wave of his hand, a slight smile on his face.

Spencer coughed in surprise and Gemma staggered a little, still clinging to her father's sleeve. "You… knew?" she managed weakly. "How?"

Mr. Templeton smiled and patted her cheek. "Because he wrote to me shortly after he started courting you, pet. Asked for discretion for both of you, so I gave it." He pried her fingers out of his sleeve and chuckled. "Really, it was quite properly done, Gemma. You're not nearly as shocking as you think." He turned and left the hallway, while Gemma gaped behind him.

He knew? All along?

"Come in here!" her mother screeched, shaking her out of her stupor.

Gemma rushed into the sitting room and went to her mother's side as she reclined on the faded brocade divan.

"You're engaged to Blackmoor?" her mother asked, squeezing her hand, her eyes alight.

Gemma smiled for the first time in minutes and nodded. "Yes, Mama. Is that all right with you?"

Her mother's plump face broke out into a beaming smile. "Dearest girl, I could not be more delighted! But is it all right with you? You seem a bit… hesitant."

"Well," Gemma said softly, "I…"

"I cannot believe you all are considering this!" Spencer broke in with a hard laugh. "Blackmoor? He's a murderer!"

Gemma whirled at once. "He is not! How dare you!"

Her handsome brother-in-law sneered viciously. "Has he told you that? Was that part of his courtship? Explaining how all of those rumors got started?"

This was not like Spencer at all, and it puzzled her, but her rage was not going to take the time to ask about it. "If there were any truth to those rumors, don't you think he would be barred from Society?" she retorted.

"It's a fair point," her mother mused in an odd, dreamy tone, turning them both. "Lady Raeburn would never let a real murderer in her house. Her second husband *was* murdered."

Gemma sighed and put a hand to her brow. "No, Mama, that was Lady Hendershot. Lady Raeburn's second husband choked on a bone."

That too-familiar glazed look overtook her mother's features, and Gemma hid another sigh. At one time in her life, Theodora Templeton had been a sharp wit and a great beauty. Now she was a slightly addled, unwell, ridiculous woman with only scant moments of her old self shining through.

"But I thought it was murder," her mother said faintly. "Everyone always said so. Lady Wiltshire's husband died in a duel, Mrs. Campbell's husband had apoplexy…"

"Enough about the widows of London!" Spencer snapped, again acting out of character. "We cannot have Blackmoor in the family! It is entirely unsuitable!"

"For whom?" Gemma responded with a defiant tilt of her chin. "I like Blackmoor. I like him very much. He is a good man, a good friend, and he kisses like an angel."

Spencer sputtered furiously and fumbled over an appropriate response, but Gemma was not about to give him the chance to do so.

"And furthermore," she continued, "he *wants* to marry me. So you may bite your tongue, Spencer Hammond, because nobody asked you!"

He gaped at her for a moment, then looked down at his mother-in-law in disgust. "You cannot agree to this, Theodora. I will speak to Templeton about it before he comes tonight, but you cannot want this for her."

Her mother shrugged, the ribbons of her lace cap bouncing. She picked up her embroidery and sighed, "Well, if the Gerrards think well of him, I am in no position to judge him. He detests Lady Greversham, which makes me think highly of him indeed."

Gemma rested a hand on her mother's shoulder, relief washing over her.

Spencer grunted in irritation. "And when your daughter is dead will you think so highly of him?"

That drew a screech from Gemma and she marched over to shove her brother-in-law, who tumbled backwards into a chair. "You are more likely to die at his hands than I, you blundering blockhead, if you continue to spout your infernal rumors about him! Ask your brother on the subject, and see what the earl says, as they are neighbors!"

With a disgusted huff, she stormed out of the room, more determined than ever that this marriage *would* occur, no matter what London, or her idiot relations, would say.

Spencer watched Gemma march away, and tossed a grin at his mother-in-law, not quite so far gone as anybody thought. "Well, I think I have pushed her far enough."

Theodora chuckled and set her embroidery down. "I'd say so. Any doubts she had about the marriage are quite gone."

He hummed in satisfaction. "Good. Nathan says he's a rare sort of man, and his friends consider him an ally. No matter what the world says, I think Gemma could do worse."

"I'd venture she could not do better," she replied, scratching idly at her cap. "It takes a very patient sort of man to put up with her, and the viscount seems to possess an astonishing amount of patience. Why do you think Gemma's father lets her run wild? He cannot handle her."

Spencer laughed and drew a knee up. "Should I warn Blackmoor, then?" he asked. "Caroline thought it might be necessary."

Theodora shook her head at once, eyes wide, smile bright. "Gads, no. We need the girl married! He can find out afterwards when he cannot escape."

Chapter Seven

There was not much for Lucas to do in the following days, as the wedding plans were swept out of his hands, and he was grateful to give them up.

He'd dealt with one wedding already, he really would prefer not to endure details of another.

He shook his head as he sat back in his chair at his club. He could not compare Celia with Gemma, and he had to avoid ever doing so.

They could not have been more different.

This was not the same thing at all.

He spun the glass in his hand against the table absently, lost in thought. Gemma's family were thrilled to have her married, and seemed equally as delighted by him as the prospective bridegroom, though he failed to see how that could be possible. Her brother-in-law was a bit more wary, but pleasant enough. They'd met occasionally since the engagement, and while he could not yet consider him a friend, he rather thought that one day Spencer Hammond might be among his closest.

He had not yet determined why it was that Gemma edged closer to him when Spencer was around, nor why she glowered at him so, but Spencer always smiled at it, which only made Gemma more irritated.

Mrs. Hammond, her sister, was immediately friendly with him, though it seemed she had been warned by Gemma about his reserve, for she had never been overbearing in her attention to him. He could see the resemblance between the sisters easily, and he could also see why Caroline had always been the more favored of the two in looks.

She was a perfect picture of an English woman, and, even after three children, hardly bore a strain or change in her appearance at all. While she could not have passed for a girl in her early Seasons, she would not have been suspected of motherhood of such a length either.

The relationship between the sisters was strong, but he could see a certain tension in Gemma on occasion, particularly when Caroline would tease her about something or other. Her family seemed to forget her age, and it was not uncommon for them to treat her as one of the older children.

It surprised him that she did not resist any of this, but he suspected she was being a dutiful daughter. Still, he did not like seeing her diminished in such a way, and he would have to do something about that.

It had been an interesting experience for him to see such a family, to become part of it. He'd never known a family with such easy manners and lightness, even if Gemma suffered on occasion for it. Good manners, warmth, and gentility abounded, including the three rowdy children of the Hammonds.

The children adored Gemma, and she them. She was playful, exuberant, and gave each child the individualized attention to make them feel important. It was her nature to be so, and she worked the same magic on him.

He would try to return the favor to her. He might not be the sort of man she deserved to have for her husband, but he would do everything in his power to ensure that she never had reason to regret marrying him.

Society would give her reason enough as it was.

He'd been relieved when Gemma had informed him that she had no desire for banns to be read. She declared she had no need of anyone's approval on the topic but her own, and she was not about to give anyone an excuse to say something. Therefore, he would have to procure a special license for them.

He had been tempted to kiss her quite soundly for that, but as they had been before her family, he'd settled for squeezing her hand. And his heart had felt the same pressure when she had squeezed back.

Gemma had also insisted that they not be married with the haste tied to a special license, and he had agreed. He wanted her to have the full wedding experience she deserved, had she married any other man. Her excuse was that the stigma of a special license was generally that the persons were marrying quickly for suspicious reasons. As she was not ashamed of anything, she proclaimed, she would be married in the same amount of time as anyone else might have.

She was determined to prove a point with her three weeks, and he adored her for it.

Private moments had been few and far between for them since their engagement, and he was beginning to grow desperate for them. Something about his intended rejuvenated him, chased the shadows from his mind, and set him at ease. It was becoming harder and harder to return to himself after leaving her, and most certainly harder to maintain his composure when he was around her.

She was light itself, and he'd had too much of darkness.

But would his darkness overwhelm her? Would she grow dimmer and dimmer under his gloom until nothing of the girl she was remained?

No. He shook his head again, more firmly. No, he would never let himself poison her in such a way. He would take himself away and suffer the rest of his life with the parting from her if he had to, but she would not suffer in such a way.

"You look delighted by your prospects," came a cheery voice.

He looked up to see Kit approaching, and he pushed a nearby chair out with his feet. "I am."

Kit frowned and sat, folding his arms. "I was being facetious."

"I know."

His friend groaned. "Blackmoor, if you don't want to marry her…"

"Why would I not want to marry her?" he demanded, forgoing his usual politeness.

Kit's brows rose, and his mouth worked silently. "Well, I don't…"

"I *do* want to marry her," Lucas insisted firmly. "Very much." He ran a hand through his hair, which made Kit's eyes widen more, as it was so out of character for him. "More than I thought I would have."

"So what is the problem?" Kit asked, his surprise fading into concern.

Lucas managed a hard laugh. "The problem is that I *will* marry her, unfortunately. She's quite determined about it, and I won't try to dissuade her."

Now his friend frowned and leaned forward. "Why so unfortunate? Why should you dissuade her?"

Lucas looked at him for a long moment, disparaging. "Because it's me, Kit."

Understanding crossed Kit's face and he exhaled slowly. "I see."

That said enough of itself. Lucas leaned his elbows on his knees and put his face in his hands. "What am I doing?"

"Taking your chance at happiness, I gather," Kit replied calmly, "and there is no reason why you shouldn't."

Lucas looked up at him in disbelief. "No reason? I can give you several."

Kit shook his head with determination. "No. You have suffered enough, Lucas, and I would venture to say needlessly. I am not about to argue with you about your decisions," he said, holding out a hand to ward off Lucas's forthcoming protests. "You did what you thought was best, and you are somehow still a gentleman despite all of that."

Lucas grunted a dismissal, thinking his friend too kind, but he was hardly going to argue the point now.

"Marry Gemma," Kit urged softly. "You deserve her."

Lucas chewed his lip for a moment and slowly sat back.

"She'd have your head if she knew you were reconsidering," Kit added in an undertone.

Lucas nearly cast his friend a bitter smile. His statement was not only wrong, it was ignorant. Gemma would not have his head; she would be hurt. How hurt, he dared not imagine, but it would be enough to damn him to hell for eternities. She may pretend at boldness for all the rest, and she was indeed an outspoken creature, but she was also in possession of a very soft heart. She'd merely learned how to secure it to the point of near invincibility.

"I'm not reconsidering," he murmured. He couldn't help but to smile as he thought of Gemma becoming his wife. "I'd be an imbecile to not have her as my wife."

"True."

"I only have reservations about the man she's getting for a

husband."

Kit nudged his chair with a boot. "I don't."

Lucas shook his head and toasted his friend, then downed the remainder of his drink. "Will you stand up with me?" he absently inquired as he slid the glass back on the table.

"Of course," came the reply. "I would be honored."

He snorted softly and fidgeted with his cravat.

"And if you want Gemma to enjoy being married to you," Kit drawled easily, "you should probably start considering yourself in a different light. At least out loud."

He flicked his gaze to his friend and saw the warning in the smile. "She'll see my faults soon enough."

"But she doesn't need them magnified beyond their true dimension."

Lucas growled a little uncomfortably. "Why are you being so damned optimistic?"

Kit chuckled and flagged a servant for a drink. "Because you're getting married, Blackmoor, and to a person I happen to like very much. I am filled with good cheer." He grinned and seemed to take great pleasure in his discomfort. "And it is my duty, now that I am a groomsman, to defend and support the bridegroom, even if from himself."

Lucas shook his head and rose, a trifle amused. "So be it. I shall find myself married in another two weeks, and I shall endeavor to enjoy every moment I can."

"And said with such enthusiasm." Kit tilted his head. "You do need Gemma. She'll brighten you up."

"Unless I dampen her," Lucas muttered, scowling again. He nodded to Kit and turned to leave.

He'd made it no more than ten feet before he was stopped by two young dandies he had never seen in the club before, and looked as though they ought to have had parental supervision in this adult place.

They attempted to look intimidating and imposing, but only managed to look ridiculous.

"Can I help you?" Lucas snapped, glancing between the two of them impatiently.

"A word, Blackmoor," the taller one said in his attempt at a gruff voice.

He barely managed to avoid rolling his eyes. "Yes, so I assumed. Pray, get on with it, I have better things to do."

The smaller pup looked rather put out and thrust his chest out more. "We do not like this engagement between you and Miss Templeton."

He quirked a brow. "No? Pity we did not ask you then."

A muted chuckle from behind him colored the lad's cheeks and he looked away.

The first lad glowered at him, then at Blackmoor like a spoiled child. "We will not stand for it, Blackmoor. You shall not have her. You shall not take a girl from our circle."

Slowly he turned his direct and disgusted attention to him. "Oh, really?" he said slowly. "Well, forgive me for not giving the dirt under my boots to care, but as neither of you, nor any other man in England, has seen fit to try for her, I must resign myself to joining whatever circle you think Miss Templeton belongs in. But only long enough for you all to realize that she is far, far above it."

He nodded stiffly and pushed between them with ease, noticing then that the entire room had become aware of the conversation.

"Anyone else have a problem with my engagement?" he demanded, looking about them all.

Eyes were instantly averted, and it was not long before conversations resumed.

Lucas met Kit's eyes across the room, and saw his friend nodding in approval.

Well, that was something.

He returned his nod, and turned from the room, wishing it was not too late to call upon Gemma.

He could have used her soothing touch.

"I think I've made a mistake."

Lucas slowed beside Gemma as they walked the park. "Really?"

His tone sounded discouraged and she looked up at him in confusion. Then she realized how her statement must have sounded and she laughed. "No, no, not about that!" she protested with a smile, holding his arm a little tighter and leaning against him. "I can assure you, I am still marrying you. You'll not lose me that easily."

She did not expect the rush of air that escaped him, nor the muttered, "Thank God," but both made her smile. Silly man, did he truly think she would back out?

He cleared his throat faintly. "Then what mistake have you made?" he asked politely, as if he'd not just displayed more emotion in that moment than he had in their entire first week of courtship.

"Making us wait," she moaned, rolling her eyes. "Mother is going to drive me to my wit's end and you will have an idiot wife."

He made a soft noise of amusement that she had learned to love, and not charge him for. "Well, I can think of worse looking idiots I could be saddled with."

She elbowed him hard and again came the almost-laugh. "I am serious, Lucas!"

His hold tightened at the sound of his name and she smiled. "All right, what has your mother done now?"

"It's our wedding!" Gemma cried, throwing her free hand up. "She's fussing over everything! I've had so many potential wedding dresses that I am tempted to tell her that I shall be married in this muslin rather than any of her grand concoctions. But as it is *your* money, as she points out, why not find something extravagant? Ridiculous woman."

Lucas stepped away to examine her a bit boldly and she blushed at his expression. "You would make a very fine bride dressed just as you are," he murmured. "Very fine."

She found herself giggling and looked away, but tugged him closer to her side. "Stop that," she scolded, her cheeks burning.

"You will have to get used to it, Gemma," he told her, keeping his voice low as a couple and their daughter passed. "Compliments may be infrequent enough for you from other sources, but they will not be so from me."

"Then you shall have a continually blushing idiot wife," she teased.

"I can be content with that," he mused thoughtfully. "My wife has some very pretty blushes."

"Lucas!"

"Yes?"

She laughed merrily at his drollness, and grinned up at him. "You will not let me be distressed, will you?"

His eyes were intense in an instant. "Not for a moment."

Her breath caught in her chest and she was strongly tempted to kiss the man, but they were in public, and she doubted he would have appreciated the display.

The action, perhaps, but not the display.

He knew her mind, she saw, for his throat worked once and then he looked away and their pace quickened ever so slightly.

"At any rate," Gemma said as brightly as she could when she recovered herself, "I should not be surprised that my mother cannot decide which gown suits me best. Everything works against me in this."

Lucas glanced over at her. "What exactly do you mean by 'everything'?"

She shrugged her shoulders, smiling. "The current styles in high fashion do not suit my frame and form. Not all bodies were created equal, I'm afraid."

Lucas suddenly stopped and turned to look at her, his expression cloudy. "Explain."

Curious as to his brusqueness, Gemma slipped her arm from his. "I am…" she began, hesitating. "I am not exactly the shape of the ideal woman."

A furrow formed between his brows for a moment, and he took her arm, his hold surprisingly gentle as he steered her off of the path and into a nearby stand of trees.

"Lucas?"

He shook his head, and released her when they were secluded. He stared at her for a long moment, shaking his head.

"What?" she asked, rubbing her arms.

"I have always found the notion of the ideal woman to be

ridiculous," he said in a low voice.

She cocked her head and leaned against a tree. "Have you?"

He nodded slowly. "Who is to say what is ideal and what is not? Perhaps if all men had the exact same preferences, it would make sense, but they don't, and it doesn't."

He walked to the edge of the stand of trees and looked out at the Serpentine. "Who is to say that a man may not prefer a tall woman over the classically short? Why should a figure be a certain way and all women must strive for it? Dark haired or pale; slender or voluptuous; finely dressed or simple; plain or exquisite… What does it matter? What does any of it truly matter?"

Gemma watched him as he spoke, his deep voice almost melodious in its speech, his expression far away. Had any man ever been so handsome in reflection?

"We like what we like," he continued, shaking his head. "Why find fault where there is none? Just because it is not to our preference does not make it wrong. Beauty is in the eye of the beholder, and each one may behold something very different."

He paused and leaned an arm against a tree, his expression now half hidden from her.

"None of it truly matters. Outward appearance is not the crux of any woman." His voice suddenly sounded harsh, almost cold. "There have been many a great beauty with a heart of stone. Evil to the core, manipulative and cruel. Nothing of beauty or worthy of praise in them at all." He swallowed harshly and straightened a little. "And some of the plainest women I know have been more beautiful at heart than a diamond of the first water. That is not to say, I suppose, that all beauty is to be distrusted, not in the least. But there is more to a woman than whether she fits within the constraints of what a group of airheaded fools think to be ideal."

Gemma bit her lip, wondering if she should interject yet.

"The only ideal I can find," Lucas said on a sigh, "is whether or not a woman suits a man. Appearance, figure, form, nature, all taken together, does she meet with his preferences and needs? Is her heart what ought to be? Does she make him strive to be better? If she does, in those respects, who can tell him that she is not ideal simply because she is shorter than average or anything else?" Again, he shook his head, his expression distant and stark. "More than what a man wants, however, is how she sees herself. If we have confined women to think they must meet certain standards in looks or fashions or accomplishment, then we have done them all a great disservice. A woman ought to be as she is, with no one to tell her she is imperfect for being such."

Gemma found herself unaccountably emotional, and she had to swallow several times before speaking was possible. "Do you know, Blackmoor," she finally managed, "I think I like you very much."

He blinked and the shadows vanished as he turned his head to look at her, a faint smile forming, but not quite reaching his eyes. "Well, that is a relief, considering you've already agreed to marry me."

She laughed softly and pushed off the tree, advancing carefully. "I've never heard you speak so much at once," she told him lightly. "What on earth prompted such a speech from you, sir?"

He turned as she reached him and held out a hand, which she took at once. "My betrothed seemed to think she was somehow lacking. And it was my duty to assure her that she is not."

She smiled up at him and stepped closer. "I never said I was lacking," she chided. "Merely that I do not meet the shape of today's ideal woman. Not all fashions are suitable for every form, and others not suitable for my taste." She winked, which made him smile. "I rather like being a little short and having a little more to my figure than others. And while my face not be as pretty as others, my smile suits it perfectly."

Lucas reached out to touch her cheek, where the corner of her smile lived. "Indeed it does, my dear." His fingers brushed lightly against her skin, and he laid his hand alongside her face. "I find you to be perfectly ideal, Gemma. I need you to know that."

Impulsively, she leaned more fully into his hand. "Nobody's ever said that to me before."

"It should have been told to you every single day," he whispered harshly. "I should not be able to have you."

"But you do," she said simply, daring to reach out and touch the lapels of his coat, "and I am glad for it."

Something flashed in his eyes and she was pulled to him suddenly, his lips finding hers in an instant. His free hand soon joined the first on her face and curved perfectly around it, gripping her hair slightly. His lips were insistent, demanding and powerful, and she clung to him for fear of wilting under the intensity. She tried in vain to match him, somehow unable to grasp the emotion and passion she could feel from him, and the distress her failure raised within her was acute.

He must have sensed it, for he soon gentled and soothed her, then wrapped his arms tightly around her, resting his chin on the top of her head.

"Someday I will learn to kiss you properly," she muttered against him.

"You kiss me any more properly than that, love, and we will need to be married much quicker than two weeks from now," he returned with a laugh, his arms tightening.

She snickered and buried her face against his coat.

She felt him kiss her hair and smiled at it.

"Find a gown that suits *your* taste, Gemma," he murmured. "Not your mother's. I don't care if she likes it or not. I don't even care if it is the simplest day dress. Nothing matters to me but that you will be my wife by the end."

Gemma pulled back to look up at him, smiling gently. "I will, Lucas. You'll not be rid of me."

He smiled and kissed her again, this time lightly. "Good."

She narrowed her eyes at him for a moment. "Why are you marrying me? It is not save me from destitution, is it?"

He reared back in surprise, his arms still fixed around her. "Is that what you think?"

She shrugged, no longer afraid to ask. "Only wondering. It doesn't change my mind one way or another. But I am curious, as you've been around for all of my Seasons, and nothing prompted you before."

He shook his head, exhaling. "No, Gemma, I am not marrying you to save your fortunes. It was nothing about money, I promise. I am marrying you for no other reason than because you are you, and I cannot resist that."

She laughed and took his hand, pulling him out of the stand of trees. "You are getting to be nonsensical, and I can't have that. I am to be the mad one, not you."

Lucas followed, his hold on her hand secure. "Why are you marrying me, then?"

She gave him a rather coy look. "Because you are an attractive and eligible bachelor who offered, and I rather enjoy making you smile. My chances of doing so are far greater if I marry you."

"Indeed they will be." He looked speculative and his lips quirked. "So you are marrying me for *my* money, is it? For your precious wager?"

"Perhaps." She sighed and took his arm. "But you've proven yourself more than your money, and I am inclined to consider us well suited."

He shook his head and looked away. "Oh, my dear Miss Templeton, what am I going to do with you?"

"Whatever you like, I should think," she said happily. She frowned in thought and looked up at him. "Why are you marrying now at all, Blackmoor? You've never done anything to indicate you wished to marry again."

His jaw tightened and he was suddenly tense. "Things change."

"What things? Not you, surely."

"Just… things." He swallowed and said, "Don't ask me, Gemma. Please."

It was then that she realized that there were some things in her betrothed's life that she might not be privy to, now or perhaps ever. He liked her, and very much, from what she could tell. He had revealed more to her than she had ever expected, but there was more, so much more. She could see it in his eyes, in every feature, in the stiff posture he adopted in such moments. He could not share it, and that pained her.

Someday, she vowed, he would trust her enough to let her in.

But for now, she would let him hide that place, so long as he did not live there.

"What shall you wear to the wedding? Shall I ask my mother to help you find something suitable as well?" she asked brightly, moving past the darkness, grinning at his accompanying groan.

Chapter Eight

*I*t had been a perfect day for a wedding. Abundant sunshine, clear blue skies, and warmer than average, and the wedding itself had been full of guests who seemed to truly wish them well.

None of those things had kept Lucas's palms from sweating or his throat from feeling constricted by the proverbial noose, but it was noted all the same.

Only a handful of the people at the church had been there for him. The relatives that nobody knew about; Marlowe and his associates, though none of them sat near each other; former schoolmates that he would not have missed but had been pressed to invite… Kit had stood with him, and his wife had sat with the rest of their friends, whom he supposed he could count as his own, though his association with them was limited at best.

He cared little for any of that. He could have done with a small ceremony in a drawing room with only a minister and witnesses. The fuss and noise, the flowers and the church, the guests and this ridiculous spectacle of a breakfast, were all endurable, however, for the woman that was now his wife.

She was a vision; his very own ray of sunshine. Her gown had been of a simple form, but of the highest quality and suited her to perfection. She had informed him a few days before that she and her mother were both satisfied with it, which was a miracle, and she had conceded to the slightly more detailed veil, to please her mother and sister.

He echoed their wishes, just this once.

Had any bride stolen the breath from her husband in such a

manner?

Her brilliant smile had lit into him as fire, and he could scarce believe that this woman, a far more bewitching and delightful creature than he had ever predicted, would have found something in him worth admiring. And to consent to marry him, beyond that! To be paired with her forever, to see such a vision of cheer and loveliness daily… Could he ever hope to deserve such a privilege?

The rational man within him knew that all of this would fade, that it was only the newness of it and the surprise of being so fortunate. Once this day, and the days following, had commenced, it would all become routine and mundane. He was fully aware of that. This was only sentimentality flooding him, and it, too, could pass. He could even admit, though it irked him, that Celia had been a more classically beautiful bride than Gemma.

His first wedding day had been overcast, ironically enough, and far more grand of a spectacle, which he had expected, given her tastes and her family.

This, all of it, was far more suitable.

He watched Gemma as she mingled with guests at the wedding breakfast, milling about and smiling brightly for everyone. She had rid herself of the veil and excesses, and no one knowing she was the bride would ever have guessed, but for the flowers dotting her golden hair. He'd given her the family diamonds to wear, and they suited her far more perfectly than he'd thought.

He'd not recollected the diamonds until recently, and as soon as he had, he'd wanted Gemma to have them. There was not much of his mother's that was worth passing on, but these he treasured. And Gemma had borne them with such reverence, though she knew nothing of his mother or the past, never knew just where the jewels had come from or their significance. She only knew they had been his mother's, and that had caused emotion enough.

And he'd never informed Celia of their existence.

He had an inkling of what that meant for him, but refused to dwell on it.

Could he really keep the darkness of his life from tainting his new wife? There was so much, too much, and now that he knew her well, cared for her more than he thought possible, he hated himself for the prospect before them.

He'd expected several voices to protest the wedding, yet none had. Gemma had given her vows with clear answers and bright eyes, and a teasing wink for him as he gave his own. Their kiss had been sweet and stirring, despite the polite briefness, and her soft sigh of delight had nearly buckled his knees.

She was too good for him. Too good, too much, and it was impossible to imagine life with her as his wife.

It was more impossible to imagine any life without her.

He was trapped between heaven and hell and there was nothing to do about it.

Gemma looked over at him from where she was and her smile softened. She continued to listen to the others, but her eyes never left him.

Slowly, his weight and anxiety ebbed away, and his breathing came easier. Doubts and fears faded to the background of his mind, the future and all its facets vanished, and all he could see was his lovely, vibrant, vivacious wife, radiant with joy.

How did she know he had needed the relief that only she could provide?

When had she become the only consolation that could reach him?

He felt himself exhale, the last of his tension evaporating from his shoulders. Gemma saw it, and her smile grew just a touch. She held out a hand, tilting her head in question.

He was moving to her side before he decided he wanted to, and seized her hand at once.

Collecting himself, he gently brought it to his lips, and turned to pretend to join in the conversation, tucking Gemma's hand safely in his arm.

It seemed her relatives had come out of the woodwork for her wedding, though none had ever given her a moment's thought before, from what he could tell. She did not seem to mind, nor did she question his lack of family in attendance.

When would the questions start? He knew they would have to at some point, she was far too curious and intuitive to let things go entirely. But how long would her patience hold out?

And when the day did come, what would he say?

"You're drifting," she murmured, tugging at his arm.

He shook himself and looked down at her. "Was I?"

She nodded, rubbing the place where her hand rested. "What's troubling you?"

He opened his mouth to deny it, but stopped when he caught her expression. She knew him as well as anyone in the world, for all his secrecy and reserve, and she would not believe him. He shook his head slightly. "The past is haunting me, I fear," he finally said, covering her hand with his.

She twisted her hand to intertwine their fingers. "Don't let it, Lucas," she pleaded, looking up into his eyes. "Not today."

He gave her a regretful look. "It's not something I can easily dismiss."

She sighed and touched his jaw with her free hand. "I'll get rid of those shadows, just see if I don't." Her voice was fierce and a little sad, and he couldn't have that.

He turned to kiss those fingers, and felt his lips curve. "If anyone can, it's you."

She brightened, and her expression turned teasing. "Won't you smile on our wedding day?"

He reached out and touched her cheek. "Does it count that I feel like smiling whenever I look at you?"

She beamed and leaned closer. "Not for the wager, but it certainly counts with your wife."

"Well, as her opinion is all I care about," he told her in a very low tone, brushing his lips across hers, "I can be content with that."

Gemma made a soft noise, and pulled back, her eyes narrowing. "You still should smile. You wouldn't want people to think you are displeased with me, would you?"

He snorted. "I just kissed you in public. Is anyone going to question that?"

She shrugged, her golden tendrils of hair bouncing near her ears. "How should I know? People question all sorts of things, but never a smile."

His lips quirked, and he shook his head slowly. "Oh, Gemma, what am I going to do with you?"

"You keep asking me that, and I keep saying you may do whatever you please," she responded lightly, turning him so they might go speak with others. "What is it about me that seems to confuse you?"

"I ask myself that daily."

"And?"

"And I married you."

"Poor man."

"Thank you."

She elbowed him swiftly and he laughed in spite of the pain, which made several turn in surprise. Gemma, however, only beamed in delight and held his arm tighter, keeping him close by her side at all times.

And he almost smiled for the rest of the day.

"Tell me again."

"Gemma, we will be there any minute."

She glowered and poked her husband in the side. "Lucas Sinclair, you made me spend my wedding night in an inn. The least you can do is tell me more about the house where we will be staying for the next two weeks."

He grabbed her hand and yanked it from his body, holding it tightly in his much larger hands, and giving her a mock severe look. "I didn't make you do anything, Lady Blackmoor," he said pointedly. "I remember distinctly asking if you wanted to push on to Thornacre and arrive around breakfast or if you wanted to stay at an inn for the night. You wanted the bed instead of the carriage, that is not my fault."

She frowned at him and tried to pull her hand away, but he held it fast. "You were supposed to claim husbandly authority and tell me to shush and do as I'm told."

He laughed once. "I'll never tell you to shush and do as you're told, and even if I did, you would never do as you were told."

"That is beside the point."

He pulled her hand to rest it on his chest, over his heart, and she stilled at the warm, steady cadence beneath his shirt. "You didn't seem to mind," he said softly, his eyes trained on her face, though her eyes were fixed on her hand. "I don't remember hearing a single word of complaint."

She flushed until she was sure her face was scarlet.

She hadn't minded. Not in the least.

And she'd only slept in the same bed as her husband, curled against him. It wasn't the typical wedding night, given what did *not* transpire, but her husband… it still sent odd shivers of delight and disbelief through her to call him that… insisted on taking her all the way to their estate before that took place. And she was grateful for the additional time to prepare herself.

But she could not deny that she had been a little… well, disappointed.

For all his saying she lacked nothing and was his ideal, she knew full well she was not particularly desirable. She only wished her husband, who viewed her with such intensity and depth, who kissed her so delightfully, had been different in that regard.

This morning had improved matters somewhat, as Lucas had been rather demonstrative in his attempts to wake her, and she could quite get used to mornings if the pattern was to be followed.

And the playful mood of her husband today as they travelled boded well for her this evening. Assuming it took place.

"You're somewhere far away," Lucas murmured, touching her chin. "Tell me."

There was absolutely no way that she was going to tell him that she was thinking about the night before them, though the color of her cheeks probably did that for her.

"Gemma…"

She looked away, focusing her gaze out of the window. "It's nothing."

He replaced his fingers on her chin and turned her face back towards him, his expression serious. "No, it's not," he said, shaking his head. "Don't hide from me, tell me."

"I just hope that I…" She broke off, biting down on her lip, then lowered her eyes in her embarrassment. "I hope that I can… please you. As your wife. That you won't be disappointed with me. In anything I do."

His hold on her chin was suddenly harder and he tilted her chin up more, his eyes suddenly blazing. "Is *that* what you think?" he asked. "That last night… That I wasn't…" He could not seem to find the words and his evident distress both comforted and worried her.

"I'm sorry," she whispered with wince.

"Don't be sorry!" he cried, releasing her chin and taking her arms. "Gemma, I…" He laughed breathlessly and shook her the smallest bit. "I am already beyond pleased with you as my wife. I could never be disappointed in you, and as for *that*… I was trying to make you comfortable and be understanding. I can assure you, I want you in every way that a man should want his wife, and when we get to Thornacre, you will understand *exactly* what that means."

The promise in his words made her heart race and her cheeks heat and she giggled nervously. "Should I be nervous?" she asked between giggles.

He yanked her to him and kissed her hard, and quite thoroughly. "Yes," he rasped against her lips. "You probably should. It will be a very short tour of the house."

She reared back, eyes wide. "What, you mean… You mean not tonight?"

He slowly shook his head, a rather wicked smile forming. "Not tonight. Or rather… not waiting until tonight. My wife seems to doubt my affections, and I cannot have that."

Gemma swallowed hastily and raised a hand to her cheek. "Remind me to keep my mouth shut more often, and to never, ever, provoke you."

He laughed and pulled her into his arms, enveloping her. "I like you just as you are, Gemma." He kissed the top of her head, and let her feel the frantic pace of his heart. "And I rather liked sharing my bed with you last night."

She snuggled into his chest, smiling and sighing. "It was rather nice, wasn't it? We should do that more often."

"Every night, I think."

She gave a hard laugh and shook her head. "Not every night, surely."

Lucas tightened his arms. "Every night," he repeated firmly.

She glanced up at him curiously. "Married couples have separate bedchambers, Blackmoor."

He returned her look. "We don't. I have no desire to spend a night away from you." He hesitated, then added, "Unless you truly want them."

Her breath caught at the open, hungry expression, and she felt herself melting just a little at his uncertainty about her wishes. She arched up to cup his cheek and kiss him, which she could tell pleased him.

"Together, then," she whispered, stroking his jaw. "Though we may scandalize everybody if it gets out."

He flashed her a grin that nearly blinded her in its brilliance. "I already scandalize everybody. It will be nice to have some company from now on."

That drew forth laughter and she nestled against him with a smile. "Tell me about Thornacre again. Why have I never heard of it?"

"Because no one ever comes there," he replied as he slowly ran his hands up and down her back. "It has been in the family for centuries, and it has been a long time since anyone inhabiting was interested in company. Considering the reputations of the families, it was hardly a place anyone wished to see."

"What reputations?" she asked, leaning her chin against him to look up. "I only know yours."

His jaw tightened and he shook his head. "It is too involved to go into now, but we've not been a popular set for some time. However, the house is without blemish despite our best efforts."

Gemma frowned at his dark tone, but he was studiously avoiding looking at her, and it went unmarked. She sighed with a bit of resignation and nudged him. "Go on, tell me about it. Is it very grand?"

He relaxed and one hand began tracing circles on her back and shoulders. "Yes, I'm afraid it is. And spacious. The grounds are some of the finest in Hampshire, if I may be permitted to admit it."

"I think you may," she quipped with a grin. "I've only seen Beverton House in Hampshire, and it's very pretty, but slightly wild."

Lucas grunted and glanced out of the window. "We are not so wild at Thornacre, but the tone is roughly the same. The house could not be more different from the stately edifice of Beverton House, but... Well, see for yourself." He inclined his head towards the window and Gemma clambered over him excitedly, drawing a low chuckle from him.

She drew in a sharp breath at the sight that met her eyes.

The pale limestone glinted in the bright sunlight, and the massive building seemed to glow with it. It was the sort of place every girl dreamed of seeing, with tall windows and turrets and gables and columns as far as the eye could see. It seemed to be the perfect combination of ancient castle and romantic country estate. Queen Elizabeth herself might have lived in such a place, or any of the Tudors, should they have been so inclined.

The grounds were as breathtaking as the house, and the gardens she could see were immaculate and pristine, every detail exact and perfectly suited to the house. The house itself spread out before her as far as she could crane her neck as they pulled into the elegant circle drive, seeming out of place and time in its appearance and beauty.

And this was now to be *hers*?

"Well?" Lucas asked in a low, amused tone, nudging her with his knee.

She slowly turned to look at him, not bothering to hide her astonishment. "You live in a castle?"

He smiled at her, which did nothing for the anticipation swirling within her stomach. "*We* live in a castle. For now."

Slowly, a wild grin spread across her face. "I think I rather like being married to you, Blackmoor."

He threw his head back and laughed heartily, and her heart fairly sang with a grand orchestra of joy at the sight and sound. "I am delighted that thirty hours of marriage has given you such pleasure," he said as his laughter subsided, shaking his head as the carriage stopped and a footman stepped forward to open the door.

Gemma glanced out of the now open door to see an army of servants streaming out and forming perfect lines. She looked back at Lucas a little agape. "It comes with people in it, too?"

Lucas snorted and tapped her nose. "Cheeky. You'll have to get used to excesses, Lady Blackmoor. We may not be elaborate, but there is no scrimping here."

"I think I can manage that," she muttered as he disembarked and reached for her.

He helped her down and proudly led her to the staff, introducing her to the butler, a somber but pleasant looking man named Hardy, and the housekeeper, Mrs. Riggle, who had warm eyes and a kind smile. The rest of the servants were resolutely emotionless, but could not contain the curiosity from their gazes as they looked at her.

Lucas said a few brief words, then led Gemma into the house, and she very much feared she would injure her neck as she tried to catch everything.

Even the doors to the house were ancient, yet in perfect order. They could have very well been Queen Anne's own doors, but far more masculine… King James, perhaps.

Lucas did not give her time to examine the door, however, as he tugged her along, her hand tight in his. Their hats and cloaks were taken and the servants began their duties, unloading carriages or returning to whatever they had been doing before. Gemma tried to take in the vestibule, a grand marble expanse that prompted soft voices and reverent tones, but she was soon tugged along once more.

"I want a tour!" she insisted, resisting the agitated pull of her husband.

He stopped and looked back at her. "A tour?" he asked.

She nodded firmly. "This place is magnificent, Lucas. Beyond imagination. I want to see it. And you promised."

His brow furrowed and his mouth became a thin line. "Right." He turned back and continued to pull her through the house. "The tour. Entrance hall." He waved his hand as they entered a majestic and vast room with unconscionable ceiling height and dark wooden paneling.

"Hallway," he said with the same faint gesture as they passed one. "Sitting room. Portraits. Stairs. And up the stairs…" He paused before the grand staircase and turned, quirking one brow at her.

She looked at him in disbelief, a wild urge to laugh forming within her. "Are you serious?"

His expression was serious and polite, but the smile that played at his lips was anything but. "The next floor is truly remarkable. You must see it."

Gemma folded her arms, unable to resist smiling at him. "What are you doing?"

He raised his brows in mock surprise. "Being husbandly. I took vows. Love, honor, cherish, seduce…"

She let out a surprised and breathless laugh. "That is not one of them!"

He shrugged. "I think it's implied." He inclined his head towards the stairs, starting towards her. "You'd better start moving."

Nervous and wild energy flooded her as she started backwards up the stairs, with him slowly pursuing her, a hunter stalking his prey. "I don't know where I'm going!" she managed, giddy and quite sure she would stumble over her own feet if he kept this up.

He seemed to give that just a moment of thought, his eyes never once leaving hers. "This is true. In that case…"

Without warning, he scooped her into his arms and carried her the rest of the way up the stairs, without any difficulty at all.

And she was laughing far too much to protest.

Chapter Nine

$\mathcal{A}$s it turned out, it was another day and a half before Gemma got the tour she had been hoping for. Not that she minded, for she had been quite pleasantly occupied during that time, and she was convinced without any trouble that married life quite suited her.

Or perhaps it was simply her husband.

Lucas had been transformed by their time here already, becoming playful and attentive, smiling and easy and warm. Yet he was still the same man who had courted her, the same one she had married. Now, it seemed, he was… more.

And she was reeling with delight at every revelation and insight into his soul.

He took her around Thornacre eventually, with her incessant prodding, and proved to be a very thorough and well-informed guide. He knew nearly every detail of the house, the restorations, the history, amusing stories… and what he didn't know, Hardy did. Gemma felt almost like an outsider as she wandered along the grand rooms and halls, afraid to touch anything or behave improperly for fear of being dismissed.

Lucas seemed to know, and did everything in his power to put her at ease.

"I'll be all right," she had assured him with a loving pat to his chest. "It will only take some time to adjust. I've been living in a far different manner my entire life, and this is all… overwhelming."

He hadn't liked that, and invited her to rearrange the sitting room in which they had been in.

She'd tried to demur, saying it was perfectly arranged as it was, but he refused adamantly.

"I don't want it to be perfect," he'd informed her. "I want it to be yours. Then it *will* be perfect."

That had earned him a sound kiss and a bit of distraction before she'd gone ahead with moving things around.

Since then, she'd been invited to rearrange anything she liked and even refurbish some of the more outdated rooms.

Mrs. Riggle had been pleased with that idea, as she had apparently wished for some updating, and they were to discuss ideas and suggestions whenever her husband decided to let her out of his sight.

It hadn't happened yet.

But she was not about to complain about that either.

The only thing Gemma was not permitted to change were the gardens, and that was completely out of Lucas's hands. The head gardener, a Mr. Chase, was fiercely protective of the gardens and grounds, and apparently lorded over them all. Not even his lord and master could exert authority over him where they were concerned. Suggestions were welcome, but could also easily be ignored.

Apparently one got used to this, but it seemed the oddest sort of arrangement.

But as the gardens and grounds were incomparable, no one was willing to argue the point.

Thornacre was perhaps even more magical than she had initially thought, Gemma considered as she wandered some of the house she had not seen yet. There were secrets here, and she was wild to uncover them. While the outside of the house seemed a mystical castle, the interiors were surprisingly modern in their tastes. Some of the details were older and there were some wonderful relics and tributes to years and family members past, but for the most part, it was not unlike other fine country estates she had seen.

Though none were of this caliber and high quality.

That caused a stirring of pride within her, and she glanced over at Lucas to tell him, only to find him staring at the one of the portraits in the gallery in which they were standing.

She followed his gaze to the portrait in question, and it was of a beautiful woman, her eyes and hair as dark as the night, her complexion nearly exotic in coloring. Gemma had never seen anyone as exquisitely arrayed with natural beauty in her entire life. And she bore a curious smile, as if she knew a joke that no one else did.

Lucas was fixated on her, his expression vacant but for the deep furrows between his brows.

Gemma looked between the two, and though she suspected she knew the identity of the woman, she was not at all tempted to ask about it. The look on his face was enough.

She wandered further down the gallery, and found a portrait of a very young Lucas. She knew it was him, as she had seen representations of his brother and the two hardly resembled each other. She smiled at the serious nature of her husband in the painting, even as a child.

She glanced down the gallery at Lucas, and he was still staring at the portrait. Gemma frowned, then laughed, clearing her throat. "Good heavens, Blackmoor, is this you?" she called.

That shook him from his reverie and his expression cleared as he came to her, looking at the painting. He winced, but took her hand and held it close to him. "Yes, unfortunately. Surly child, am I not?"

She laughed, half with relief that he was returned to her and half amusement at his words. "You are darling."

He snorted, his thumb absently stroking her hand. "Hardly. I look like an old man."

Gemma turned to face him and took his other hand in hers, interlacing their fingers. "Well, I hope that our sons look just like you," she murmured, going up on her toes to capture his lips in a gentle, teasing kiss.

He hummed a little and followed her as she lowered herself, kissing her twice more, and taking his time to do so. "I hope all of the children look like you, love," he replied, with the faintest of third kisses.

She shivered and pulled away just slightly, exhaling dramatically. "I don't know that I will ever get used to that," she mused, smiling up at him.

He chuckled and tugged her back until she was flush against him. "I hope not. And yet I hope so. I hope you get used to not being used to it. To me."

Gemma bit her lip, shaking her head. "You, dear husband, are the best sort of puzzle."

He quirked his brows and sighed, looking around the room. "Let's find somewhere else to be. The gallery makes me uneasy."

She frowned in confusion, but let him pull her away.

Her puzzling husband was certainly allowed his mysteries.

Someday, perhaps, he would trust her with his shadows.

But for now, this was enough.

"Where to?" she asked brightly, holding his arm and playing with their twined fingers. "We've seen the entire house, haven't we?"

He squeezed her hand, unconsciously pleased with her change in subject. "How would the stables do for you? We have some of the finest, and our horses are the best quality. You could ride any of your choice."

She wrinkled up her nose and clicked her tongue. "I don't know how to ride."

He paused and looked down at her in surprise. "You don't?"

She shook her head, shrugging. "We don't have a country house, remember? We've been in London as long as I can remember, and though I visit Beverton House occasionally and other estates when invited, I've never ridden. I always found a reason to avoid it to prevent having to explain myself."

He looked at her closely, his eyes warm and surprisingly tender. "Would you like to learn?"

She nodded, suddenly shy. "Would you teach me?"

"Of course." He kissed her nose. "It would be my pleasure. Any excuse to put my hands on your ankles. Or any part of you."

She barked a laugh and stepped out of his tempting hold. "You are incorrigible. What has come over you?"

He shrugged, smiling easily as they left the gallery. "Perhaps I enjoy being married to you."

She grinned and allowed him to take her hand again. "I enjoy being married to you as well. Though it's been less than a week, that's hardly enough time for anything."

"I mean to improve with time." He sobered as they descended the back stairs. "I cannot promise that being married to me will always be like this, Gemma. But I intend to live in this interlude for as long as possible."

She looked up at him, touched at his soft admission. Despite the brief nature of their courtship and nearly as brief tenure of their acquaintance, she had come to know him better than she'd known another living soul on the earth except for her family. Even then, she felt she knew him better.

He would never have admitted something so emotional before.

And that said a great deal about their relationship.

"So do I," she murmured. Then she tilted her head at him. "Are you trying to disillusion me already, my lord? Are you not the majestic man I've imagined you to be?"

His smile was swift and vanished with the same speed. "No, you must have misunderstood. I intend for you to always see me with a bit of a halo, slightly aglow whenever I enter a room, and in possession of no faults at all."

She nodded obediently, pretending to think on it. "I shall endeavor to perceive such things all my days, provided I am not blinded by your brilliance. And how shall you see me, my lord?"

He stopped and looked her over with the same intensity and thoroughness that robbed her of sense whenever he employed it. He shook his head.

"What?" she asked softly.

"You are sunlight," he replied in soft tones. "Loveliness and goodness, as bright as a morning in spring. And my better half by far and away. There is nothing to be disillusioned about there. Only truth."

She blushed and turned away, pulling on his hand to continue walking. It was not uncommon for him to say extraordinary things like that, but the hearing never got easier. And when they were not in their bedchamber, wrapped in each other's arms, it was more difficult to hear. There, at least, he might be excused his effusive views of her. Out here in the open, proper and composed, it was too much.

She believed him, absolutely; Lucas was no flatterer and was incapable of exaggeration. He truly meant every lovely and touching thing he said to her. But compliments and such lofty sentiments were a weight on her, and an odd choking sensation accompanied them. Flustered and blushing, she would search for anything to shift topics to something less dangerous and disconcerting.

And Lucas knew it.

"You also are the best bedmate I've ever enjoyed," he added lightly, drawing her hand up to kiss it. "I should have married you ages ago. I am almost faint with anticipation for tonight."

"Lucas!"

"Did you know you talk in your sleep?" he asked in response. "Very entertaining. You recited poetry last night. It was lovely, particularly when you snored in the middle."

Inordinately pleased by his lightness, and growing ever more delighted by his teasing, she giggled and leaned against him, letting him lead her wherever he wanted to.

Yes, married life suited her quite well.

It did not take long at all for Gemma to pick up the fundamentals of riding, and even less than that for her to be comfortable upon the horse itself. He had walked beside her as the stable master led the horse around the paddock, and he'd kept his hand on her leg the entire time.

For balance, of course.

He mentally grinned at the blatant lie. He would use any excuse he needed to touch her. He couldn't help it, any more than he could suddenly smile with ease.

Gemma was turning him into a much younger version of himself, but even that was a stretch, for he had never been like this.

He loved being married to her, though she was right that it was barely enough time for anything, and he knew everything would change with time. But he intended to enjoy this bliss while he could.

He would let the sunlight warm him.

The clouds would return soon enough.

Gemma had finally begged him to ride with her and to venture beyond the paddock, to see more of the estate. He'd had to remind her that she was not in a riding habit, only to be told quite pertly that as she had never ridden before, she did not *have* a riding habit.

Properly put in his place, he'd had his horse saddled and brought out, and now they rode together, slowly for her pace, but he was content with it.

He could have done without the stable master asking if his injuries were healed enough to ride, considering Gemma had been nearby and heard it, but the man had not pressed when Lucas had nodded in response.

Now they ambled along the property, not far enough to visit tenants, but enough that they could no longer see the house, thanks to the rolling hills and lush countryside.

"Why did Mr. Fletcher ask about injuries?" Gemma finally asked him, having dispensed with her cheery chattering minutes before.

Lucas closed his eyes and exhaled through his nose. How was this conversation going to proceed? Did he tell her everything that had transpired from the injuries? Did he tell her nothing?

He could not lie. He would not.

Lies had played enough part in his life without his adding to them.

"Lucas?"

He looked over at his young wife, knowing the moment he saw her face that he would tell her the truth. All of it.

"Seven months ago," he began, keeping his voice controlled and as easy as he could manage, "I was riding the estate, and riding hard. No reason, just mad and desperate to do something wild. I led my horse through trees and over jumps, growing more and more reckless. Then a neighbor shot a rifle without warning, and the horse threw me at the largest jump. I could have broken my neck, but somehow managed to only injure my back and my leg."

"Lucas!" Gemma gasped, wide eyed and suddenly raking her gaze over him as if the injuries were fresh.

He smiled tightly, her late concern oddly touching for its uselessness. "I couldn't move, but I had feeling in all my extremities, so I felt some consolation there. It was only when the horse returned itself to the stables and people came looking that I truly felt the pain, as they had to move me. I didn't know it at the time, but I had several lacerations that could have been dangerous, had they become infected."

"Where?" Gemma whimpered, holding her reigns limply.

He gestured to his left side. "Across the back and hip here, and the leg." He winced in recollection. "I fractured the leg and possibly the hip, and was bedridden for weeks. It was agony. I refused laudanum."

"Why?" she cried, the thought apparently distressful. "Why would you do that?"

He shook his head, not ready to reveal that much of his dark past. "It makes no difference, but I would not take it. So I was left to endure it without that, and most of the lacerations needed stitching, so there were tugs and pulls and bandages, and…" He shook his head in disgust. "All because I decided to act out against nature and myself. But it led me to some good."

Gemma gasped and sputtered. "What good? Darling, you must have been in anguish!"

His head swam at hearing her call him 'darling', and he sidled up next to her and took her hand carefully. "I am well now, love," he soothed. "The scars are barely noticeable. I hardly feel anything."

Her brows snapped together. "Hardly?"

"It does twinge on occasion," he admitted reluctantly.

She tossed her head and her jaw tightened. "I am seeing to them tonight, no excuses."

He almost grinned at the thought. "If you insist."

She narrowed her eyes at him, but her lips quirked. "Insolent man. Well, are you able to ride without pain?"

"Not a single twinge," he assured her. "I can do everything. And anything."

Her mouth quirked again, and he suddenly had a glimpse of what frustration she must have felt trying to get him to smile. She refused to do so now, and it was maddening.

"Now, tell me what good," she said primly, her eyes severe. "I don't believe it."

He sighed and looked away again. "That experience was what prompted me to think seriously about marriage. I had nearly thrown my life away, and no one would care. The estate would pass to my idiot cousin Lewis, and all would be ruined. I had worked too hard for that, and… I didn't want to be alone anymore. I needed to marry and have an heir, and soon."

He didn't have to look at her to know that she had stiffened in her saddle.

"So that is why you suddenly pursued me right at the start of the Season," she finally said, her voice as stiff as her posture.

There was really no way around that but to answer. "Yes."

"I asked you why you wanted to marry me, and you said it was because I am me. Was that true?"

He turned almost fully in the saddle to look at her. "Yes. It was always going to be you, Gemma. I couldn't… I could not imagine anyone else."

She watched him with steady eyes, and it frightened him. He'd just borne his soul a little and she had no response?

"But the prompting for it was the desperation for a wife and an heir." Her tone was clipped, and he swallowed hastily, nodding in response.

She huffed and rolled her eyes. "Well, why didn't you just tell me that? I am perfectly capable of bearing an heir, why not tell me?"

"I didn't want you to think I was courting you for your breeding abilities," he muttered with no small amount of chagrin. His motives were honest, but now they seemed rather… weak.

Gemma snorted softly. "Oh, you fair flatterer. But now I know what is expected, I shall keep you apprised of the situation."

"Don't do that," he insisted, losing some of his patience, but still quite calm. "Don't pretend this changes things. I am in no rush for an heir. So long as I don't meet an untimely death, it's of no real concern as yet."

Gemma gave him a derisive look. "Every woman knows she must bear her husband a son, Lucas. I'm no mess of distraught tears here. But if you say anything about your untimely death ever again, you may find you meet one at my hands."

Had his perfect little wife just threatened to kill him? For mentioning his own death? He couldn't help it, he smiled. "You can't kill me before there's an heir."

Gemma screeched and looked away. "If I could gallop away from you to gather myself, I would do it, Lucas Sinclair! But doing so would make me lose control of the horse, and you would have to save me, and that would be unbearable when I am mad at you."

He didn't care, he still smiled. "But I'm smiling, Gemma. Is that not something?"

She sniffed. "It just means that you owe me money. Stop being happy, I'm not speaking to you until we get home."

His heart tightened at the word 'home' and he had the mad desire to sweep his wife onto his horse and show her just how much it meant, but she was mad at him, for now, and it would not help his cause.

But the rest of the silent ride back to the house, he smiled to himself.

And when they returned to the stables, and once again entered the house, he ignored protocol and propriety and tossed his wife over his shoulder, ignoring her protesting and squawking.

By the time they reached the bedchamber and he had closed the door behind him, she was laughing breathlessly and had stopped pummeling him. He tossed her easily onto the bed, then crawled up after her, sliding his fingers between hers as he loomed over her.

"What is my balance so far today, Lady Blackmoor?" he asked, nudging his nose against hers.

"Oh, it's exorbitant," she informed him, her tone cool, but teasing. "You smiled the entire ride home, you offended your wife, you laughed on the stairs… You're being careless, and it would take me hours to calculate it properly."

He leaned down and brushed his lips along hers, smiling at the faint gasp.

"Well," he murmured, "let's see if I can bring the balance to a more reasonable level, shall we?"

Gemma grinned unabashedly and raised her chin. "Well, you may try."

He grinned in return, and proceeded to kiss his wife most thoroughly.

And try he did.

Chapter Ten

*E*ventually, they settled into a fairly regular routine. Despite his efforts, Lucas could not spend every moment with Gemma, as there were duties that had to be tended to. He had never grumbled about his duties before, and it was strange and foreign to him to be reluctant to act on his responsibilities.

Gemma had rolled her eyes and told him to get on with it, which her husband had not appreciated.

But it did make him smile.

She grinned to herself as she stretched her toes into the rug of the lady's parlor, quite possibly her favorite room in the house, least of all because it was specifically hers.

Lucas had been wonderful in the days they had been here. He saw to her care by day, and even more by night, any reserve or control gone as he asked her nightly of his balance, amused by her recitations of his bill, and then proceeded to attempt to pay the balance in his own creative ways.

Who would have thought that beneath the cool and composed exterior of Lord Blackmoor lived a man who was playful, affectionate, and brimming with good-humor?

What was equally as shocking to her had been the dawning of realization that she needed Lucas. She had needed him for ages and had not known it. He answered the questions she had not known to ask. He relieved her worries and soothed her fears, he teased her into peals of laughter, he held her for hours on end so that she might never be alone.

And he did not know, could not know, just what that meant to her.

She did not bother restraining a sigh as she thought through on their time together at Thornacre.

Long walks throughout the estate, hand in hand, simply dressed. Lazy mornings spent in bed full of affection and laughter. Riding across the hills as he encouraged her newfound skills and joy in it. Swimming in the pond…

She snickered at that particular memory. It had been a warm day, and she'd dared Lucas to do it. He'd blanched at first, but a bit of coaxing from her had him splashing her and daring *her* to join him.

He might still be the proper and composed man she'd always thought him, but that was certainly not all there was.

There was little that she truly did know about him, if she were to be honest. She knew the sort of man he was, his temperament, what would amuse him, how he took his tea, which meals were his favorite, that sort of thing. Very wifely things. But as far was *who* he was, his past and his deeper, more complicated parts, she was almost entirely ignorant.

He hid a great deal from her, and that made her uneasy.

She tried not to show it, as he was so giving and generous, so very attentive and sweet, and she had no regrets at all about marrying him. She was falling in love with him, for heaven's sake. But the shadows that crossed his face concerned her. The avoidance of certain topics concerned her.

His sudden intensity bordering on desperation concerned her.

He always seemed to be afraid of losing her, and she had no idea why.

She was not going anywhere.

If he would ever come out and say what he was afraid of, she would have told him so.

But he did not confide in her about anything that truly mattered. Ever.

Oh, he'd told her all about the estate and the tenants, the ones that would plague them with needs incessantly, the ones who truly needed their attention, the ones who had been there the longest… He knew every detail of every family, which spoke well of his nature and his views of his responsibilities. He was a very active sort of viscount, and only yesterday he had come home covered in dirt and sweat, sleeves rolled to the elbow and cravat completely gone. When she had asked about it, he'd simply said one of the tenants needed a hand before going on his way to wash.

She rather liked that sort of earthiness about him and had convinced him to wear his fresh clothing in the same style for the rest of the day.

He seemed to enjoy it as well, once she told him why she wished it.

She shook her head, smiling fondly. Her husband, for all his faults and secrets, seemed as mad about her as she was about him. Would this delirium ever truly fade? It had to, surely. When they returned to London in a few days… and the thought made her groan in anguish… he would be polite and proper once more in public, but would he change in private?

Would he always be this husband to her, or would he go back?

London had never been kind to him, yet he continually returned. She'd brought that up the other night, but he would not be swayed from it. He wanted her to reap the benefits of the Season, wanted to show her off a little, and wanted her to take advantage of the change in her situation while she could. It appeared he was going back to London for her, yet she had not asked and would be perfectly content to remain at Thornacre.

He was the one who insisted on going back. She couldn't have cared less about it.

If he wanted to return, she would go with him. London was where they began, where she first began to like him. Surely it could not be that dangerous for them.

Still, without knowing the demons her husband faced, how could she know how they would fare?

Gemma gnawed her lip and glanced out of the window, as if she would see her husband there. Then, before she could question herself, she sprang up from her chair and took the stairs two at a time up to the gallery.

Lucas would be meeting with his solicitor all day. She had hours before his return. He had studiously avoided the gallery since they had visited the first time, but her curiosity had only grown more rampant.

Mrs. Riggle had given her very few insights into the family, and she was not about to divulge anything, which Gemma found rather touching, if frustrating. But loyalty was so rarely to be found when Lucas was about, given his reputation and the general distrust of him, that even the frustration was worth it.

Gemma wandered the gallery with more care than she had done before, trying to absorb the details of every member within it.

She knew from the brief moments that he had spoken of his family that his brother Robert had been older, that they had never been cheerful or friendly children, and that the family had always been unpopular. She suspected that he had been close with his mother, given the way he treasured her diamonds and had shared them with Gemma on their wedding day.

He'd told her that they now belonged to her, but it seemed a trifle awkward when she did not know anything about the woman.

And Gemma had never really been one for jewels.

But that would remain *her* secret.

And one she felt sure could be persuaded to change with time and practice.

There were very few portraits of Lucas amongst all the rest. Whether that was by design or by providence, she could not have said. There were plenty of portraits of his brother, who was darker in features and perhaps more attractive than Lucas, but she did not like his looks. He was far more of a dandy than Lucas was, finely arrayed in every portrait and smirking dangerously. He was a man that was not to be trusted. Or rather, he had been.

And from the looks of things, Robert had been a favorite of his parents. Or perhaps he simply enjoyed the process of having a portrait done, or several. Robert had died before his father and thus never possessed the title, which, she'd come to understand, had been quite a fortunate thing.

She caught brief glimpses of Lucas's father, the previous Lord Blackmoor. He seemed a very cross sort of person, but with the same sort of puffed up energy of his elder son. And rather rotund, and quite overbearing. He was a man who was obeyed with precision, and his features seemed to be curved into a cruel sort of sneer.

And this was from whom Lucas had descended?

She shuddered and rubbed her arms as she moved on, glaring briefly at the portrait of the beautiful woman from before. It could only be Lucas's first wife, and Gemma's envy of her festered. What was the true story there? She shook her head and moved on.

Older relatives and family members graced the walls, their scowls and excesses the most common thing among them. She could see physical features that Lucas had inherited, and he had perfected the family stoicism, yet he graciously seemed to have been spared the desire for excesses. Given what she was gleaning just from studying these portraits, it was a miracle her husband was as wonderful as he was.

Aside from the occasional family sitting when the boys were very young, she could not find a portrait of Lucas's mother. She seemed frail and weak, but soft and warm as well. Her eyes were Lucas's eyes, but she seemed somehow more lifeless in the paint than any other person.

Finally, Gemma caught sight of a very small portrait that was nearly indistinguishable from the grandeur of the rest.

A delicate oval frame around a small watercolor portrait of a young woman, but there was no mistaking the eyes or the soft curve of her cheek. That was Lucas's mother, possibly from her early days of courtship or marriage to the late Lord Blackmoor. She was a beautiful creature, and a hint of mischief lay in her eyes.

Ah, so that was where he got it, was it?

She smiled at the young woman, sad to notice the discrepancy between this fresh young woman and the wasted creature she appeared in the family portraits. The smile forced, the features more stark, the posture rigid… She had become completely altered from her marriage, from her life.

Gemma fought hard to keep her tears at bay, and reached out to touch the frame gently.

"I'll take care of him," she vowed, somehow sensing the connection that had once existed between the sad woman and her stoic son. "I promise you, I will bring him joy."

Though it was silly to think it, she imagined the girl in the picture smiled just a bit more.

And Gemma returned it, nodding swiftly, then glared viciously at every other portrait. She might not know the history of these people, but there was no explaining the darkness that weighed upon one's self when studying them.

She would take care of Lucas. None of them ever had, but she would.

Whatever shadows existed in his past, she would chase them away. She would replace them with only good things. She would remind him of the man he had been here with her, and nothing that London or life could hold would change that.

She nodded once more and strode from the gallery, wishing her husband would not be gone quite so long so that she might hold him.

She would let herself fall in love with him, being more than halfway there already. She would trust him to share the private details of his life with her when he was ready. And when he did, she would help him to carry the burden and lighten his load.

He took such care with her, and of her. She would do the same with him.

He might think all of the care ought to be on his side, thinking little enough of himself. But that was her job now, as his wife. He was hers to nurture and take care of, to see to his wellbeing, to make his happiness and peace her chief concern. He needed her as much as she needed him, and probably more.

And he would realize it himself before long.

He had been counting the hours since breakfast, and every passing one had felt an age. He fully expected to see Gemma graying and wrinkled when he returned home, and he had no doubt she would be just as lovely to him as before. But he'd rather she remain young a while longer.

He craned his neck painfully as he returned to the house, pleased they had finished earlier than expected, and determined to take advantage of the few hours before dusk.

Matters of business were never so irksome as when they kept a man from his wife.

But it had been necessary, and things were now in fine order, which meant he could return to London without fear.

Well, without worrying over his estate at any rate.

London would always be fearful for him.

He paused as he caught sight of his wife out in the garden, free of bonnet, wandering with a basket half-filled with flowers. She had won over Mr. Chase, which was a miracle of truly biblical proportions, and while he would not condone her altering the gardens, he let her pick from it and offer suggestions.

It seemed Gemma had magic over them all.

She seemed at this moment as though she had been brought up in that garden, a flower in her hair and her countenance easy and gentle, her gown the exact shade of blue as the blooms in her basket. She could not have been more charming or pretty, or more enchanting. She smiled softly as she bent to smell a fresh bloom, and he found himself smiling with her.

Had simple pleasures ever stirred him so?

Was there a simpler pleasure than looking at his wife?

He doubted it, but he was apparently biased, and growing more so by the day.

He waved down a passing servant and gave instructions to her for the kitchen staff, then ventured out into the gardens to his captivating wife.

Gemma beamed at his approach and kissed him with enthusiasm in greeting.

"Well, this is a pleasant surprise," he mused when she relinquished him, wrapping his arms about her waist.

She smirked a little and leaned against him. "I missed you," she said simply.

He kissed her head and rested his chin there. "I missed you more. It was the longest day of my life, I am sure of it."

Gemma snorted and whacked him lightly on his good hip with her basket, pulling away. "You are tiresome," she teased.

He shrugged and took her arm to walk the garden with her. "You will get used to that."

She snickered and tucked a loose tendril of hair behind her ear.

"What did you do while I was away?" he asked politely, picking another flower for her.

"I consulted with Mrs. Riggle about some of the rooms," she recited, toying with the flower in her hand. "I wandered the house looking for mysteries. I stared at portraits of you in the gallery."

He frowned and glanced at her. "There aren't many of those," he said carefully.

"Yes, I know," she huffed with impatience. "We need to get a fresh one. When I want to think on my husband in his absence, I would much prefer an adult portrait rather than child one. It just seemed wrong to pine after the young version of you."

He barked a laugh and brought her hand to his lips. "Fair enough. Though I hate standing for portraits. What did you do to make up for the inconvenient lack of proper portraits?"

She lifted her chin with a proud smile. "I walked to Beverton."

He stopped and turned to look at her. "That is four miles," he marveled, looking her over and expecting to find her tired or injured.

"I know. But it is such a pretty walk." She frowned in disappointment. "Moira was not in, she's stayed in London. Nathan is only here for a few days and then he returns, but it was good to visit all the same. And don't fret, he made me take a coach back."

That settled him some. He would have to remember to thank Beverton for that. Gemma was independent enough to do as she pleased, and he would not stop or restrain her, but another protector in the area would set him at ease.

"Oh, and someone wished for me to give this to you," she said suddenly, pulling a sealed note from her apron. "I tried to get his name, but he did not seem to hear me. I didn't recognize him from our visits, but he was headed towards the tenant farms." She shrugged and handed it to him. "It did not seem important to him, so I have no idea what it could be about."

Neither did he, but he took the note all the same, the handwriting unfamiliar, and tucked it in his pocket.

Gemma quirked a smile. "Aren't you going to read it?"

"Not now," he said with a shake of his head, returning her smile. "I am going to have a picnic with my wife in our garden."

She grinned broadly. "Really?"

He nodded, thinking he could do some very astonishing things for that smile. "I've already had directions given to Cook. Shall we see to it?"

In short order, they were seated on a blanket in the middle of the garden with an array of food around them, and Lucas, having filled himself with the excellent fare, sat back on his hands and watched his wife steadily, every movement and nuance, every hint of expression fascinating to him.

"Lucas," Gemma suddenly murmured softly, her tone inquisitive.

He tilted his head, wondering at her averted gaze. "Yes?"

"Tell me something about your family."

He stiffened and his jaw tightened, his hands tensing against the ground. "Why?"

She shrugged, suddenly looking very small. "I don't know anything about them. I'm curious."

He wet his lips, wondering what she had heard, what she knew, if she knew anything at all. Carefully, he cleared his throat. "What would you like to know?"

She peered over at him, her clear eyes wide and entreating. "Tell me something about your mother."

He stared her for a long moment, then exhaled. His mother was a relatively safe topic, all things considered. And if she did not ask for the story, he did not have to share it. "She always smelled of lavender," he said quietly, his eyes losing their focus as he thought. "I never knew why, but she always did. And she loved roses. White ones. Mr. Chase used to take extra special care with those every year."

Gemma smiled and reached out her hand to cover his. "What was she like?"

"Gentle. Soft. And sad." He swallowed and shook his head. "I…"

She suddenly squeezed his hand, cutting him off. "It's all right. That is enough." She smiled and pulled her hand back. "Do you have any family at all, Lucas? I know you have that idiot cousin who will inherit if I don't do my duty." She snorted and rolled her eyes, making him smile. "Is there anyone else?"

He hesitated, considering revealing another secret, this one that hardly anybody knew. But this was his wife, and this secret was harmless.

He could tell her.

"Do you remember my full name?" he asked with a hesitant look.

Her brow furrowed in thought. "Lucas James Riverton Sin…" Her eyes widened and she looked at him in shock. "No…"

He nodded, his mouth forming a firm line. "Yes."

"The Rivertons?" she squeaked. "As in… the Rivertons?"

He nodded, amused against his will. "The very same."

"How?" she cried, smiling. "How and how does no one know?"

He shrugged. "My mother was the sister of Lord Riverton. The match with my father was not a favorable one, but she was in love. She was practically cut off after the marriage, as no one wanted to associate with the Blackmoors. Things got better after… well, she could at least correspond with her brother. But we've never publicly acknowledged the connection. And with everything else that happened, it seemed best to leave things as they stood."

"Do you see them often?" she asked, her voice small and careful, as if she knew he was nearing the end of his willingness to speak.

"Sometimes." He gave her a bland look. "But in private. I rarely go to their events. It is easier that way. They came to the wedding, you recall, but sat on your side, as your mother invited them. But they would like to know you better, so we are invited to dine when we return."

Her grin was quick and mischievous. "Really? I've never been to the Rivertons."

"It's quite the ordeal," he said with a sigh, looking away.

Again her hand covered his, and squeezed softly.

For a moment, nothing was said. And then she cleared her throat.

"When I was a child," she began, her voice a little husky, "I used to romp and play outside on fair days. Just in the garden, nothing too extreme. But we visited some cousins one summer, and it was a fine day, and I went out to play with the other children. We started hiding and seeking, laughing and running, and getting further and further from the house."

She swallowed suddenly and her hold tightened on him.

"I began to explore on my own, and was so engrossed in it that I did not notice the others leaving. It started to grow dark and I became quite lost." She shook her head, her voice quivering as if she were still the little girl lost on an unfamiliar estate. "I tried to find my way home, but it was impossible. I sat down amongst some rocks in a makeshift cave, knowing my family would come searching for me, and I ought to remain in one place."

A feeling of dread welled up within him and he turned his hand so he could hold hers.

"Darkness fell completely," she continued, "and I realized that no one was going to find me. My little cave suddenly became oppressive and terrifying, and I fled from it. I had never been so frightened in my entire life, and I think that fear carried me back, for I did not have the energy myself."

Unsure why she was sharing this story, but sensing it mattered a great deal to her, he remained silent and kissed her hand.

She cleared her throat and tossed her head. "The house was soon in sight and I wept with joy and relief, my fear finally fading. I knew they would be relieved at having me back and all would be well." Her voice broke and she frowned at it. "I made my way back inside and found that no one had left to look for me. They were going about their usual business as if I had been there. Then my father saw me, and he said… He said 'Oh, I forgot all about you'."

Lucas closed his eyes, a flash of pain spreading across his chest.

"I'd been lost for hours," she whispered. "Terrified and alone, and a child. And no one knew I was missing. No one was looking for me." She sniffed and looked over at him with a small smile, despite her tears. "I've never told anyone that before."

Understanding dawned on him and he couldn't manage to speak. He pulled her into his arms and held her close, burying his face in her hair. He had shared details with her, hardly his most unpleasant but against his nature all the same, and she had revealed secret details of her past as well, and probably *her* most unpleasant. The amount of trust that placed on him was immeasurable and he felt the weight of it. More than that, he felt honored and touched by it.

"How long were you scared for afterwards?" he whispered, stroking her hair.

"A while," came her soft response. "Darkness was difficult for a time. Now… well, I still prefer to avoid dark enclosed spaces. Can't abide them." She tucked herself more securely against him. "And I hate being alone," she admitted in a half whisper.

He bit back a groan and tightened his hold. "You'll never be alone again, love," he assured her, kissing her hair. "I'll always be here. I'll always miss you. And I will always look for you. You're not alone anymore."

She sighed and wrapped her arms around him, clinging just as tightly. "Neither are you," she replied.

He closed his eyes and pressed a soft kiss against her skin, wondering if that could even be possible.

Chapter Eleven

$\mathcal{V}$ery early the next morning, Lucas slipped from the bed quietly, careful not to jostle anything. Not that it would have mattered, Gemma slept more soundly than anyone he'd ever known and he suspected war could break out and the cannons would not even give her a stir.

He dressed with quick efficiency, and had his horse saddled. If all went accordingly, he would be back before Gemma woke, and he could have the pleasure of waking her himself.

Mornings with her were his favorite.

But he had matters to see to, and she could not know of them.

The morning was still and hung with a heavy mist, the sun just barely breaking through. It would have been a perfect opportunity for a long ride and contemplation, but he was only going four miles.

Beverton House soon loomed before him, and he grunted in discomfort.

He'd battled with himself over this course for quite some time last evening, but it was the only solution that made any sense.

He knew the earl from their dealings with the landowners in the area, and knew him to be a man of sense, wisdom, and discretion.

And he had a vested interest in Gemma, which made Lucas inclined to trust him more.

He could be of some assistance in this.

A stodgy but remarkably alert butler showed him into the quiet house, and he faintly wondered if the earl would need to be woken for this interview.

That would hardly be a good way to start.

But a few moments later, Beverton walked in, casually dressed, and looking mildly curious.

"Blackmoor," he said in greeting as he came and took his hand.

"Beverton," Lucas replied, shaking firmly. "I hope I am not come too early, I do not wish to disturb."

Beverton shook his head and waved him to a nearby room. "Not at all, I had just finished breakfast."

Lucas nodded, satisfied that his instinct had been correct.

He glanced around the room, a comfortable and masculine study that reflected a taste similar to his own. Simply furnished, classically designed, and free of distraction, with plenty of books lining the shelves. The massive desk was organized and at the moment bore several sheets of parchment with details and plans very similar to the ones Lucas had been poring over with his solicitor for the past few days. It seemed that the problems plaguing his tenants were not limited to his lands alone.

"Did you come to examine my study, Blackmoor, or is there something else?" Beverton asked, his tone polite but amused.

Lucas turned to look at the earl and found him leaning against the wall, arms folded, watching him carefully. The man was direct, but he appreciated that. He rather preferred frankness and honesty, and saw no need for inflation in word.

"There is a… private matter," Lucas said carefully, clasping his hands behind him. "One that I would prefer my wife not become aware of, and though we are not close, I trust your judgment."

"I am glad to hear that, I feel the same way," the earl replied. "Why can Gemma not know?"

Lucas exhaled slowly. "It may be a dangerous sort of matter."

Beverton stiffened at that and his brows rose in surprise. "What sort of danger are we talking about? Are you into something…?"

He shook his head at once. "No, nothing of the kind. I cannot even say for sure what it is, but…" He trailed off, not knowing how to describe what he was feeling, the foreboding that seemed to seize the breath in his chest.

"Why me?" Beverton asked in a low voice. "You have better acquaintances than I, other men you can trust."

"All true," Lucas replied with a nod. "But you are here. And you value Gemma on a personal level. And that is all that I need."

He received a firm nod in return. "I'd say I'm honored, but at the moment, I think I will reserve judgment." There was a quick smile and then he was serious once more. "You may tell me whatever you wish, and it will remain between us. I will do what I can to help. What is it?"

Despite the oddity of coming over to this man's estate early in the morning, of desiring to confide in a man with whom he had only ever done business, and acting in a manner completely unlike his usual behavior, his natural reservation was suddenly there in full force.

Beverton waited patiently, apparently feeling no need to rush him.

There was nothing for it, he supposed. He needed help and his resources were limited.

"When Gemma came to visit you yesterday," Lucas began on a reluctant exhale, "she was approached by a man. She did not recognize him, and he gave no name. He only asked that she give this to me."

He reached into his pocket and pulled out the missive, handing it out.

Beverton took it, his brow furrowing. "Did she read it?"

Lucas shook his head. "No, she said it did not seem important, and almost forgot about it. I treated it with little importance for her sake and did not read it myself until much later."

Beverton opened it and read the contents, then frowned more. "'Mind your valuables'." He glanced up. "Is that supposed to mean something to you?"

"Not really," he said, taking it back. "I have no valuables at Thornacre. Nothing of significant monetary worth, nothing I would miss, nothing anyone would gain by stealing." His jaw tightened and he met the earl's dark gaze steadily. "Except my wife."

Beverton stilled completely, every feature suddenly hard.

"I cannot say for certain that is what was implied," Lucas continued, his voice markedly lower. He folded the missive and replaced it in his pocket. "But I have thought on it over and over, and it is the only thing that makes sense."

"Why would it make sense?" Beverton asked, moving to sit in a chair and waving Lucas into one as well. "And why would a threat of any kind be made towards you? Who wishes you ill?"

Lucas sighed as he sank into a chair. "It would be easier to list the people who do not wish me ill than the alternative. The rumors surrounding my person continually over the last few years see to that quite handily, and I have seen no reason to refute the onslaught of them. I do not care, you see. To be perfectly blunt, I care for nothing of Society and none but a scant few individuals. Gemma is the chief of those. Anyone who would truly wish me ill could hurt me the most through her."

The earl swore softly and ran a hand through his hair. He shook his head, then looked back at him, placing his hand near his mouth thoughtfully. "But why threaten you at all?"

Lucas chewed on the inside of his mouth for a moment. "What do you know of my family's history, Beverton?"

He shrugged, his eyes steady. "Only the rumors. And what is said out here."

That was to be expected. His own tenants did not trust him, but as he had proven over time to be a most capable and considerate landowner, they remained and had confidence in his abilities. None of them would be speaking well of him in other respects, but neither were they fleeing the county with horrifying tales to tell.

"My family has been living at Thornacre for centuries," Lucas told him, settling into his chair. "The ancestry was once respectable, but wild behaviors and a taste for excesses soon rid them of that. My father inherited those same behaviors and tastes."

He snorted and shook his head. "For all of his claims of important peerage and parading his title, he ruined the family more than anyone else in the past combined. The only way to salvage anything was to marry an heiress, and he managed to persuade one that he was in love with her."

"Your mother," the earl murmured, keeping his voice low.

He nodded. "Not a pleasant match for her family, but her heart was lost to him. And soon, so was her fortune. He never loved her, never treated her well, and we watched her suffer for it. None of her fortune went to restoring the estate and the lands, it went to my father's pockets, and then to the tables and pockets of other men. And women."

Lucas ran a hand over his face, suddenly fatigued. "My brother was the same sort of man. Reckless, wild, extravagant… Cared for absolutely nothing but his own satisfaction and pleasures. I was the only remotely sensible one, and they knew it. I was the one who worked with the solicitor to try to salvage things. I was the one who wanted to restore whatever shred of decency our family ever had. I was determined that at least one of us would amount to something."

"Sounds reasonable," Beverton commented with an amiable shrug.

Lucas did not respond to that. "Because they knew my nature, they could use me to their ends. My brother refused to marry, had absolutely no interest in anything of the sort. He and my father made enemies faster than I could attempt to resolve matters. Not that it would have done any good, I am not exactly adept at dealing with people." He broke off for a tight, humorless smile, which Beverton returned without comment.

"The only way to salvage anything," he continued with a harsh sigh, "as any one saw it, including myself, was to marry an heiress. Again. My brother wouldn't, and for that all of England ought to be grateful. So it came to me to save the family, and I did it. I would be a credit to my family. I married an heiress with popularity and a respectable pedigree. Her fortune, however, was mine to control and not my father or brother's. I put it to use for the estate and built up what I could."

"And then what?" Beverton asked when Lucas did not continue.

He snorted again. "And then three months after my marriage, my brother died of an overdose of laudanum while intoxicated in a brothel. My father died a few months after that in a duel over a horse he had bet on. The rumors festered and grew from there, but I can honestly say most of the things they say about my family are true. Even with my own rumors, I am still the most respectable one. Not that anyone else sees it that way, it just proves their point about us."

He shrugged and rubbed at his eyes. His life was one exhausting tale of disappointment and failure after another, and the telling only reinforced that. "So you see, the idea of a threat is fairly second nature by now. I am surprised it has taken this long for one to appear."

Beverton whistled low and shook his head. "I never imagined anything like that. What a waste." He sat forward, his eyes focusing on Lucas. "What can I do?"

Was it really so simple as that? He told one of the darkest parts of his history to this man, and there was no judgment or recrimination? Merely an offer of his help and support?

It was astonishing beyond measure.

"I must protect Gemma at all costs," Lucas said, feeling a bit dazed. "I don't even know if the threat is legitimate, or if it is truly regarding her at all. I do not have the ability to glean information as easily as others. We are returning to London shortly, but the threat was issued here. If you could keep your ears open, apprise me of anything you hear… I do not hear all that I should, and I listen even less. I would not trouble you if it were me alone, but with Gemma…"

Beverton held up a hand, shaking his head. "Say no more. I would be happy to. I happen to have some gossiping tenants, and I've been wondering what to do with them. Good people, honest workers. I can see what comes up." He tilted his head just a little. "What about London? Do you anticipate trouble there?"

Lucas glowered and slowly rose. "I always anticipate trouble in London," he muttered darkly, "but there, at least, I have some resources."

The earl rose and extended his hand. "You may consider me one there as well. Whatever I may offer, I do."

Lucas shook his hand, the unfamiliar sensation of gratitude swelling within him. "Thank you. I hope this all proves unnecessary."

"As do I."

Lucas nodded and walked for the door.

"Blackmoor?"

He turned slightly and only raised a querying brow.

The earl was facing him, arms loosely folded across his chest. "What happened to your first wife?"

He had expected the question earlier, and with more finesse than that. But the earl had been an army man before he inherited, and Lucas's experience with him had only proven the man to be open and forthcoming. He tried to ignore the irritation at being questioned thus, as it was hardly a comfortable thing, but he did have validity in asking. Considering what help he had offered and the willingness with which he had listened, Lucas would allow it.

But it did not mean he would be forthcoming in return.

He offered a bitter hint of a smile. "She died. That is all I have ever said on the subject."

Before he could be questioned further, he nodded and quit the house, desperate to be rid of the shadows that had descended.

He needed to go home and hold his wife.

While he still could.

"I have never been this nervous in my entire life, and I once played for a royal prince."

"Did you really?"

"He was ugly and fat and an unimportant cousin," Gemma snapped, fidgeting with her silk. It would take some time for her to become accustomed to the finery she was now dressing in, and on a night like this, even the smooth silk was chafing. "And if anybody had mentioned that to me before my performance, I would have felt much better about it."

Lucas plucked her hand off of her skirt. "I am sure you were delightful. Now, why are you nervous?"

She looked up at her husband incredulously. "We are about to meet your closest relatives, who just happen to be the most influential members of Society. The fact that you are as calm as you are is absolutely ridiculous."

He chuckled and squeezed her hand when she tried to drag it back to her dress. "They are my family, love. I am not intimidated by them at all. If it weren't for you, I would not even be seeing them tonight." He frowned in mock consternation. "Though I don't understand why you agreed to come our first night in London. You haven't even seen the house yet. I had a grand tour planned."

Gemma's cheeks flushed but she glared at him all the same. "I may be new at being your wife, Blackmoor, but I certainly know a duty when it is presented. We are paying our respects to your family, and considering the imposing nature of said family, I am quite terrified, so you might as well stop teasing me and set me at ease!"

Lucas slowly released her hand, and she was quick to begin examining her gloves. They were a pristine white, but she still felt as though they were tainted with age, as all her previous ones had been. And she could not go to the Rivertons with aged gloves.

"You're right." Lucas murmured softly. "I am sorry."

Unwilling to give in to emotion, for fear she would never recover, she nodded just once, readjusting her gloves for the third time.

Her husband released a heavy sigh beside her and reached out to graze her cheek with his bare fingers. "I miss life at Thornacre already."

Gemma's eyelashes fluttered as his touch soothed her more effectively than any word could have, and memories of Thornacre flashed across her mind and heart with surprisingly painful clarity.

She took his fingers from her face and kissed them gently. "So do I," she whispered.

There was nothing else to say on the subject, and they rode the rest of the way to the Rivertons' in silence, a thick, unspoken emotion between them.

The last three days at Thornacre had been some of the most treasured, and it pained Gemma to leave. London was a return to the reality of life while Thornacre had been an idyllic fantasy for them both.

Lucas had been free of care and worry there, for the most part, and she had grown closer to him than she had dared hope. He'd shown her places he'd found as a child, including some ruins of an ancient monastery, had raced her across the estate on foot, waded through a stream with her… Everything she had ever wanted to do as a wild young girl, he had known and fulfilled. He had chased her through the house, lay with her in the grass as they watched clouds pass, and loved her long into the night with more tenderness and feeling than she could ever have imagined. Tears had been shed on her part, much to her chagrin, but he had merely kissed them away and held her closer.

Thornacre would always be home.

Nerves faded and she leaned her head on Lucas's shoulder, and was rewarded at once with his arm around her, pulling her close.

She said nothing, and neither did he.

They pulled up to the impressive estate, just on the outskirts of London, and Gemma moved away from Lucas with a faint gasp of astonishment.

She had never seen any building look as grand as this, and all alight as if expecting the high Society of London to flock unto it. The windows were large, but fine and clear, the stone polished and smooth, and the candles within only highlighted the perfection of the edifice. If the exterior could be so impressive, what would within be like?

"A bit much, isn't it?" Lucas muttered dryly. "Not sure whose idea it was, but they do enjoy making a statement."

Gemma turned a critical eye to him, only to find his lips twitching a little. "You like them," she pointed out, smiling herself.

He shrugged, but she could see it in his eyes. "They are family."

"So why not acknowledge it?" she asked with narrowed eyes.

Immediately his expression shuttered and he shook his head. "Not now, Gemma. Not tonight."

"But…"

"I mean it."

She clamped down on her lip and stared at him for a moment, noting the tension in his entire frame, but especially in his jaw. The coldness in his eyes, the furrow between his brows… She had never seen him so serious and focused, and she knew she had pushed too far. Which seemed odd, as she had not pushed at all.

But patience would be rewarded.

She hoped.

She nodded with an apologetic smile. "All right."

He kissed her swiftly and then disembarked, helping her down. "Are you ready?" he asked, leaning down to whisper in her ear.

She shivered and clung to his hand. "As I will ever be, I suppose."

He squeezed her hand and led her up the grand stairs to the entrance.

Her first impression of the Rivertons was that they were surprisingly... normal. Elegant, refined, perfectly cultured, and she would never manage the grace Lady Riverton exuded if she worked at it every day of her life, but all of that aside, they were no different than anyone else she had ever met.

Well, perhaps a little better.

Lady Riverton was a beauty, even at her age, and she kissed Lucas on each cheek with a fond smile, which made Gemma positively beam. Then she took Gemma by the arm and conversed with her steadily until dinner was served, only introducing her to her new daughter-in-law, who joined them.

She did not even meet the cousins or Lord Riverton properly until dinner.

But no one seemed to mind. On the contrary, they were warm and easy, remarkably relaxed, and, except for Lucas, smiled a great deal.

She kept a steady watch on her husband throughout the meal, as he conversed with his uncle and cousins, expressionless as ever, but more at ease than she had ever seen him in public. The men seemed to pay him a marked degree of attention and respect, and she wondered at that.

Her hand was suddenly covered and she looked over at Lady Riverton, whose dark eyes shone brightly in the candlelight. "We don't see him nearly enough," she murmured, indicating him slightly with her head. "When we do, it is quite a treat."

Gemma opened her mouth to say something, but then smiled and exhaled in relief. "There are not many who feel that way," she replied carefully.

Lady Riverton scoffed and went back to her meal. "Yes, unfortunately. And Lucas is too proper, too polite, and too much of a gentleman to do anything about it."

Gemma looked over at him again, smiling with the warmth she felt inside. "Yes, I know," she murmured.

He eventually saw her looking and his mouth quirked as if he would smile, then he turned back to Captain Riverton by his side.

"Well, now, that was an interesting sight," his aunt mused slyly.

Gemma glanced back to see the older woman smiling at her

nephew. "What is that, my lady?"

The dark eyes settled on her and the smile grew. "That is more emotion than I have seen Lucas display in years, my dear. You must be very good for him."

Gemma felt her cheeks heat and she looked down at her plate. "I try, my lady. It is all very new, but…" She trailed off, unsure of how exactly to finish.

Lady Sheffield, the wife of the viscount, chuckled softly from where she sat across from her, and Gemma glanced up at the woman with a bashful smile.

She had never been well acquainted with Sophie Bruce before her marriage to the viscount, but she had been pleasantly surprised by the woman, and if she remembered correctly, she had been quite firmly on the shelf before the viscount made his suit.

Now that she met her, she had no idea why that should have been.

"Personally," Sophie said, still smiling, "I've never known Henry or Will to look so interested in anything. They are quite bored by Society as whole, you know. Henry always said the only girl who ever held any interest for him was Mary Hamilton, as she was then." She glanced down at her husband slyly. "I like her immensely, but I'm very glad their tastes did not converge at that time."

Gemma laughed and shook her head. "Yes, can you imagine what poor Mr. Harris might have done then?"

The ladies laughed to themselves, which made the gentlemen look over warily.

"I never trust laughter amongst ladies," Lord Riverton said, giving his wife a mock warning look. "It generally means they are up to mischief, and I don't like that at all."

Lord Sheffield, who took after his father in the darker looks that Lucas also bore, somberly shook his head. "I would not have believed it before marrying last year, but I, too, find that is the case." He cast a faint wink at his wife, who rolled her eyes in response.

Gemma giggled, sitting up a little bit. "I am never up to mischief, my lords. I am always perfectly behaved, and composed at all times."

Lucas barked a laugh and turned it into a cough at her look, which set his cousins to laughing uproariously, while his aunt and uncle looked bewildered, but pleased.

When he had composed himself, he fixed her with a very polite stare. "Yes, indeed, you will never find a more dignified, tranquil, docile woman than my wife. We are very boring, the pair of us."

Gemma nodded soberly, though the table snickered, knowing better. "We are so very tiresome, it is a wonder we manage to stay awake in each other's company at all."

"I wondered about that," Captain Riverton said from her side, glancing at Lucas with a grin. "How do you manage to bear his company, Lady Blackmoor? I rather thought a lie-down might be more beneficial to your health."

Gemma bit back a snort, and Lucas raised a brow at her, daring her to reply.

She gave his cousin a doleful look. "I have worked very hard to find his charms, Captain. And if one will work at it, they will find enough to make him amusing. For a quarter hour, at least."

Laughter rang out and Lucas narrowed his eyes at her, but his lips twitched and she saw the pleasure in his eyes. She smiled at him and caught the flash of heat it rendered in him, and returned to her dinner with more focus.

"Lucas, why don't we see you more?" his aunt simpered a little, looking quite as if she yearned for it. "If we might just acknowledge the connection…"

"No, Aunt," Lucas said, cutting her off with astonishing coldness. He shook his head firmly. "No."

"But…"

"Anna," Lord Riverton said gently, his eyes on his nephew. "It is his decision. We will respect it."

Lucas barley glanced at his uncle as he nodded once. "Thank you."

Awkwardness settled heavily for a moment on them all.

Gemma stared at her husband with concern, but he studiously avoided looking at anyone. There was much she wished to know, and so much that was not being said. She was all confusion, uneasiness, and astonishment that it was Lucas who did not want the connection known.

Why would he want such a thing when they cared about him so?

But now was not the time for that, and Gemma could not have this disquieting sense among the group. She had always been the one to put people at ease, and now she would do so again.

She turned to Captain Riverton, who really was quite a towering man, and fair as his mother, and she smiled innocently. "Tell me, Captain…"

"Will," he corrected with a quick smile. "If it pleases you, my lady."

She nodded once. "Gemma, then."

He grinned broadly and tipped his head to listen more closely. "Tell you what, Gemma?"

She waited just a moment, seizing the attention of the table, then ventured, "Is there a particular young lady that strikes your interest? I have it on good authority that there is a hefty wager on you."

As the poor man squawked in protest, his brother grinned evilly, and his parents and sister-in-law joined in the good-natured ribbing.

And eventually, Lucas rejoined the conversation, his tension only slightly abating.

Chapter Twelve

$\mathcal{L}$ondon, with all its wonderful ugliness, wasted no time in reminding Lucas just how mutual the dislike of each other was.

It started off well enough, a small gathering at the home of Kit and Marianne Gerrard to welcome them back to Town, and only their friends and family had been invited, so he was the most comfortable he was likely to ever be in London.

And it did his heart good to see Gemma interact with her friends. It was in her nature to be friendly and warm, and as such, she had many who enjoyed her company. But true friends she had very few of, and Lily Granger and Marianne Gerrard had done her a world of good.

He did not miss how Gemma glared at Thomas Granger, Lily's husband, who had become more reticent and aloof than anyone had ever expected since his unfortunate financial distress and subsequent marriage. He'd always thought extremely highly of the man, though they were not friends, and he did not see why the marriage should be an unfortunate one.

He knew better than to ask Gemma on the subject, however. The way the marriage had come about had been poorly handled where Lily was concerned, and Gemma was too loyal to hear any argument on the subject.

He could hardly fault her for that.

Conversation had been limited with him, but what did occur was pleasant enough. Invitations were extended for various things, and he was noncommittal with them all, as he was wont.

The following days were filled with the flurry of activity that others usually endured during London Seasons, but he never had. Oh, he still had his usual things, and there was nothing to truly find displeasure in there. But with Gemma as his wife, he was experiencing an unusual view of the Season.

He suspected she was being invited as a novelty, but he patiently went along with her to everything he was permitted to.

She thrilled with the flurry of things, just as he knew she would, which is why he had insisted on coming back to London. He could have stayed at Thornacre for the rest of his life in a blissfully reclusive state, but he could not subject her to that.

He spent his days managing his business affairs or at his club, and had occasionally fenced with his cousin Henry or young Bennett Stanford, but the mindless nature of each day gave him too much time to think. With Gemma being taken on shopping excursions with Marianne or Caroline, or being invited to tea, or whatever else she was engaged to do, the house was too quiet and it unnerved him.

He did not used to mind it as such.

And now, of all horrid things, he was back at the theater, having escorted his wife to a new play. Her pleasure at the outing had ebbed away his reluctance, but as he stood by the wall, watching her mingle with others during the intermission, he felt the oddest desire to escape the scene altogether.

It could have been the number of people staring at him and then subversively looking away. It could have been the people who watched Gemma with a mixture of pity and derision. Or it could have been the people who avoided coming near them altogether and took great pains to find alternate routes.

He was used to being ignored for the most part.

Suddenly he was back on display.

His cravat suddenly seemed to be strangling him and it took his considerable control not to tug at it.

Gemma's musical laugh wafted over the general steady din of the crowd and his stomach settled, the tension in his shoulders easing.

"She looks well," Kit said, coming up beside him. "Hampshire agreed with her?"

Lucas nodded once, keeping his gaze fixed on what he could see of his wife. "With both of us."

"I haven't been to Thornacre in years. Have you made any changes to it?"

Lucas shook his head.

Kit waited a moment, then shifted a little. "What troubles you?" he asked, keeping his voice low.

"Why do you think something troubles me?" Lucas returned, matching his tone.

Kit snorted softly in response.

He supposed that had been a pointless question. He knew he'd been growing surly of late, and he couldn't help it. The wariness he had felt since receiving the threat in Hampshire had not abated in London; on the contrary, he was feeling it in extremes, seeing threats and trouble everywhere he went.

It made no sense, as nothing remotely resembling the missive had been seen in London, and nothing had been untoward at all.

But he could not shake the feeling that he was being watched, and by something more than the usual awkward stares of Society.

And then there were the rumors…

He would not tell Kit all of that. Not here, not now, not until it became necessary. The fewer aware of it, the better.

He shook his head. "Just waiting for the storm to commence," he muttered. "It cannot be long."

"It was interesting while you were gone," Kit told him, nodding politely at a passing acquaintance.

Lucas glanced over at his pristine friend. "How so?"

One shoulder lifted slightly. "Marianne has the ear of everyone, and her aunt beyond. Then there is my brother…" He snorted again and rolled his eyes. "At any rate, there was much speculation surrounding you two. I imagine there have been a shocking number of invitations?"

"Too many," Lucas confirmed, pretending to adjust his gloves. "It unnerves me."

"It probably should." Kit cleared his throat and straightened. "I don't know what it means, Blackmoor, but the conversation was all regarding the pair of you and your marriage. I don't imagine you will be escaping it soon."

Lucas swore under his breath, tempted to drag Gemma out of

this horrid theater at this moment. "What do I do?" he asked quietly.

Kit hesitated, then exhaled. "As you have done, I imagine. Surely it will pass. The Season is full of scandals, and it is early."

"Patience is not a virtue I possess."

"I know."

They both watched Gemma for a moment, and caught sight of two women skirting her presence in a wide arc, painfully obvious to everyone except Gemma, who had not noticed.

Lucas ground his teeth together so hard his jaw ached.

"Consider it watching and waiting," Kit muttered, his brow furrowed in irritation. "Strategy. She'll win them all over, you will see."

"She can't erase the past," he hissed, his blasted cravat feeling tight once more.

There was a long pause, and then Kit's response came: "No, but she can shape the future."

He did not want to hear optimism at this moment. Kit, for all his wisdom and loyalty, had no idea, could not possibly imagine what it felt like to be in his position. "Leave me," he grunted, desperate to be alone in his disgruntlement.

He never did notice when Kit did so, his entire being focused on Gemma, watching and waiting for any sign that she experienced any upset.

He never saw it.

So he did as his friend had instructed. He watched, he waited, and when the intermission ended, he escorted his beaming wife back to their box.

But not even her good humor could take away his darkness this time.

Gemma had never been this sought after in her entire life, and it was as invigorating as it was nerve-wracking.

She knew full well that it had nothing to do with her and everything to do with the man she had married. There was no possible way she had suddenly become so interesting and exciting, let alone for her popularity to have risen from her own merits. No, it was the same crush of insipidness that had made Marianne Gerrard so wildly popular after her infamous foiled elopement-abduction scandal.

She was a novelty and nothing more.

But she would put it to whatever good use she could.

She smiled and laughed and behaved with the perfect amount of politeness, allowing for her usual spattering of wit and boldness, but to a more refined degree.

After all, she was a viscountess now. She must be positively regal.

And given the fact that her husband was one of the most reserved and aloof men to ever call himself an Englishman, she could hardly be the wildly carefree Gemma Templeton, though the temptation was strong at times.

Particularly when dealing with the societal gargoyles who only wanted an excuse to hang her with their silken cords.

She flatly refused to give them an inch.

Her friends rallied around her, and she was grateful for that. Marianne understood navigating Society better than anyone she had ever met, and Lily was a calming influence. Between the pair of them, and the connections of the Whitlocks, Bevertons, and their friends, things had not been nearly as bad as they could have been.

But she could hardly miss the looks and whispers, and the people who shied away from her entirely.

And this was what Lucas dealt with on a regular basis?

Her heart swelled within her with such pained emotion. And yet he did not seem to care about it. He had no doubt learned to be resilient and immune to it by now, but he should not have had to.

Why would they not see in him what she did?

He had been so quiet of late. He accompanied her to everything suitable, but he was somehow more stoic than the man who had courted her. He still held all of the warmth in his eyes, but he looked at her so infrequently that it was difficult to see.

He did not touch her as much, had not held her in days. But his words, when he spoke, were as lovely and warm as ever.

But not so playful.

Never that.

And he would not talk about it.

"Nobody frowns so at a card party," Lily murmured from her side, nudging her a little.

Gemma shook herself and forced her expression to clear.

Marianne sat across from her, absently laying down a card, her eyes fixed on Gemma. "What is it?" she asked quietly.

Gemma shook her head, glancing at the fourth person at their table, the elderly and delightful Lady Cartwright, whose party this was.

She sensed their attention on her and waved her hand with a small smile. "Please, ladies, my husband used to work for the Foreign Office. And I have the ear of all Society. I know more secrets than the government. Pretend I am not here. I shall thank you to keep laying your cards, though. We'll let Mrs. Granger appear to win this time, hmm?"

And with that she plastered a blank look on her face and discarded, waiting for Gemma to take her turn.

She did so, then looked at her friends. "Something is troubling Blackmoor," she finally said on a soft sigh. "And he will not talk about it."

A slight furrow appeared on Marianne's face and her lips turned down. "Yes, I wondered if that might be it."

"Meaning what?" Gemma replied, wondering what she had missed.

Marianne twisted her mouth and looked at Lily, who only shrugged.

"What?"

Lily gave her a hesitant smile. "You and Blackmoor were the chief topic of conversation while you were away. Stories flew about with such speed and with varying levels of ridiculousness that it was dizzying. It made Marianne's adventures look rather boring."

"Excuse me?" Marianne huffed, but she smiled and wrinkled up her nose in delight.

"What did they say?" Gemma whispered, feeling the color drain from her face.

Lily shifted uncomfortably in her seat. "There was some speculation as to whether you would come back at all. That you would end up…" She grimaced and waved awkwardly. "You know."

"Dead," Gemma replied flatly.

Lily only nodded.

Marianne cleared her throat. "Others thought you must have been far more wicked and perverse than they'd thought, that Blackmoor had compromised you beyond a hope of recovery, that you were a desperate fortune hunter who only wished to marry, and that the pair of you would end up killing each other before the month was out."

"And then some said that suggested you might…" Lily blushed and wrinkled her nose. "Well, that you might have… helped him. With his first wife."

Gemma gaped at her friends in shock. No one ever had ever spoken of her in such horrifying terms before. She had certainly been gossiped about on occasion, but with pity or sympathy and a hint of a smile. Never like this.

"I heard that you were sold to him for salvation of your father's debts," Lady Cartwright mused as if speaking of the weather. "Discard, if you please, Mrs. Gerrard."

Marianne did so, smiling at Gemma kindly. "It isn't that bad, Gemma. Really."

"Not that bad?" she choked, the room seeming to spin about her. "It's horrible!"

"Considering what is being said about your husband at any given moment," Lady Cartwright said in her offhand way as she discarded a card of her own, "it is really quite tame."

Gemma glared at her, though she did not know her well enough to do so. "You are not helping, madam."

Lady Cartwright cracked a smile. "I never said I was. Discard."

Gemma flung a card out moodily.

"Straighten up," Marianne hissed through her false smile. "Smile. They can't touch you, remember?"

Instinctively, Gemma obeyed, though it felt like a complete betrayal to her husband to smile at a time like this. "So why invite me anywhere if I am so horrible a creature?" she asked, looking politely at Lily.

Her friend patted her knee under the table. "Because everyone wants to see. They want to know if your husband has corrupted you or if you might give them anything to gossip about. You haven't, which is brilliant."

"They are very upset with you, my dear," Lady Cartwright said softly, nodding at Marianne to play. "You aren't supposed to be happy."

"Well that is rather unfortunate for them, because I am," she snapped.

Lady Cartwright gave her a half smile. "Too right, my lady."

Marianne cleared her throat in the most delicate manner possible. "Now, what about Blackmoor is worrying you?"

Gemma chewed her lip gently, glancing over to where her husband and the other men had retreated into a separate card room. "He is just so quiet now," she half-whispered.

Marianne let out a rather indelicate snort for her perfect persona. "Darling, that is the nature of Lord Blackmoor."

"I have only heard him speak a handful of times myself," Lily added.

"With *me*," Gemma clarified irritably. "He has never been this quiet with me."

Marianne's expression cleared and she gave a soft "Oh," of understanding.

Gemma released a sigh. "Something is troubling him, I know it. But he will not discuss it. Adamantly refuses. And that was all right for a while, I assumed that patience would reward me."

"It still might," Lily said with gentle hope.

Gemma laid down a card she didn't even look at. "I know that. I do. But it was easier to wait when he was… there."

Marianne pursed her lips. "Might I offer some advice about being married to a reserved man?"

"Please," Gemma begged, knowing she would seem desperate.

"Let him have his reserve," Marianne urged softly, smiling with only a little force. "You knew he was a reserved man when you married him, and you still married him."

Gemma nodded, her brow furrowing. "But he was not as reserved with me."

"No, and nor would he be. And compared with what he is like

in public, Gemma, he is undoubtedly still not as reserved with you." She flicked her glance to the gentlemen's card room, then back to her. "He does not like London. And knowing what he faces when he comes, I can't say I blame him. He will tell you in time, I feel certain of it. But when you are at home, do not press him. Let him open to you in his own way."

It was excellent advice, and she wished she had considered that herself.

"You think he will?" she asked in a small voice.

Warmth hit Marianne's eyes and she winked. "I think he will, when he can. You've only been married three weeks, dear. It will take longer than that for Blackmoor to let himself be vulnerable."

"Especially after years of being so guarded," Lily murmured sympathetically, blinking when their three husbands entered the room together.

Gemma could not take her eyes from Lucas as his tall and imposing form entered the room. Even in this small gathering, the conversation softened at it.

But, true to form, Lucas did not react. He merely turned his head to listen more intently to whatever that horrid Mr. Granger was saying.

"Why can't they leave him alone?" Gemma whispered before she could stop herself.

Lily covered her hand and Gemma glanced at her. "He has done well enough with it. Perhaps it only takes some getting used to."

Lucas had said the same sort of thing only weeks ago, and Gemma had doubted it at that time. Looking back at him, knowing him now as she did, caring for him as deeply as she did, she was even more certain of herself.

"I shall never get used to it," she hissed, her eyes burning. "He is my husband, and I will not stand for it."

"Don't make a scene about it," Marianne insisted, though she bore a faint smile that she shared with Lily. "Nothing will do the trick like supporting your husband and behaving as though it cannot touch you."

Gemma frowned. "That seems counterproductive."

"Our instincts will us to act," Lady Cartwright said with a sigh, "but all it does is whip people into more of a frenzy."

She wondered what on earth *that* could mean, as she had never heard a single breath of anything remotely shocking about the Cartwrights, but now was not the time to ask.

"So I am supposed to stand idly by and do nothing?" she groaned, looking around at them.

All three were nodding, although how Lily could do so was beyond her. Everybody loved her husband except them and Lily was declared the most fortunate of women, despite the fact that her heart broke a little more every day.

"And smile," Lily suggested as she did so. "No one will argue with your smile. You've done a marvelous job so far, people are beginning to talk for other reasons."

"Good," Gemma sniffed.

"And I think that would help your husband, too," Marianne mused softly, a small smile on her face as she dealt a new hand of cards.

"Do you?"

She nodded primly. "The way he is looking over here now, Gemma, I think he is very concerned about you. The pair of you will worry circles around each other."

Gemma glanced back to find Lucas's gaze on her with such intensity that her breath caught. She knew how to read his expression and his eyes so much the better now, and for all the outward stoicism, she could see the concern and warmth and apprehension in his gaze. And she was forgetting to be composed while chatting with her friends.

What had he seen? He could not have heard, but what would he think?

Somehow, looking at him made smiling easier. The pain in her chest, though her heart still ached for him, for them. But her friends were right. If Lucas could stand all that was said about him, though it must pain him somehow, then she could bear it as well.

It may bristle her, it may take every ounce of resolve she had, but she could act the part. For him.

After all, she had been acting for the world for most of her life.

Now, however, she would not have to do so alone.

She tilted her head, and let her lips curve into a small smile, her eyes softening.

The change in Lucas was astonishing, though she doubted anyone else would see it. His face relaxed, his eyes lost their wariness, and a hint of the playful man from Thornacre appeared.

Then, impossibly, his mouth curved just a hint, and her heart threatened to burst completely.

"Oh my," Lily murmured, an obvious smile in her voice. "I feel very much like an intruder at the moment."

"I do believe I owe you a pound," Marianne said with a laugh.

"Not yet," Gemma murmured, her smile deepening with pride and emotion as she watched her husband and he watched her. "I can do better than that."

As if he knew what she had said, Lucas cast a very faint wink at her.

She suddenly felt the urge to laugh.

"My dear Lady Blackmoor," Lady Cartwright huffed with a teasing smile, "do cease flirting with your husband and lay a card before I do it for you."

Gemma winked boldly back at her husband, and returned her attention to whatever game they were playing, feeling a little better.

Perhaps they could weather this storm after all.

Chapter Thirteen

$\mathcal{S}$he may have been mistaken in her optimism.

A scant three days after Lady Cartwright's card party, Gemma was beginning to wonder if she had married a stranger after all.

She only saw him at meals, and that was only if she could be so fortunate as to find him there when she arrived. She had actually been reduced to sending him missives by one of the servants, as she had no idea where he was or what he was about.

The first day she had scoured the townhouse for him, only getting lost twice, and then asking the severe housekeeper of his whereabouts, which had only earned her a pitying look and a useless answer.

She knew better than to think he was upset with her. She hadn't done anything that anyone could construe as being in error or improper. On the contrary, her behavior had been more perfect than it had been in her entire life.

But Lucas was absolutely nowhere to be found when she wished to. There were no notes for her, no indication of where he might have gone or what he might be doing. She imagined he must have some pressing matters of business, but was it so much that he could not speak to her about it?

Or inform her of his plans?

She had received more invitations since Lady Cartwright's card party, but hardly as many as she had been receiving. And they were beginning to be most curiously addressed.

To her alone.

Not her husband.

That had made her frown and she really did need to speak with him about it. She could hardly represent them well if she did not know which invitations to accept and which to decline.

As he had been so remarkably absent, she had been forced to use her best judgment, which had never been perfect where Society was concerned. Thankfully, her sister, Marianne, and Moira, Lady Beverton, were of much use there. She'd been seen out in public with them on various excursions, earning stares and whispers as she did so. She smiled serenely and even dared to meet some of the gawkish looks, which only led to flushed cheeks and sputterings on the part of the others.

She'd seen Lucas do that on occasion, and she suddenly understood the appeal of such an action.

It was great fun.

And she *would* have shared her amusement with her husband, if only he would be available to do so.

This morning, however, she had no errands, no appointments, and nothing to divert her. As she had done at Thornacre, she had gone over each of the rooms and determined their state and any changes needing to be made, whether out of necessity or her own tastes. But the rooms were in perfect order and only slight alterations were needed. She knew each member of the staff and had been perfectly cordial and warm with all, but they seemed more inclined to be reserved, as their master.

Only her maid was the least bit chatty, and Hattie was hardly someone she could sit and have conversation with without a reason. She was a maid, not a companion, and there were other things she needed to accomplish with her time than humoring the mistress of the house.

She wandered the house aimlessly for a moment, then frowned to herself. This was ridiculous. She was moping around her house because she had nothing to do and her husband was avoiding her.

A grown woman with an independent spirit should not be prone to such silliness.

Lady Raeburn's musicale was approaching, as was Miranda Ascott's a few weeks after. She could select numbers to rehearse in preparation. It seemed an age since she had played, and even longer since she had done so for her own enjoyment.

The music room in their London house was a very open room, allowing for as much of the natural light that London could offer, which generally did not amount to much. Today, however, the sunlight streamed through the windows and there seemed to be a glow about everything within. The gilded enhancements on the walls and ceiling transformed the room into an almost mystical place, and Gemma sighed in contentment.

She pulled out her violin, tightened the strings, and began to play scales and light pieces to warm her fingers and the instrument.

Then, when she was ready, she started a few pieces she knew already and had practiced before she had left for Thornacre. She struggled to find something that was adequate, as nothing seemed to suit her anymore. These pieces were innocent and delicate, simple and light. She could play any of them at this moment and receive her due praises, but she was not that girl anymore.

She fumbled through some other pieces, finding a few that would be more of a challenge for her, and one she thought could pair well with Lily's playing and Marianne's voice, if they were so inclined. Marianne was still relatively timid with her musical abilities, but with the proper encouragement and the support of her friends, it might not be so terrifying.

She found another piece in her collection that she pulled out with a smile. It had at one time seemed so difficult for her inexperienced fingers, and she'd worked at it for weeks without feeling comfortable with it, and had shoved it away.

Now, however, she had the skills for it, and if she remembered correctly, the song was haunting and poignant and just what she needed at this moment.

She set the music on her stand, scanned the lines, and with a faint smile, began to play.

Softly, sweetly, the beginning notes rang out, innocent and sad. She smiled at the irony in that. Then they changed and deepened, and the melody flew from her violin, mingling with the magic of the room. In her mind, Gemma could hear the accompanying pianoforte, and the emotion suddenly came easier. The notes appeared in her memory and she closed her eyes, moved by the poignant strains.

Other strings joined in, an orchestra to the music she led with her simple violin, as if her heart played all the rest. All of her pain, her confusion, her hope, her love… It all poured forth freely, set to the exquisite music of her soul, now filling her and the room around her.

She felt herself moving with it, lost in the world of the song, to the instruments only she could hear. The music seemed to yearn with her, to feel everything she felt, expressed in a more evocative manner than she could ever speak.

As the tempo increased, she moved more, and the imagined symphony moved with her, a strange but fulfilling unison of form and feeling. She was dramatic and dynamic, open and alive, in agony and in ecstasy, no sign of the proper posture or poise that she had perfected for performance. This was music spreading the wings of her soul and she was helpless to resist its lure.

Then the song slowed, sobered, and one by one the other instruments faded into the background as she and her lone violin sadly, solemnly, finished the last few notes, which hung in the air as a fog over morning dew.

She exhaled and dropped her bow, fighting back tears that she didn't know had sprung into being. She lowered her head and forced them away, blinking hard. When they were at last gone, she pulled the instrument away from her and turned to replace the music and find another.

She caught sight of the open door and jerked with a gasp.

Lucas leaned upon the doorjamb, perfectly proper but for his lack of jacket and his slightly untidy cravat. His eyes were wide and his breathing seemed unsteady. His gaze was riveted upon her, more intense and potent, somehow, than any look he had ever given her.

How long had he been there?

Long enough, it seemed, for he regarded her in a sort of wonder.

She blushed and swallowed hard. If he had witnessed the entirety of that piece, he had seen her, and she had hardly been composed or refined. She could not have said how it must have looked to anyone else, no matter how freeing it had felt. The awkwardness that had existed between them of late was suddenly present within her in full force, no matter how remarkable the change in him was now.

Lord only knew what he must have thought of her.

"I…" she began, stumbling over the words. She cleared her throat. "I imagined I was being accompanied by several others." She gestured to the open, empty room, then shrugged. "It all sounded very grand in my head."

"I heard it," he murmured, his lips barely moving.

She frowned and cocked her head. "Heard what?"

"The rest," he said simply. "All of it. I heard everything." And he sounded as awestruck as he looked.

Gemma's eyes widened and she faltered a step. "You did?" she whispered, her voice carrying somehow.

He nodded slowly, his gaze still fixed on her. Then he shook his head just as slowly and pushed off of the doorjamb, coming over to her. Gently he took her face in his hands, staring down into her eyes.

"You are breathtaking," he told her, stroking her cheeks. "I could hardly move when I heard you. When I saw you." He shook his head again and pressed his lips to her brow, then leaned down for the softest, gentlest kiss.

Gemma released a sigh she did not know she had been holding, and looked up into Lucas's face. "Thank you," she whispered, smiling.

"For what?" he asked, still staring at her as if she were beyond imagination.

She turned her head and kissed one of his palms. "For hearing me."

That earned her another soft kiss, and then his brow furrowed just a little.

She could not bear for this moment to turn so suddenly. "What?"

"I told you once that we weren't friends," he said, sounding more like himself. "That we could not be, and you knew why."

Relieved, she nodded quickly. "Yes, it made perfect sense, once I considered it."

He shook his head once. "I was wrong."

She widened her eyes, confused. "Were you?"

"Completely, horribly wrong." He cupped her face more tightly, his eyes suddenly intense. "We are friends, Gemma. I think… I think you might be the closest friend I have." He swallowed and stroked one cheek softly. "Certainly the dearest. And absolutely my favorite."

"We're friends?" she asked with a beaming smile and a little laugh.

He returned her smile with just a slight one of his own. "The best."

Her eyes filled with tears and she couldn't blink them away this time. "Oh, Lucas."

"What?" he asked, concern wrinkling his face and softening his tone.

She let a watery laugh escape and stepped out of his hold just to lay her instrument down, then came back to him. "Your closest, dearest, favorite friend would very much like to kiss you quite soundly."

A spark of amusement lit his eyes. "Would she?"

"Yes. Please."

He stepped closer, sliding his arms around her waist and pulling her nearly flush with him. "I always try to accommodate my friends."

She snorted and slid her hands up around his neck. "Such a gentleman."

"Always," he murmured as his lips descended, and Gemma, for all her desire to kiss her husband soundly, found herself rather swept away by his kiss instead.

Lucas clutched the note in his hand so tightly he thought the parchment might tear beneath it.

Not here, not now.

But the proof was before him.

One word this time. *Penance.*

The handwriting was the same, but there was nothing at all distinctive about it. It could have been anyone's hand, and it was executed with perfect precision.

He was tempted to crumple it up, to burn it, to tear it into shreds, but he was wiser than that. He knew better.

He slid it into the drawer of his desk, where the other lay hidden, and slammed the drawer shut, covering his face with his hands.

Penance.

The single word had sent a chill to his heart. Penance for what? Despite his many failings, his past, and his reputation, he had nothing to make penance for. He had not grievously abused any person on earth, had always been honest in his dealings, and took great pride in being a gentleman, regardless of what anyone else said.

But somehow, he knew none of that would matter.

Just as he had known the first missive had not been regarding true valuables.

He slid his hands up to grip his hair, trying to steady his breathing. Gemma had been wondering about his solitude and his surliness, he knew that, but God help him, he could not tell her. He could not bear to let her know what nightmares plagued him both night and day. His life was one of darkness and isolation, and he would not let her succumb to it as he had.

He'd meant to remain as aloof and reserved as he had ever been, and then the other day she had played her violin with such passion, such emotion, it stirred his very soul, and he had been powerless to resist going to her, to take her into his arms, if only briefly. To confide in her the barest, briefest glimpse of what she meant to him.

Friends, he had called it.

She was his friend, and had been.

But she was so much more than that.

He sat back in his chair and yanked at his cravat, loosening it further still. Gemma was the breath and life for him, and he loved her with a fierceness that unsettled him.

He'd loved her from the very beginning. It surprised him how easy it had been to admit it to himself once he'd realized the truth. He suspected it was entirely pointless to have attempted to resist it, but as he had given himself up to the joyous fall of it, he could not say for certain.

Gemma.

What was he going to do about her?

He had heard plenty of the rumors swirling about her, now that she was his wife. They angered and irritated him more than anything that had ever been said about him, including the murder allegations, but he knew better than to do anything about it. He could not refute, defend, or make any sort of action that would in any way be construed as aggressive. It would do more harm than good and bar him from polite society even more.

And, by extension, Gemma. Which was worse.

He glanced back at the drawer, brow furrowing. Who would hold a vendetta against him and for what? How far would they go?

How much would they dare to threaten?

He shuddered faintly at the implications he dared not consider.

Gemma had been so warm and sweet, so artless since they had been in London. And he had been occupied with his thoughts, leaving her to her own affairs so as not to taint her in public.

Somehow, that had continued into life out of the public eye, until the moment with the violin. It pained him to do it, but ultimately, it would be better for Gemma if he maintained a little distance. She could move and behave as she wished if he were less present.

He could not leave her alone and unprotected, particularly with the mysterious notes and threats that he could not stop. But if he could somehow lessen the consequences of his life for her, he would consider that saving her as much as anything else.

Gemma was a smart woman, and clever beyond reckoning. And sensitive. She would fight it, would be confused by it, and press him. She was a persistent creature and would not accept any attempt at avoidance.

It was for precisely that reason that he had avoided being at home. If she could not see him, she could not ask him.

He should not have said anything when he'd watched her play. He should have left before she had seen him, then his feelings might not have shown and he might not have given her hope.

But he had been transfixed and there was no chance of moving in any direction but towards her.

He'd faintly hoped that he could somehow manage while keeping her as close as he wished, but he knew it was folly. Especially with this new threat against him, whatever it meant.

He'd gone back to his polite distance since then, and it seemed to be working. But nights were the torment. He had been coming back to the house late at night after wasting hours at the club and sleeping in one of the guest rooms so she would not know.

But he was not foolish enough to think that she did not suspect something.

As long as she never confronted him, he would never have to lie.

If lying were even possible where she was concerned.

A knock sounded at his study door and he frowned. He was generally not disturbed when the door was closed, as all knew he valued his privacy highly. "Come."

Gemma entered, looking uncertain, but beautiful. "Lucas?"

He managed to smooth his expression, but his heart pounded harder. She was supposed to have been out with her sister today, and the house to have been empty. He would never have been here if he had known.

"Weren't you to be out with Mrs. Hammond?" he asked politely, rising from his desk.

She smiled tightly and entered the room more fully. "We are delayed, I am to meet her shortly." She looked down at her hands for a moment, then up at him. "We received an invitation to the Rivertons."

Lucas stilled, his chest tightening. "Did we?"

She nodded, giving him an odd look. "Their first ball is in two weeks. I thought it best that I speak to you before accepting."

He lowered himself into his chair and shook his head. "Don't accept."

Her brow wrinkled and she stepped closer to his desk. "You don't want to go?"

He shrugged. "I rarely attend events there at all."

"But they are your family."

"And you are the only one who knows that."

She stared him for a long moment and he could see the thoughts whirling behind her eyes. "You… won't go?"

"No."

She had, no doubt, expected more of an answer than that, but he would not say more. "May I go, then?" she asked impatiently.

A sick feeling suddenly hit his gut, but he masked it by leaning forward. "I would prefer if you did not. But the choice is yours."

He saw her answer the moment he said the words. Her shoulders slumped a little and she tried for a smile. "Then I suppose I will send my regrets," she said, turning from the room.

"Don't bother," he told her, ignoring the flash of pain. "I never do."

She turned before she reached the door, her eyes sad. "Why won't you let them acknowledge you, Lucas?"

He closed his eyes briefly, and sighed. "It is easier that way."

"For whom?"

He tilted his head and looked at her exasperated face with what he hoped was sympathy. "For everyone."

She chewed her lip for a moment. "Why is it you that refuses to acknowledge it? They are willing, they said so themselves."

Darkness unfurled in his chest and he looked away. "There is too much in the past. They are a respectable family of high standing. I will not taint that with my association."

"Lucas…"

The emotion in her voice would have undone him, but he shook his head forcefully. "No. No, Gemma. Please, don't accept the invitation, don't send a refusal, and just let things proceed as they have done. Don't ask why."

She said nothing for a long moment, but he could not bring himself to look at her.

"When you decide you are going to trust me," Gemma said in a very low voice, "I will be ready to hear. Assuming you decide to trust me at all."

Lucas closed his eyes against the pain as he heard the door to his study closed.

He reached into the desk drawer and pulled out the note, reading the line again.

Penance.

Nothing could be worse than the penance he was already paying.

The question that plagued him was if his wife, the woman he loved, would ever forgive him.

His suspected answer terrified him.

Chapter Fourteen

S omething was bothering Lucas, and it was going to kill her to remain ignorant.

She tugged at her white elbow gloves irritably as she stood without partner yet again along the walls of the Duke of Eastbourne's extravagant ballroom. Lucas had danced the first dance with her and then fled the premises, as he had done so many times in the past, but never when they had been together. He'd said no more than ten words to her today, and less than that for the past five days.

He was not angry with her, which was her only comfort. She suspected she had very little to do with his black mood at all. It was as if the shadows she had been glimpsing in him had become rolling, overbearing thunderclouds that consumed him.

She wished that he would let her in. Surely nothing could be so bad as to burden him so completely.

But he had been alone for so long. So misunderstood and practically exiled, she doubted he knew just how to manage whatever darkness that was affecting him.

Trust was not easy for him and she knew it.

There would be some difficulty in her gaining, or sustaining, any form of trust of him when he almost continually avoided her.

He had ceased with his poor pretending at avoiding sharing her bed, and now they parted after dinner. Privacy was something he was used to, so she allowed it without any sort of argument.

But the loneliness in the night was deafening.

She shivered in the warm room and gently tucked an errant curl behind her ear. She could not think such things here and now. She was Lady Blackmoor, who must be all grace and poise, who must represent her stoic and reclusive husband well. Everyone was watching her at all times, quite literally everyone, and she would give them nothing at all to comment or speculate on.

It would have gone a lot further if her husband had remained with her, or looked pleased to be anywhere at all, but there was no changing his personality.

And she did not wish to change him.

She loved him, despite the madness of everything and his current distance, and she would wish for nothing more than for him to be the man she knew.

Loving him so freely and then being expected to be virtual strangers was painful beyond belief.

She watched the dancing with a bit of ambivalence now, pretending to smile as if she had intended to stand here without partner. She was a married woman now, after all. Partners would not be as available to her as before, as they would be intent on wooing the young ladies. And when she considered who her husband was and what the reputation of the pair of them had become, it was hardly surprising.

Marianne, she could see, was dancing with her husband, and they were lost in each other, as usual. The sight gave her hope. Kit Gerrard was a very reserved man himself, and he had rarely danced before his marriage. Now he was seen more, smiled more, and danced a great deal more, usually with his wife alone, but there were some exceptions.

Surely Lucas could be so altered with time. Not to change his nature, but to be seen in such joy.

Perhaps when his shadows were vanquished, he would feel free enough to do so.

Or perhaps he would always be as he was.

She winced a little at the thought. She did not want a distant husband, one that avoided her and had become even more reclusive than normal.

She wanted…

Thornacre.

Her heart gave as she recalled those blissful days, the love and energy that had filled every moment, the deepening feelings and blatant flirtation…

That was what she had always imagined a marriage ought to be like. She never expected it for herself, but it had been her dream of one all the same. To have anything else, now that she knew what was possible, was nothing short of cruel.

But how did Lucas feel on the subject? He was no actor, could not pretend at anything. He had felt the same things she had at Thornacre, had been just as eager and willing and light. Despite his reserve and disinclination toward expression, he was a man who felt things very strongly, and he had lost what they'd shared, too.

Was he suffering for it as she was?

Why then the distance?

She shook her head slightly, smiling when Marianne and Kit came towards her.

A slight furrow appeared between Marianne's delicate brows. "What's that for?"

"Just thinking," Gemma said lightly, shaking her head again. "Never a good thing in my situation. Why are you dancing, Marianne? In your condition…"

"It was the last time," she laughed with a slight roll of her eyes. "I told Kit that at least four times in the dance."

"One can hardly blame me for my concern," he muttered, smiling with warmth that was unfamiliar on his features. He looked at Gemma, and held out a hand. "Would you care for a dance, Lady Blackmoor?"

Gemma grinned and placed her hand in his. "I would be delighted."

To her surprise, Kit chatted amicably throughout the dance, and she was instantly at ease and warming to the dance within moments. Not that she had expected the dance to be unpleasant, for he had always treated her with respect and kindness. But he was not the sort of man who would converse endlessly about nothing, and yet here he was doing so. It was rather endearing, and she was very glad that he was a friend to Lucas, and that his wife was a friend to her.

It was a reminder that she was not alone in this, and there would always be allies.

"Where is your husband?" Kit asked as he escorted her back when the dance was completed.

She shrugged one shoulder. "You would know better than I."

He frowned a little.

"Do you know…?" she began hesitantly.

"No," he said, cutting her off. "No, I don't know what this is. But I hope you will not take it as a reflection upon you or your marriage, Gemma. He cares for you very much."

She smiled fondly and squeezed his hand. "I know."

Uncomfortable with emotion and warmth as ever, Kit looked away quickly, but Gemma saw his mouth quirk. "Refreshment?" he asked in a stiff voice that did not fool her.

"Please."

Though it was hardly the usual thing to do, the Duke and Duchess of Eastbourne used a far corner of their ballroom for lemonade and some light refreshment. They had servants who wandered the place with trays, but the intrepid soul could fend for themselves if they so chose.

Kit escorted her over and she patiently waited, glancing around the room aimlessly, taking note of the wallflowers and unoccupied gentlemen with amusement.

Some things did not change.

"The father was quite the horrid man himself, you know. The late Lord Blackmoor? He was barred from London functions before he married his wife."

Gemma's ears perked up and she glanced over at the collection of ladies seated nearby.

"Whom did he marry? I don't recall."

"Nobody does. They never appeared together in Society, not even once. No one would have them. Reclusive bunch, that family."

"Didn't the late viscount have a bit of a reputation?"

There was a derisive snort from one of them. "A bit? The man was a drunk and a gambler, and it was usually other people's money he gambled with. He never had half a crown to his own name, and the debts were extreme. The family was hardly in a fine position generations before, but there had never been a Lord Blackmoor so ruinous as he. Every estate was lost saving for the family holdings, which were left in a bad way."

"Is it true they had to do away with maids in the house because of him?"

"Oh, yes. Him and his son."

"The current viscount?" someone asked with a gasp.

Gemma went cold at the blatant suggestion.

"No, you goose, his brother! That one gave his father a run for his money with bad behavior. It seemed they were determined to out-scandal the other."

"Oh, yes, he was a wicked one. He was only permitted in Society briefly until at least ten fathers of young ladies made certain accusations. And then he only lurked in the darkest corners of London, sowing temptation and ruin wherever he went."

"Surely not."

"Oh no? Don't you remember how he died?"

Gemma stiffened and her eyes focused on the pinched looking woman currently fanning herself with a poorly painted fan. She would not dare reveal any truly scandalous information at a gathering such as this.

But then, she had already said so much.

She leaned forward and Gemma had to strain to catch her words.

"He died in the Seven Dials of a laudanum overdose. While intoxicated. In a brothel."

Shocked gasps echoed around the circle, and several fans moved a great deal faster.

Sensing she had a captive audience, the cruel woman smirked. "Ladies of ill repute draped about the room, in all manner of undress. Two other rakes nearby, only slightly better off. And the rooms had not been paid for."

The women tittered and Gemma ground her teeth together.

Something brushed her arm and she jerked to see Kit there, looking murderous and cold, his eyes fixed on the women as well.

"I cannot bear it," she hissed.

"Drink your lemonade," he replied, taking a sip of his own.

She glanced down at her hand, wondering when the cup had been placed there. She was tempted to toss it aside. "I have no…"

"Do it."

She glowered and did so.

"Well, the late Lord Blackmoor died in a duel," one of the other women laughed. "Over a horse, wasn't it?"

Someone snickered. "Yes, a badly placed bet. Don't remember all the particulars, but he questioned the breeding of the horse, the honesty of the owner, and claimed he had been duped into placing his entire sum on an ill-bred nag."

"He was killed in the duel?"

"Run clean through."

"Dueling is illegal."

"It was not a matter of legality. A magistrate was there and oversaw it, for heaven's sake. The matter would have proceeded accordingly, but after the duel, he attacked Sir Preston again, and Sir Preston had no choice but to defend himself. It was no loss to anyone for the viscount to die, and they left the corpse there in the field for his own kind to dispose of however they saw fit."

"That's not polite."

"Politeness has no place with people like that. The whole family is a bad lot, and the mother died in the midst of all of that, wilted away into nothingness because of the behaviors of her family, from the shame, ignored and neglected. Weak little creature, nothing left to live for, and the will to live bled out of her slowly, and then all at once."

"Kit, I can't…" Gemma pleaded softly.

"Steady," he murmured, setting a hand at her elbow.

She shook her head. "Take me away."

He nodded once and began to do so, far more dignified and composed than Gemma could have done.

"And the current viscount?" some impertinent young woman asked.

Gemma pulled to a halt, jolting Kit beside her.

"He never did anything to stop any of them, did he? He could have done that at any time. But no, he was a passive bystander and let his family destroy itself."

Gemma snarled and turned to unleash her fury on the group of women only to find Lucas standing in her path.

"Leave it alone," he whispered, his voice hollow and his eyes vacant.

She shook her head fiercely. "No. I will not let them slander you and your family like this."

"It's all true, Gemma," he bit out, his voice catching as if someone had stolen his breath. "Every word."

Without waiting for a response, he moved past her and left the room.

She glanced back at Kit, who had also watched Lucas go. His eyes flicked down to Gemma, a question in them.

"Please," she murmured with a nod.

He dipped his chin once and made his way to follow Lucas out of the room.

Gemma put a hand to her brow and moved to a nearby pillar, leaning against it with a heavy sigh.

"Surely the viscount is more respectable than that," a quiet woman asked timidly. "I've never heard of…"

"The murder?" someone interrupted in a sharp snap. "The current viscount is exactly like the rest, my dear. He is more discreet and mysterious about it, to be sure, and who knows what sort of depravities he is engaged in? He merely learned from the behavior of his father and brother, and the ancestors before them, and has seen the effects of the publicity of such actions. Time will tell, though. All secrets are revealed at some time or another."

"You really think he is as bad as the rest?"

"Worse, my dear. He will prove to be far worse."

Gemma straightened up, clenched her hands into fists, and moved out of the safety of her hiding place. She marched over to the circle of women and faced the shrewish one who had spoken so much. The entire group fell silent, watching her.

The woman's eyes narrowed malevolently. "Lady Blackmoor."

Gemma had no idea who the woman was, nor did she care. She would not engage in politeness. After all, she was a Blackmoor. And politeness had no place with them.

"You will cease your gross abuse of my husband and his family," she told the woman, but spoke to the circle as well. Somehow, she kept her tone even and the tremors remained in her chest without spreading to her limbs. "You will behave as the proper ladies you are reputed to be and leave us alone."

"Oh, will I?" the woman sneered.

Gemma lowered her chin just a touch, her lip curling. "Yes."

The woman blinked uncertainly, and looked down at her hands in her lap.

"I know your husband, madam," another woman broke in coldly, and Gemma glanced at her. "And there is far more I could say on the subject."

"*I* know my husband, madam," Gemma snapped. "Perhaps if you knew yours, you would have a worthwhile thought to share with the world. As it is, you know nothing on the subject of any husband, yours or mine, and I will thank you to take your ignorance and…"

"My dance, Lady Blackmoor," Colin Gerrard suddenly exclaimed jovially, seizing her hand and jauntily pulling her away as if his eagerness could not be contained.

When they were far away, he let his grin fade and he shook his head a little. "Good lord, Gemma," he chuckled softly. "Did you not listen to anything Marianne said?"

"Marianne would have said worse under the circumstances and you know it," she muttered, her face flaming.

Colin laughed and winked. "True enough, but you really must learn how to contain it. Channel the rage constructively, use subterfuge, whatever you must. Blatant attacks won't work here."

"I should have been a soldier."

He grinned and tapped her cheek before taking her to the dance floor. "Aye, that would have been a fine fit for you. But this is an entirely different sort of battlefield. And at the moment, looking happy and smiling and dancing is going to help your cause more than dealing with those women."

It felt false and betraying to smile at the moment, but Colin was right. He knew Society and its navigation like no other, and would it would be wise to heed his counsel.

For now.

She stayed as long as she could bear to, and then a few moments longer, before finding Kit, who informed her that Lucas had left the ball when he had stormed out, but the carriage was still available for her use. She had suspected as much, knowing her husband. He would not be able to stay after hearing such things, especially given the shadows she had glimpsed in his eyes.

It was all true, he had said. But how could that be?

She wondered on that the entire ride home. It could not be. It was too horrible, like the lurid details of a particularly salacious novel that no sensible person ought to enjoy. Surely they were mistaken.

She disembarked from the carriage and hurried into the house, mind awash with the information she had received tonight.

What horrible details to live through, what misfortunes to endure… What was truth and what was not?

No matter what Lucas said, it could not be all truth.

She let the maid help her with her cloak and tugged her gloves off. "Where is he?" she murmured.

The maid looked at her with wide eyes, then folded the cloak over her arms, lowering her gaze. "The gallery, madam."

Gemma nodded, thanked her, then made her way quietly up the stairs in the darkened house.

The gallery spanned much of the second floor, and there was no light at all within but the moonlight through the windows.

It took Gemma a moment for her eyes to adjust, and then she saw him.

He sat in a chair, but only at the barest edge, his elbows on his knees, head in his hands. He was without coat, cravat, or waistcoat, and there was no hint of the fine man that had been seen in the Eastbourne ballroom hours ago.

His hands slid from his head across his face, then flopped loosely before him, his head dropping. He looked somehow small and diminished thus, his shoulders slumped as if the entire weight of the world rested on him.

The sight of him sent her heart to her throat. This was a man tormented beyond belief, haunted by something far worse than shadows. In that moment, she knew that he had not been mistaken at all. Every word of that horrible conversation *had* been true. It was inconceivable for him to be so pained if it had been anything less.

These were the horrors he lived with and faced on a regular basis. And when confronted by them, he brought himself here to surround himself with the likeness of the very people who had driven him to this.

She had been so wrong about him, about the darkness that wore on him. He bore a heavy burden, several of them, and the weight was crushing him.

He seemed to shudder a little, and she clamped down on her bottom lip to keep her distress contained.

How he must suffer! He was so proud, so strong and immovable at all times. This was sheer and utter anguish, and witnessing it was too much.

Feeling it could only be infinitely worse.

Slowly, not wishing to startle him, Gemma moved further into the room. He gave no indication that he noticed her in any way, but she was undeterred. She walked carefully over to the chair until she was directly before him.

He did not raise his head; he did not stir in the least. His breathing was unsteady and his shoulders seemed to shake with tremors, but no sound emerged from him.

Tears filled her eyes as she reached out gently and touched his hair. He stilled beneath her hand, but made no move. Encouraged, she began slowly running her fingers through the dark locks. She stepped closer and let both hands wander through his hair, stroking and soothing, his fingers barely brushing the edge of her skirt.

A soft exhale escaped him and he seemed to lean into her touch. She smiled through her tears and continued the strokes, letting him nuzzle as he would.

His hands slid up and rested on her hips, pulling her closer. He pressed his face against her stomach, releasing another harsh breath.

Gemma slid her arms gently around him, cradling his head against her, fingers still running through the dark tresses. Tears began to trickle down her cheeks, and her heart filled with love for this man in her arms. She would hold him for the rest of her life if he would let her. She would have borne his burdens if he would share them.

But this was enough.

After a few long moments, Lucas lifted his head, resting his chin against her and looking up into her face, his expression worn and weary, lost and alone. His eyes were soft and tender, so gentle and open, her heart broke anew for him.

She brushed a hand along his cheek, his jaw, meeting his eyes gently as her other hand cupped the back of his head, toying with the locks there. Gracefully her fingers stroked along his face, lightly scratching the stubble at his jaw and his chin, tracing his ear and cheekbones, memorizing every feature.

His breathing deepened and he slowly rose, his hands still on her, his eyes never wavering. Her hands slid to his neck, one moving to rest on the exposed skin of his chest, where his erratic heartbeat pounded.

Lucas cupped her cheek, his thumb brushing over her cheekbone, making her eyelids flutter in delight. He leaned down and captured her lips gently, slowly taking them again and again, exquisite playing that made her knees shake and her heart race. She pressed the back of his neck, and he responded, taking her deeper, longer, receiving her kisses as earnestly as she was his.

His arms tightened around her, pulling her so close she hardly knew where she ended and he began, and her body thrilled at the familiar pressure. His mouth slid from hers to her cheek, her jaw, down the column of her neck to the barely exposed shoulder. She cradled his head against her as her breath raced, as her heart soared, as she turned to kiss his neck in return.

He worked his way back up, taking her lips once more, hot and tender and wrenching all at once. A hand slid into her hair, tangling within it, and she gasped in delight.

He paused, his lips barely touching hers.

She waited, heart frantic.

Then he scooped her up into his arms, and his mouth was on hers again as he carried her from the room, her arms twining around his neck as her tears renewed. And when he had kissed those away, he kissed her still, carrying her all the while.

Chapter Fifteen

$\mathcal{E}$ventually, Lucas had told her everything he could about his family. Things he had never told another living soul, the childhood he suffered through with the members of his family, watching his mother waste away under the abandonment and disregard of his father… It was gut wrenching to relive, but she was steadfast and sure throughout the telling, never once offering him the pity he feared or the disgust he expected.

She listened patiently, holding his hand, and when he had told all, she had curled up beside him, rested her head on his chest, and held him, scattering soft, fleeting kisses where she could.

Just once, she whispered, "I am so sorry."

But other than that, the subject was never breached again. No probing questions, no sounds of distress, no recoiling.

Gemma was an inquisitive person, and an emotional one. Yet she had somehow contained all of that and let him get through his confessions without interruption for her comments, questions, or expressions. And then, remarkably, she had soothed him, just as she had last night in the gallery.

He fought a lump in his throat as he sat in his study now, in the early morning hours. She was a remarkable woman, and the love for her that he had felt before, seemingly a fervent and abiding adoration, was suddenly eclipsed by the depth and breadth of what the dawn had found in him. She was everything, and by some miracle, she was his.

He had meant to tell her about his past and his family at some point, when he had reconciled the idea in his mind. He would never have imagined all of that to be trotted out at a public event for her ears so unprepared and unaware. It was not fair for her to be bombarded in that way, no matter how true the unpleasant details were.

His wife could very well have left him after having heard the horrors of his family. The heritage was not one that anyone would wish for, and it was that reason that kept him from discussing it with anyone, let alone being upfront with her before the marriage. His family had little enough to do with him… he had truly been the passive bystander as they ruined themselves… but he alone had to live with the repercussions. He had been the one to pick up the pieces and try to salvage something.

No woman would wish for such a life.

But Gemma had been unfazed by the revelations, thinking only of him and his comfort, welfare, and well-being.

He did not deserve her.

And she did not deserve this.

He frowned as he sat back in his chair. Why were these things being discussed again? It had been years since anyone had thought of his father or brother; no one ever talked about them. He thought they were long forgotten.

Why now?

It was unsettling, to say the least.

What else could come out?

He shuddered as the image of Celia flashed across his mind, laughing and taunting as she always had been.

He ought to tell Gemma about her. The truth. But doing that would expose him in such a way that he was not sure he could bear it.

Gemma thought his family's past was all the horror he lived with.

She had no idea how much worse it got.

Lucas shook his head as he slid some papers to the corner of his desk. He ought to tell her, she deserved the truth from him.

But how?

A small note, sealed as unobtrusively as ever, unaddressed, appeared from under the documents he had pushed aside and he stared at it, his breath catching painfully.

It had been over a week since the last.

Penance.

He had paid penance every day of his life, and more yet again only last night.

Fingers unsteady, he reached for the missive and broke the tiny seal.

The same scrawling hand had penned the words, *Is it enough?*

Lucas dropped the note with a harsh exhale, staring at it as though he could engulf it in flames by doing so.

Is it enough?

Is *what* enough? His misery? His life?

His eyes widened. Whoever was behind this had begun the rumor mill about his family again. It was a deliberate provocation to him and to Gemma. It was intentional and personal, a move calculated to make him suffer as much as possible, knowing his predilection for privacy and his reputation of not speaking about any matters of his past.

It was cruel and twisted, and damned effective.

If they were aiming at wounding him, they would do well on this vein.

If their aim was Gemma…

He ran his hands into his hair. Who knew what would finally make Gemma see the truth of who and what he was? It was only a matter of time before she realized what a foolish choice she had made in accepting him. In caring for him.

He couldn't tell her about Celia. It would break the fragile link that existed between them, and she would be worse off than before.

So long as she was with him, she would suffer.

He could not break out of the marriage, it would kill him to do that, but he could at least protect her from the worst of it. The world hated him. They only pitied her.

He could live with that.

Could she?

A soft knock at the door brought his head up and Gemma stood there, sleep rumpled and innocent, her wrap cinched loosely over her nightgown.

"I thought we dealt with shadows already," she murmured,

folding her arms as she looked at him with concern.

The rough timbre of her voice broke him and he rose, stepping around the desk. "We did," he assured her.

She tilted her head back as he approached, her blond curls falling tangled and wild down her back. "Then what are these?" she asked, reaching up to stroke the skin beneath his eyes.

He drew her fingers down and kissed them gently. "Remainders," he whispered, nuzzling his stubble against her soft palm.

Gemma tilted her head sadly. "What can I do?"

He exhaled and pulled her tightly against him, securing his arms about her as though his life depended on it. "Stay," he ground out, squeezing his eyes shut. "Just stay."

She did not comprehend, he knew, but she said nothing in response as she wrapped her arms around his back and held fast.

He needed nothing else in the world but her.

And if she would forgive him for what he must do, he would spend the rest of their lives ensuring she never had cause to forgive him again.

But he could not know how long her generous heart would hold out, how far her loyalty would extend. Another man and another woman might have found a different path through all of this, but he knew no other course. There was too much at stake, and now the dangers were increasing, perhaps even to a physical level. He would not risk her or her happiness. She could find joy in their life despite him, and he would see to it.

If she stayed, he would find a way.

But that was the question, wasn't it?

Could she care for him enough to remain?

He held her tighter and buried his face into her hair, terrified to the bone of the answer.

"Blackmoor, I would have a word with you."

Lucas huffed in irritation and raised his head to look at the woman standing in the doorway of his study. "Marianne, I don't have time for this."

She folded her arms and raised a brow, perfectly mirroring the exact arch of the feather curving out of the hat precariously perched on her towering curls. "Your wife is out of the house with her sister at the moment, and I will be making an unannounced call upon her shortly after she returns. You will make time for me now."

He threw up his hands and sat back in his chair. "Fine. As if you would listen to me anyway."

Her lips quirked into a pert smile and she entered the room with the procession of a girl being presented at court, and she sat just as regally.

He snorted. "Do you always make an entrance like that?"

"If I can help it, yes."

"And does your husband know you have come to call on me?"

"Yes. He is currently speaking with your valet. Something about the way you wore your cravat intrigued him."

Lucas was tempted to grin outright. That was highly unlikely. Kit Gerrard had no interest in fashion whatsoever; this was his way of letting Marianne have her word out while staying well shod of it.

Traitor.

"A gentleman rises when a lady enters a room," Marianne chided with another swift smile.

Lucas gave her a wry look. "Does he? Pity I have never been accused of being such a thing."

Marianne gave a light laugh, and then sobered, giving him a calculating look.

He stared back rather frankly.

But Marianne was a stubborn woman with no small amount of will, and she did not give an inch.

Finally, Lucas sighed and drummed his fingers on the arms of his chair. "Are you going to stare at me until I confess my sins, or do you have a point?"

"What are you doing to Gemma?" she asked in a voice that was much smaller than anything he had come to expect from her.

He felt his jaw slacken. "What do you mean?"

Her delicate brows lowered. "Don't play games with me,

Blackmoor. She is one of very few friends that I have, and she is worried sick over you. And you are not helping matters by being aloof."

He glowered and looked away from her too-knowing eyes. "You don't know what you are talking about."

"Don't I?" she snapped. "I may not know you as well as my husband, Blackmoor, but I do know you. You think nothing of yourself, which is why you let the world speak of you as they will. But you are also a little bit of a hero, and no one else is permitted to suffer by your hand or while you can do something about it. So what are you doing and why?"

Lucas had looked back at her at some point, stunned that this woman he'd only known a year, if that, had pegged him so perfectly. He knew that he had underestimated her at first, but he had hardly expected her to be so observant as this.

She rolled her eyes. "Oh, for heaven's sake, get over your shock and tell me. I don't want to sit here all day."

"I am not telling you anything."

She glowered impressively, reminding him of the expression he had often seen on her brother's face. "Why not?"

"Because believe it or not, Mrs. Gerrard, you do not need to be aware of everything that goes on in the world you seem to rule."

She gave him a hard look. "Don't be rude."

He shrugged. "Don't be impertinent."

"Blackmoor, I am concerned for you and for Gemma!" she protested. "You know I think the world of you, no matter how I may insult you. And I love Gemma dearly. I don't want the two of you to be unhappy!"

He raised a brow in disbelief. "Why should you think we will be unhappy?"

"I saw her face yesterday. And I am seeing yours now. What in the world is going on?"

He watched her for a long moment, chewing the inside of his lip. He'd maintained a distance for three days now, and it was torment. Sheer, bloody torment. But he was not ignoring her, he could not. They had meals together, and polite conversation ensued, and he tried to be attentive without being invested, avoided touching her as much as he could, which was proving harder than expected.

He was being a perfectly cordial husband.

And it was damn near killing him.

"On second thought," Marianne murmured in a surprisingly hoarse voice, "I don't want to know. This is beyond me."

He swallowed hard and nodded once. "Thank you."

She rose as gracefully as she had sat, and came over to him, covering his hand with hers. "Promise me Gemma won't be hurt."

"I can't," he whispered, meeting her eyes. "I'll try, but I can't promise. You know I would never hurt her if I could help it, it would kill me. But things as they are..."

A slight wrinkle appeared between her brows. "Promise me you won't be hurt."

He snorted softly and pulled his hand out from under hers. "I'll not promise that either. Don't set your heart to bleeding for me, Marianne. It's not worth it."

"Don't say that."

"It's not." He shook his head. "But take care of Gemma. I don't know what is going to happen, but..."

Marianne searched his eyes for a moment, then nodded firmly. "You have my word, of course, but who is going to take care of you?" She raised a questioning brow and swept from the room.

"Ideally, my wife," he muttered to the empty room as he rubbed at his face, then pressed his hands over his eyes.

"I'm really very sorry about that," Kit's voice said from the doorway. "You know Marianne, I couldn't control her."

"Go away," Lucas ordered from behind his hands.

Kit scoffed and his footsteps retreated down the hall.

He was really going to have to speak with Rogers about letting people into the house without his permission.

It was some time before he could get Marianne's words out of his head, and he was grateful for the silence to dwell on them. He knew full well that he'd revealed too much in his expression, but it couldn't be helped.

He would need to control that. Vulnerability was not something he could afford.

A soft knock at the door brought him up again, and wildly he looked up to see who had disturbed him this time.

Nothing could have shocked him as much as seeing Caroline Hammond standing there, looking markedly uncertain and timid.

"Mrs. Hammond," he greeted curiously, rising and coming around the edge of his desk. "I thought you were out with Gemma."

She nodded once. "I was. We have finished our errands, and she is with Marianne now. I was halfway home when I realized…" She trailed off, frowning.

Lucas had not interacted with his sister-in-law a great deal, but uncertainty was not in her nature. "Realized what?" he prodded as gently as he could.

Caroline raised her dark eyes to his. "I have never spoken with you about my sister, and I feel that I need to."

"Did something happen?" he asked, his voice rising with an edge of panic, suddenly gripping her arm.

She looked down at his hand, then up at him in surprise. "No, everything is fine. At least, it seems to be. She is a little downcast, but Society will do that to people if given an inch."

Lucas released a slow breath, steadying himself as best as he could. "They will, I'll not deny it."

"May we speak openly, Blackmoor?"

He nodded and gestured to an open seat. "Please."

Caroline sat and waited for him to do so as well, and he opted for a seat close to her instead of behind his desk once more.

She looked down at her gloved hands, her complexion only marred by the furrow between her brows. She really was a beautiful woman, and he suspected she would always be the envy of many, but she lacked Gemma's mischief and sparkle, the life that danced in every feature, the magic quality that made her so exquisite.

But he could hardly blame Caroline for what she lacked, given that she was a remarkable woman in her own right.

"Gemma is a special person," Caroline murmured softly, twisting her fingers. "Far more so than anybody ever thinks or supposes. Everybody has always liked her, they cannot help it. She has a pull about her."

This was true, and he made no attempt to comment.

"She has always been that way. She is the favorite of our cousins, has always charmed anyone who met her, and has the amazing ability to make people smile or laugh." A faint smile lit Caroline's face. "The trouble is that it also makes her easy to take for granted, and people do, myself included."

Again, she was not saying anything that Lucas was not already fully aware of, so he remained silent.

Caroline looked over at him briefly. "Gemma tries to hide that it bothers her, but… and this is what I wanted so speak to you about… she cannot hide anything."

Ah, now that was an interesting point to bring up, and he sat back in his chair.

"Try as she might," Caroline continued with a swallow, "Gemma cannot hide any emotion. You can see it in her eyes, in her expression, in her manner… Her words and her tone may be passably convincing, but anyone paying attention would know the truth. Every emotion, every hurt, every irritation is there in her eyes."

"I know," Lucas said quietly, remembering the way his wife's eyes had dimmed this morning at his dismissive tone. He was being a horrible brute, but it was necessary.

Caroline smiled slightly. "She will never be able to lie to you."

That drew a snort from him, and her smile grew.

"She cannot be dishonest," she went on. "Her heart is too tender, and she is not at all convincing as an actress. Gemma has no deception within her. I have never met a more genuine person in my life, and I am her sister, I know her better than anyone."

Almost, he thought with a mental smirk.

Caroline sighed and turned to him a little more fully. "I just wanted to ensure that you knew the sort of woman you had married, Blackmoor. Not because of any doubts or concerns, but because I care about my sister, and I wanted you to know this much at least."

"I appreciate your candor," he said politely, "but may I ask why now?"

"I ought to have said something before the wedding," she sighed with a shake of her head. "I don't know you well, hardly at all, but my sister cares a great deal for you, anyone can see that. And as her sister, I only want to be sure that you will take as much care of her as she will try to of you."

Inexplicably, his throat tightened and he could not speak.

"She is the rarest sort of person," Caroline murmured as if lost in thought. "No artifice or deception about her in anything. She has far too much heart and the determination to let it lead. She is…"

"Gemma is exactly who she is," Lucas overrode in his own bemused tone. "Without apology or excuse, she is nothing more or less than herself at all times."

Caroline was silent for so long that Lucas had to turn to look at her, and found her smiling softly.

"What?" he asked, a bit bluntly.

"I can see that my concerns are unnecessary," she said, her lips curving further. She rose, still wearing that peculiar smile.

He awkwardly got to his feet, unsure what had just happened.

"Thank you for indulging a sister's whims, my lord." She curtseyed politely, and he bowed stiffly, remembering at the last minute to take her hand and kiss it.

"You are always welcome," he murmured.

Caroline's smile grew and she put a hand on his arm. "Take care of her, Blackmoor. She will give you everything if you will let her."

She squeezed gently, and left the room, leaving him staring after her in bewilderment.

He ran a hand through his hair, and returned to his desk, sinking heavily into the seat.

Gemma could give him everything? He shook his head and glowered to himself.

Could no one understand that was his greatest fear?

Chapter Sixteen

Gemma tipped her head back to allow the sun more access to her cheeks, sighing softly in delight at the warmth.

Most women preferred to be pale and almost sickly, but she was not one of them. She enjoyed being a little healthier looking, even if it was unfashionable. A pink nose never cursed anyone.

She ought not to have such leisure time to sit around and indulge in her complexion, but her friends had gone without feeling the need to entertain her today, and there were no more calls to return. There were no more invitations at all. No one wanted to see her, no one wished for her company, and no one minded if she sat here in the sun.

She could have gone home, she supposed. There were many things she could see to there, as she now ran the house, and several tasks she could complete that really ought to be done.

But here she sat, taking a long moment to bask in the sun.

Because home was a miserable place.

Whatever progress she imagined from that exquisite moment with Lucas in the gallery, and the tender hours afterwards, had vanished so quickly that none of it seemed real. He was distant, aloof, and generally absent, even when he was sitting before her and sharing the same meal.

She would never have accused him of being rude or ungentlemanly, as every word he shared with her was of absolute politeness and decency. He'd never had a cross word with her, never gave her the slightest indication that he was displeased or in any way upset, and yet his expression was usually troubled when he thought she wasn't looking. He was very good at containing it, wearing a calm and implacable façade whenever they conversed or when he knew he was being observed.

She'd asked him about it only once since the morning after the ball, and he'd blandly written it off as fatigue in the most unconvincing manner possible. She suspected he was being truthful, in his own way, and was simply keeping the reason for his fatigue and distraction to himself.

He'd not hidden from her before, despite his reserve and the secrets he held from the public, but now she was just as lost as anyone else might have been.

Home with him was lonelier than any crowded ballroom or empty cave she had ever experienced.

She'd tried to be patient, she'd given him distance so he might not feel pressed, but the reality was that she desperately wanted to press him. She wanted to rage at him. She wanted to demand that he let her in and be a husband instead of a recluse. She wanted…

Well, she wanted her husband back, but she wasn't entirely certain she knew who that was.

And there was no one who could know him well enough to explain it to her.

She'd tried with Marianne, but she'd been oddly evasive about it. She did not know Lucas on a particularly intimate level, but she'd said she would have Kit see to it. And Kit had given her nothing to go on.

She'd tried to counsel with her sister, but Caroline knew even less of Lucas than Marianne, and could only assure Gemma that her husband cared about her a great deal.

That much she knew already, for whatever she asked for was given.

Except answers.

Except his confidence.

Except him.

Tears swirled in her eyes and she choked on a gasp as she tried to force them away. It would not do to cry in the park publicly, no matter how people ignored her.

"Lady Blackmoor?"

She glanced over to see a man approaching and she straightened up, fixing a polite smile on her face. He was a little familiar, but not enough that she should recognize him. He was young… whether in looks or age, it was impossible to say… and dressed a bit like a popinjay. Dark hair, dark eyes, and a charming smile, but no name came to mind.

He removed his hat in a grand sweep and bowed politely, then replaced it. "What a pleasure!" he cried, his smile crinkling his cheeks. "I had no idea you were returned to London."

Her smile turned quizzical, and she raised a brow at him. They had been in London nearly three weeks, and had attended many events. Perhaps he was only recently returned himself, though. It would explain the confusion. But as she looked at him, she wondered if perhaps his mind was not entirely adept at remembering the details.

"Ah, you don't remember me, do you?" he asked with a light laugh, correctly reading her expression.

She gave him an apologetic look. "I apologize."

He shook his head at once. "Not at all, not at all. We met, I believe, at your wedding breakfast, and that is hardly the way to begin. You are excused from remembering something so insignificant on such a day."

His superfluous nature was dizzying, but he was pleasant enough, which was a welcome change, and she could not help but to smile at him.

"Bennett Stanford," he said, bowing once more. "I am acquainted with your husband. He and my brother were schoolmates."

"Lord Oliver," Gemma recalled, her smile genuine now. "Yes, I remember him telling me about you."

He quirked a brow. "Really? And what, pray tell, did the good viscount have to say about me, hmm?"

Gemma shook her head at once. "No, I will not betray confidences."

"But I am off to fence at the club and will surely meet him there! I could have something to bait him with!" He seemed so eager that she nearly laughed at him.

"I doubt my husband would appreciate being baited," she scolded, warning him. Lucas had been acting so strange lately, there was no telling what it might do to him.

Mr. Stanford waved a dismissive hand. "Oh, he would be quite used to it from me. I'm a bit of a puppy, you see, and he only barely tolerates me. Years of practice, I am afraid." He shrugged a little. "I am a younger brother, after all, and act as such for everyone."

Gemma grinned outright. "It is a wonder Lord Oliver tolerates you."

"He doesn't." He flashed a quick grin, then let it fade easily. "But you seem, if you'll forgive me, a trifle sad today, my lady. Might I be of some assistance?"

She reared back in surprise, wondering what he had seen, what he could possible presume. "I don't think so," she managed, knowing better than to attempt lying. "It is… a personal matter."

He nodded thoughtfully. "I would never wish to pry, my lady, I only… Well, it is a shame to see so pretty a woman looking so unhappy."

"I am not unhappy," she muttered defensively.

"Forgive me," he replied with a slight bow. "I am often thoughtless with my speech."

She sighed and slowly shook her head. "No, I fear I am to blame. I was lost in my thoughts, and they are not pleasant."

"If I were a thought of yours, I should be most pleasant indeed."

She snorted suddenly and looked up at him. "Flowery turn of phrase for a puppy to use on a married woman."

He smiled brashly. "I must keep up the practice." He held out a hand and she slowly laid hers in it. He raised her glove to his lips, still smiling. "I shall tell your husband of our meeting today, and how delightful I found you. Surely that should please him."

"I cannot say if it should or not," she murmured before she could stop the words.

His brow furrowed. "Is there some… disagreement between you and your husband, madam?"

She opened her mouth, then forced a smile. "That would be far too personal a divulgence for so slight an acquaintance."

He nodded at once. "Of course. Forgive me." He flashed another smile. "Again."

She inclined her head properly in acceptance. "Of course."

"Well, at the very least, I must compliment Blackmoor for his excellent choice of wife. But I knew he would choose well, should he have married again."

She smiled reluctantly. "Did you?"

He seemed surprised by her response. "Of course. He is a most excellent man, and has impeccable taste. You and his first wife were testaments to that."

Gemma could not hide her surprise at his saying so. "You can say that, with all of the… rumors?"

"I would never say less. I pay no mind to the rumors." He leaned forward, his eyes earnest. "And nor should you."

Gemma was thrilled to the bone to hear someone say such things about Lucas, considering everything she had ever heard before, and everything she had heard since her marriage. "Mr. Bennett Stanford, I think you are a fine man. And if it will not trouble you, I could do with an escort home. If you would be so kind."

His smile was dazzling and he gallantly offered her his arm. "With pleasure, Lady Blackmoor. Though I would recommend in the future bringing a servant with you. We must maintain propriety. Reputation is a tricky business."

Gemma offered a grim smile as she rose and took his arm. "Don't I know it."

He chuckled and patted her hand. "Never fear, my lady. It comes with the territory. Now, tell me about yourself. I must reconcile your reputation with your words if I am to protect you properly in the future."

She glanced up at the taller man. "Are you to be a knight for my honor, then?"

He suddenly appeared very puffed up indeed. "I'll be the gallant knight for any pretty face, madam. Every proper lady wants one, and I aim to be the most sought after."

Against her will, she laughed, thinking this man a very ridiculous puppy indeed, but at least he was kind and amusing. And for now, that would suffice.

Closer than you know.

Lucas stared at the missive for what had to be the hundredth time that afternoon. The surprise and shock had worn off, but the anxiety was running rampant. More than a week without a word, and now this. What sort of cryptic message was this and why now? Closer how? In what ways?

Or to whom?

"I haven't heard anything in recent days, but your tenants are a little protective of you. That should be encouraging for you."

Lucas slowly raised his head to meet the quizzical look of Lord Beverton, who was situated comfortably in his study, watching him. He'd come just before the missive had to offer his report from Hampshire, which had been completely pointless and uneventful. Some had recalled seeing an unfamiliar man wandering about, but as he had not made himself known to anyone, nor left any sort of impression, there was nothing to be said about it.

"Protective?" Lucas managed, his mouth dry, his mind whirling to recall what had been said in the minutes he had been otherwise occupied. "I've never encountered any particular loyalty from them, they seem more suspicious than anything else."

The earl flashed him a quick and easy smile. "They are indeed suspicious, but they refused to tell me anything until they knew where my opinion of you lay. Said you were the best landlord they'd ever known and they'd not hear a word against you."

There was a faint tightness in his chest for a moment, but it was quick to dissipate. "That is good to hear. Thank you."

Beverton tilted his head. "I don't think your tenants are the ones you need to worry about."

"I didn't think so."

"Mine check out as well."

"Good."

"Are you going to tell me what that one says or do I need to guess?"

Lucas looked over at him warily. "You don't need to be

involved."

Beverton snorted. "I am already involved. If you'd rather it stay private, I'll say nothing more about it. But if you want a second set of eyes…" He shrugged and said nothing more.

Lucas considered telling the man what exactly he could do with his second set of eyes, that this was his personal business and not for anyone else's concern… but Beverton was right, he was already involved, and there was nothing to indicate that Lucas could not trust him further.

With a barely muffled sigh of resignation, he handed it over, and watched for the reaction.

The earl's brows rose sharply, then looked up at him. "Are there more?"

Lucas nodded once, reached into the desk drawer, and pulled out the others, handing them over as well.

It only took a moment, and then all notes were handed back to him. "I don't like this," Beverton said bluntly.

"I am not particularly fond of them either," Lucas replied tightly.

"This is more than mischief."

"I agree."

"Gemma needs to know."

"No."

That seemed to surprise him. "No?"

Lucas shook his head firmly.

He frowned. "She needs to know."

"I can't tell her. Not yet. It's too soon for… Not yet."

Beverton was silent, then just shook his head. "If you wait too long, you may be too late."

"I know that," he snapped. He sighed, rubbing his brow. "Forgive me, that was unnecessary."

"Not at all. You are under strain, and I am impertinent." He smiled easily, as if the matter truly were forgotten. "If you need me, you need only ask."

Lucas nodded, suspecting the earl knew he would never ask anything further of him. "Of course."

A knock at the door turned them both to look at it.

"Come," Lucas called.

A ray of sunlight in the form of his wife entered, looking a little smaller than normal, her smile a little too forced. "Good morning," she said softly.

He rose and offered her a bow. "Good morning."

She entered the room, her tension easing slightly. "I… Nathan?" she asked, catching a glimpse of the earl, who had also risen with her entrance. "What on earth are you doing here?"

He grinned and reached an arm about her shoulder, pulling her in for a quick hug. "Can a man not visit his favorite relation by marriage without raising questions?"

Gemma rolled her eyes at Lucas, and it reminded him so much of their earlier days that it ached. "No, he cannot. And I am not related to you at all."

"You wound me, Gemma," he tutted, releasing her. "I always thought of us as family."

"One Hammond brother is quite enough for me," she said with a smile. "Now, what brings you here?" She looked between Lucas and Beverton expectantly.

Oddly enough, Lucas could not conjure up a feasible reason for the earl's visit.

Thankfully, Beverton was a quick thinker.

"That infested crop that the Burns family was dealing with back at Thornacre?" he said easily.

Gemma nodded, looking curious.

"A few farms on my estate have suffered the same. Blackmoor and I were discussing options for aiding the families until we can determine what can be salvaged."

Lucas kept his face impassive as his wife looked at him for confirmation.

"Can they be salvaged?" she asked, truly concerned.

Trust his wife to actually pay attention to the details of their tenants' farms and understand the implications of them.

"We think so," Lucas told her, attempting to sound reassuring. "Beverton and his manager have some good ideas, we may be able to implement them."

At least, he hoped Beverton had some good ideas. Or else he would have a great deal of explaining to do later.

"And on that note, I need to go and send instructions," Beverton replied on cue. He kissed Gemma's cheek fondly and nodded at Lucas. "I will keep you informed, Blackmoor, if you would be so kind as to do the same."

"Of course."

He nodded once, then left the room without further ado.

Gemma turned to Lucas, her smile still lingering, and it caught him unawares somewhere in the vicinity of his chest. It had been ages since she had smiled at him.

It had been ages since he had given her a reason to.

"I didn't mean to disturb you," she murmured quietly, adjusting a strand of hair behind her ear.

He hated that gesture, a sign of timidity and nerves that was so unlike his vibrant, impulsive wife. He infused every ounce of warmth he could muster into his gaze and moved around his desk slowly. "Not at all. We were finished. Your timing was perfect."

His voice had softened on the last word and Gemma caught it, her eyes lighting with a hint of hope.

Unable to resist it, and her, he took her hand in his and raised it to his lips. "What can I do for you?"

The formality of the words was, he hoped, lessened by the tone he could not contain, and she offered him a small, hesitant smile. "I received an invitation for a tea and luncheon with Lady Cavendish on Tuesday."

He nearly smiled at that. "That is impressive," he mused, leaning against his desk, still holding her hand. "I didn't think you were overly acquainted with Lady Cavendish and her circle."

Gemma grinned brashly. "I'm not, but she moves in circles with Lady Raeburn, who *is* quite fond of me, and Lady Cavendish has a tendency to like anything Lady Raeburn finds worthwhile, particularly if it will gain her some attention herself." She shrugged lightly. "I've never been invited before, but with Tibby's musicale approaching, Lady Cavendish no doubt will wish to discuss my wardrobe and selection of music so she might appear to have some influence."

Lucas chuckled a bit dryly and shook his head. "Opportunistic woman." He tilted his head. "Why come to me about this? You don't need my authority or permission for your social agenda. Accept it and let the ladies fawn over you."

She twisted her lips. "Well… I happen to know that Lady Cavendish is also quite extravagantly devoted to Lady Riverton. She invites her to everything, and I believe Lady Riverton comes more often than not."

"Ah," Lucas murmured as he sat back, watching his wife.

"I… did not want to accept without consulting you, considering that fact," she said quietly, averting her gaze.

Unobserved, he smiled and let it fade before squeezing her hand. "Of course, you should go. I have no control over who Lady Cavendish invites to her soirées, and you cannot avoid my aunt at every turn, nor would I wish you to, should your paths cross naturally. Just because the family connection is not acknowledged does not mean you cannot associate with her."

She looked at him quickly, her eyes brightening. "You mean it? I don't wish to cause you any grief or discomfort."

He shook his head, bringing her hand to his lips once more, lingering. "No, love, you won't. You never could. Go and be fawned over, mingle with the high society ladies, and let the world wonder at your brilliance."

Her fingers fluttered against him and he met her eyes, choked by the warmth in her smile. "You fair flatterer," she whispered. "You will give me quite an opinion of myself."

"No more than you deserve," he replied.

She smirked a little, wrinkling her nose up. "Will you come and walk with me, Lucas? It is a fair day, and…"

He shook his head before she could finish, the reality of their situation returning to his mind. "No, my dear, I cannot. There is too much to do, and you are far too pleasant a distraction." He released her hand and moved back around his desk, clenching his hand, desperate to retain the feel of her there.

He barely caught her small sigh of resignation, but when he looked at her again, she was perfectly composed.

"As you wish," she said politely. She turned from the room, then glanced back at the door. "By the by, I met your Mr. Stanford the other day."

Lucas raised a brow as he shuffled papers on his desk. "You met him at the wedding."

"Not really. Not in a way that I recalled anyway, which he was eager to remind me of." She smiled, but not at him, and that rankled him. "He happened upon me in the park and we conversed some. He likes you a great deal, you know, and says you have always had impeccable taste in women."

"And what did you make of him?" he asked, forcing his voice to be unaffected.

She raised her eyes to his, and they were markedly unreadable. "You are quite right. He is a puppy, but an oddly charming one. I like him."

For some reason, he didn't like that she liked him, despite his own fair opinion of the man. "Good," he grunted. "I shall inform him when next we fence."

"Oh, don't bother," she replied. "He'd be insufferable if he knew I held a high opinion of him." She vanished before he could respond further, which suited him just as well.

He didn't know how he would have responded.

His wife was having a life without him. Mingling with people who would never have approached him, meeting people who had long been in his world, but never hers, and benefitting from his position without suffering the pains of it. It was everything he wanted for her.

So why did it sting so poignantly?

He sank into his chair with a groan and put a hand over his eyes. Impeccable taste in women? Idiot. He had impeccable taste in *one* woman, but his past history with the other had been a nightmare.

But no one knew that.

No one could.

A chill raced up his spine as her face appeared in his mind's eye, her laugh echoing in his ears, the coldness in her eyes cutting him just as swiftly as it ever had before. Again and again, her words replayed, calculated to wound him precisely and effectively, ever cutting and cruel.

The prodding came again, as it always did, and he fought it, distracted himself as best as he could with the matters at hand, business and properties and investitures, but he could not fight it forever. He never could.

With a disgusted sigh, he shoved away from the desk and left his study, his path and his steps sure, despite the sickening twist of his stomach. He mounted the stairs and secluded himself to the gallery once more, only giving the faintest indication to the footman that he was not to be disturbed.

For a while, at least, he would be otherwise occupied.

Chapter Seventeen

"*L*ady Blackmoor, it is such a pleasure to have you here with us!" Lady Cavendish gushed as she clung to Gemma's hand, her powder blue gown so flounced it swallowed Gemma's simple cream muslin without effort.

"Thank you for your kind invitation," Gemma replied with a kind smile, letting herself be led.

"Do you know the other ladies here?" Lady Cavendish asked with a grand gesture to the others sitting about.

Gemma's smile became a bit tight. "By sight, yes. By introduction, only a few."

Lady Cavendish took care of that in short order, making elaborate and detailed introductions that seemed to tighten the face of every woman present as one or more items listed were not entirely pleasant ones, and Gemma got the suspicion that, although there were some ladies of high society in attendance, their being present was more of an effort to not offend the hostess rather than to enjoy her company.

She rather felt the same way.

Lady Raeburn was present, as was Lady Whitlock, and a few other ladies that Gemma could mingle with, but for the most part, they were already situated in their comfortable groups, and she was left to herself for a moment, though Lady Whitlock indicated she would be with her shortly.

She didn't mind. The reprieve was a blessing.

The days had been passing in a sort of daze, nothing of true interest or significance distinguishing one from the next. Her husband was absent, then remarkably attentive, and then once again distant, and she could never manage to discover what determined the mood or change. He was so distracted, so disinterested most of the time, but there was an odd sort of longing in his eyes that she did not care for at all.

She'd tried everything she could to encourage him, but it only seemed to push him further away. He'd even gone so far as to flat out refuse to share her bed the other night, stating he was not interested in doing so at this time. She'd tried not to take it personally, but it was difficult, and she would be lying if she did not admit to shedding tears over that particular instance.

They were in a sort of neutral ground at the moment. She never sought him out and only spoke to him on light subjects when they happened to be together. He listened politely, conversed minimally, and gave her the benefit of his full attention as he always had done.

But he never smiled. Not even in his eyes.

More and more she had begun wondering about his first wife. He'd been in the gallery many evenings, she knew, and she had never disturbed him there again, given their new tension. Did he gaze up at her portrait, a rather grand and spectacular one, with longing and anguish? Did he miss her as fiercely as he seemed to?

She had gone into the gallery herself, on occasion, and stared at the previous Lady Blackmoor with an assessing study. She was trim in all of right places, and voluptuous in others. A rare, exotic beauty, dark and seductive, and she could easily see how she would charm an entire ballroom of people, men and women. She was a captivating woman, even in art, and in life she must have been a magnificent sight to behold.

How could plain, plump, forgettable Gemma compete with such a woman in a man's heart?

Oh, she was not silly enough to think that her husband did not value her. On the contrary, she knew he did. She had felt it, he had shown it, and she could not… and would not… be that sort of maudlin woman who would always doubt it. Lucas liked her, cared for her, respected her, and would always take care of her.

But would it ever be what he felt for his first wife?

Her conversations with Mr. Stanford, which had continued at

fairly regular intervals, had led her to believe that Lucas was a single-minded man, which she had suspected, and that perhaps he might be feeling some guilt for his second marriage. But she was repeatedly assured of her husband's fidelity and admiration, not that she needed any such assurances, and that he would soon get over it.

She valued his opinions greatly, and had begun to ask him what he knew about Lucas's first wife, though he had not known her well, by his own admission. He could only tell her impressions, and they were along the same vein that her own thoughts had been. Everyone had adored her, and no one understood why she had married Blackmoor when she could have had anyone. But she had made her choice and no one had ever heard her regret it. She had teased her husband on occasion, even outside of his presence, as a woman of her nature would, but she seemed perfectly content with her lot. And no one had ever heard Blackmoor utter a cross or disagreeable word about her.

It was hard to hear, but necessary.

Mr. Stanford refused to let her dwell on such unhappy things, and often set his mind to make her smile, which was a welcome respite. It was such a pleasure to have a friend, someone who could cheer her without anything feeling forced.

Of course, she had Lily and Marianne, and her sister, when she could be spared, but there was something almost magnetic about Mr. Stanford, and the surprise in seeing him was always the greater for its spontaneity. He refused to let her set a time for them to meet ever, as it would seem to be a bit more scandalous if they met by design. He was always so considerate with such things, never wishing to make it appear as though either of them were betraying Lucas in any way. He valued Lucas, and Gemma herself, far too much to even hint at such things.

Such devoted friendship for a man he only admired from a distance, save their brief interaction together.

She hoped Lucas was as loyal to the young man, as he seemed to have earned his respect somehow.

She shook her head now, reminding herself that her husband was, above all else, a man of honor. He would do his duty by his friends and his associates, no matter the cost. No matter where his heart lay where she, or his first wife, were concerned, he would always behave with respect and integrity.

He was incapable of anything less.

And oh, how she missed him.

"Oh, Lady Riverton! How delightful to see you again!"

Gemma glanced up to see Lady Cavendish fawning over the newly arrived Lady Riverton, looking resplendent in a bold emerald gown that bore only the faintest of lace detailing, strings of pearls at her elegant throat. She commanded notice with her mere presence, and had Gemma not experienced the warmth and genuine heart of the woman, she would have been terrified into stunned silence.

As it was, she recollected her duty and responsibility as the wife of Lord Blackmoor and looked sufficiently impressed that such a lady would deign to appear, knowing how important it was that they remain strangers until such a time as it was appropriate.

Hiding her relief and pleasure seemed wrong, but Lady Riverton was playing the game as well, surveying the group with a polite, if distant, smile.

"What a fine gathering," Lady Riverton murmured, though everyone could hear her clearly. "Have I missed the luncheon?"

"No, my lady," Lady Cavendish clucked with a wave of her plump hand. "We were nearly to bring it out when you arrived."

"Perfect." She glanced about the room and her eyes fell on Gemma, and there they stayed. "Lady Cavendish, I don't believe I know that young woman. Would you be so good as to introduce us?"

Lady Cavendish might as well have been asked to oblige royalty for all of her fluttering, and she made the introductions with too much flourish, too much information, and too much patronization. But it would be allowed, considering it permitted Gemma and Lady Riverton to be acquainted publicly and converse.

"Lovely to make your acquaintance, Lady Blackmoor," Lady Riverton said with an incline of her fair head. "Might I claim the seat beside you?"

"I would be honored, my lady," Gemma replied with a demure nod.

She sat beside her on the divan, and then, noting that Lady Cavendish was still hovering, gave her a warm smile. "Dear Eloise, would you be so good as to see if your cook would mind including cucumber sandwiches in the luncheon? She is so talented, so gifted, and does you such credit, it would be delightful to partake of them."

Lady Cavendish beamed and blessed herself and dashed out of the room without any sort of grace at all, entirely forgetting herself under such attentions.

"There," Lady Riverton muttered under her breath as she made herself some tea. "That should keep her occupied for a moment. Her cook hates cucumber sandwiches, but she can hardly refuse a request."

"Especially from you," Gemma replied as she sipped her own tea with a smile. "Well done."

Lady Riverton gave her a sly smile. "A well-placed compliment with sufficient flattery will get you everywhere, my dear."

Gemma choked back a laugh as she tried to maintain her composed demeanor. Several women were still staring at them, whispering to themselves about it, and Lady Whitlock herself raised an impressed brow at her.

"Everybody wants to know why you are speaking with me," Gemma murmured, setting her tea down. "Such attentions, my lady."

"Enough of that. They can come and speak with you themselves if they wish to know what I find worthwhile in you." She cleared her throat, and raised her voice just one delicate notch. "No, I will not allow such modesty. Lady Raeburn raves of your talents, and I must hear it for myself. Tibby!"

Lady Raeburn turned with a devilish grin. "Anna?"

"Am I invited to your musicale this year?"

"Of course, my lady. You have a standing invitation."

"Consider this my reservation. Myself, my husband, and our sons will all attend. We must hear Lady Blackmoor play, don't you agree?"

Tibby looked at Gemma warmly, her eyes twinkling. "Aye, we must. It is my favorite part every year."

Gemma blushed and ducked her face.

The ladies in the room began to titter and attention was at last away from her.

"There," Lady Riverton sighed, patting Gemma's knee. "Now we may talk without observation. They are going to spread the word on that and find a way to become invited themselves." She giggled softly and sipped her tea.

Gemma glanced over at the woman with a smile. "You enjoy being who you are, don't you?"

That earned her a swift grin. "It certainly has its advantages." She set her tea aside and turned more fully to Gemma. "How are you, dear? We missed you at our party."

Gemma winced, then forced herself to smile for effect. "I am so sorry about that. I… We…"

Lady Riverton smiled sadly. "Lucas said no, didn't he?"

Unable to hide it, she nodded glumly.

Lady Riverton sighed and shook her head. "I thought he might. We always invite him, and every once in a while, he makes an appearance, however brief and limited. It would be wonderful to see him more, but until he comes to terms with it…" She shrugged lightly, looking troubled.

"Why does he do that?" Gemma whispered, forgoing her polite exterior. "Why shut himself off from the world?"

Lady Riverton's eyes were suddenly fixed and intense on hers. "Is he shutting you out, too?"

Unbidden tears sprang to Gemma's eyes as she nodded.

Lady Riverton made a soft noise of sympathy. "Are you unhappy?"

"I shouldn't be," Gemma whispered, blinking back the tears before they could fall. "I don't want to be, but… I miss him so. He's so distant, so closed… I didn't make a mistake in marrying him, did I?"

"No," Lady Riverton insisted, reaching out to squeeze Gemma's hand tightly. "No, dear, you didn't. He needs you. Desperately. And I think he knows it."

"Then why?" she asked, her voice hoarse.

Lady Riverton exhaled slowly. "Do you know about his family and their past?"

Gemma nodded, pretending to sip her tea once more.

"I am surprised you know that much," Lady Riverton said with a touch of irony. "He never speaks of it. Refuses to. He is well aware of what his family was, and who. He watched them destroy themselves, watched his mother waste away, saw everything, and he was determined to be better than that. Being the private man that he is, the best way to do that was to avoid giving anyone anything to say about him. He did not discuss his family, and he did not discuss himself. When troubles came, and they always did, he retreated into himself, waited for the storm to pass, and then began again."

Gemma listened with all the energy of her heart even as her mind whirled with images of a younger Lucas trying to rise above his family and being continually dragged down by them. What opportunities had been deflected by virtue of who he was? It was no wonder he was so independent, so totally separated from anyone or anything.

He'd had to be.

"When it was only him," Lady Riverton continued, "we reached out again, though my husband had been trying for years. Eventually, Lucas allowed for private reconciliation, and when he permits it, we see him. But we cannot push, or he will disappear again. And having some of him is better than none of him."

That struck a chord with Gemma, and her chest tightened in response.

She wanted *all* of Lucas. Not just some of him.

But she would have to take what he would give.

It was better than nothing.

"What of his first wife?" she asked in a much lower voice, desperate to avoid anyone hearing this particular part of the discussion.

Lady Riverton stiffened and her gaze sharpened. "Celia? What do you know?"

"Almost nothing," she admitted. "I know she was loved and admired by everyone, and that she was a great beauty. And Lucas has only ever said that he didn't kill her."

Lady Riverton's mouth tightened and she looked away. "I don't know much more than that myself," she whispered. "All he has ever said is that she died, and Society, knowing his family and their past, took that as an admission somehow. But while she lived… I cannot say much, Gemma, simply because I do not know. I wish I did."

"Can you tell me what you do know?" Gemma pleaded softly, turning the hand she held to squeeze it. "I just… I think he may still love her, and I wonder if that might be… hurting him." She twisted her lips a little, feeling that her words were rather lame and small.

Lady Riverton met her eyes for a long moment, then dipped her chin in a small nod. "I cannot tell you if he loved her. I cannot tell you if she loved him. They almost never moved in the same circles. And given her open nature and his reserve, she was the more favored. Everyone flocked to her, as if she were an addiction. She was a bold and brazen heiress, and she would have turned London on its head had she had a full Season at her disposal. I will never know how Lucas arranged the marriage between them, but everyone… and I do mean everyone," she added, eyes widening for emphasis, "thought it a most fortunate match for him. When she did not draw him out, it was assumed to be a marriage of convenience, and that was more understandable."

She sighed and rubbed Gemma's hand gently. "She was… captivating, Gemma. And Lucas, at first, watched her with a fierceness that ought to have given some caution, but it seemed to have the opposite effect. Eventually, he stopped watching altogether. And Celia never minded, at least in public. She smiled and laughed and flirted as she ever had. Who knows what life was like at home, in private, but I often wondered if…" She bit her lip slightly, frowning. "I often wondered if she might have been… entertaining certain attentions privately. From others. You understand?"

Gemma's breath caught in horror and she forced herself to swallow and nod.

"I cannot prove it, and nothing was ever evident," she told her, shaking her head, her brow furrowing. "It was only a feeling. How she acted, the men she attracted, the looks she gave…"

"That can't have been easy for Lucas," Gemma murmured.

Her words seemed to shake Lady Riverton from her reminiscence and the older woman smiled at her. "No, I don't think it was. But again, he never spoke of it, and never acted in any way to inform the public one way or the other."

Gemma sat back, feeling surprisingly drained for having been on the receiving end of the information. "No, he wouldn't, would he?"

Lady Riverton said nothing and reached for her tea, fixing a soft, polite smile on her face.

"What do I do?" she asked her, her voice small.

"Love him," Lady Riverton replied in the same tone. "Let him have his reserve, but don't let him hide there. I don't know him as well as I would like to, Gemma, but don't give up on him. Please."

"I won't," Gemma assured her with a smile, her eyes growing misty. "I can't."

Lady Riverton smiled warmly at her, which made Gemma want to cry more, and then luncheon was served and they were forced to speak of other things with the rest of the group, which served Gemma well enough, as she had very little of consequence to say.

There was too much to think on at the moment.

Gemma paced outside of Lucas's study for so long she was beginning to feel fatigue in her legs before she felt confident enough to attempt knocking.

Her words with Lady Riverton had started her thinking of a course. She had then happened across Mr. Stanford after the luncheon, and after advising with him, only very superficially, he agreed with her course.

Faintly, the thought occurred to her not to divulge private matters of her husband with a man that did not enjoy his own confidence, but she was growing desperate. And Stanford had her husband's interests at heart, he viewed him as a brother, or nearly. Surely it would be permissible this once… And she had not revealed anything truly personal about him.

Her own heart, however, could not keep itself hidden as she talked about her husband.

And bless Mr. Stanford, he knew. He smiled and offered his advice, repeatedly stating that he had no assurances that his advice would be at all effective, as her husband was a mystery.

That she knew well.

Hence her current hesitation.

But she was not, and never had been, a ninny.

She raised her hand and knocked with as much firmness as she could muster.

"Come."

She held her breath and entered the dark, masculine room. "I bring you the greetings of your aunt, and the wishes of Lady Raeburn for your attendance at her musicale."

Lucas looked up from his desk only briefly. "And how is my aunt?"

"Very well," Gemma said with a smile. "She looked positively radiant."

"She does that," he muttered, going back to his work. "Did anyone notice the two of you being overly social?"

Gemma scoffed. "Of course they did. Lady Riverton took notice of poor Lady Blackmoor, a little nobody everyone is ignoring these days."

That brought his head up with a jerk.

"But she only paid me polite attentions," Gemma reassured him, a bit taken aback by the darkness in his gaze. "She was generous in her praises and before the luncheon was over, I had several new acquaintances and more invitations. That is all. No one suspected anything, I promise."

He stared at her for a long moment, then looked back down at his work. "Good."

"And will you come to Lady Raeburn's musicale?" she asked, wondering why his mood was so foul. "I am to be playing, after all."

"I doubt it," he said in an offhand way.

Her mouth dropped open in shock. "What? Why?"

"I don't need to give a reason."

"Perhaps not for everyone else, but I would like one," she retorted. "I have been practicing for weeks, you've heard me."

"All the more reason not to, I know how brilliantly you play."

"Lucas, that is not the same thing!"

He glanced up at her. "Isn't it? You said so yourself, you are very sought after now. I am not. It would be better for you if I left you to it."

She was shaking her head before he finished. "No, they will say what they have been saying. That you have tired of me. That I am not enough to sustain your attentions. That I have thrown you over. You have left me so alone that nobody knows what to make of either of us, and now I am talked about as much as you!"

He slowly raised a brow at her. "Perhaps you regret our marriage now that you know what it entails."

She frowned in response. "That is not what I said."

He snorted in derision and sat back in his chair. "What are you saying, then?"

His manner was so unlike the man she knew that she had no inkling of how to respond. "I… I miss you," she said simply.

A barely imperceptible twinge flickered across his face. "I am where I have always been," he replied with a slight gesture of his hands.

"No, you are so far away I hardly recognize you," she murmured. Then she raised her chin a touch. "Perhaps it is you who regrets our marriage."

He glowered at her. "Don't be ridiculous."

Something spurred her into impudence. "Am I? I never see you anymore. We never talk as we used to."

He sighed and picked up his pen, going back to his work. "I have responsibilities, Gemma. I am busy."

She would not be put off like this, to be brushed aside like some insignificant acquaintance. "Too busy for your wife?" she demanded. "You used to have all the time in the world for me."

That struck him, and he went so still she wondered if he even breathed.

"Walk with me, Lucas," she begged softly, knowing he was not as unfeeling as he was behaving. "Just the park. Please."

He looked up at her for a long moment, then sighed and stood, coming over to kiss her brow gently. "All right."

There was barely time for her heart to thrill at it before he had her out the door and walking briskly, as if that was what she meant. As if it were only an errand to be completed.

As if she were merely a duty.

They walked on in silence, side by side, but worlds apart. It was not at all what she had intended, but she would take it, if that was all he would give.

Without a word, he led her to the grove of trees she'd come to treasure, where they had once kissed and confessed all sort of things. Once safely within, the tension in him seemed to fall away. He exhaled deeply, closing his eyes.

"Lucas?" she prodded with some concern, laying a hand on his chest.

He turned and seized her face, his lips crashing down on hers with a fierceness and intensity that stole her breath. She responded in kind, fisting her hands in his shirt, passion rising within her as a torrential flood.

He pressed her back against a tree, wild and unfettered, his mouth eager and insistent. She had longed for this, dreamed of it, craved it… But it would solve nothing. Knowing this still burned beneath the surface encouraged her, emboldened her, and she took her chance.

She broke off the kiss and cupped her husband's face. "Lucas, tell me what is wrong," she whispered, her lips grazing his. "Tell me the trouble."

He instantly stiffened, jerked back, and removed her hands from his face. "No. I've told you not to ask me, and I mean it!"

He shook his head at her, then turned and strode out of the grove.

"Don't leave me alone again!" she called, her voice cracking.

He stopped at once, hands clenching at his side, then turned to look back at her.

She didn't bother to hide her tears as they began to course down her cheeks. "Don't leave me alone," she pleaded, biting down on her lip.

He stared at her for a moment, his hands on his hips, exhaled slowly, then came back to her and held out his hand. "Forgive me. Come."

She noted that he did not apologize, only asked for her forgiveness. For some reason she could not identify, that seemed a significant omission. But she swallowed back her pain and distress, took his hand, and they silently continued their walk.

He did not leave her alone in the grove, but it was not the grove to which she had been referring.

When they returned home, when this painful interlude ended,

would she be alone again?

She was very much afraid that she already knew the answer to that.

Chapter Eighteen

*N*ever in his entire life had Lucas felt this level of depression.

Considering the plethora of opportunities with darkness and discouragement that had been presented to him over the course of his life, that was saying a great deal.

There was nothing to smile about, should he have been at all tempted to do something so irrational. There was nothing to lessen the burdens currently weighing on him. There was no relief to be found, no comfort he could receive.

His wife was miserable.

And it was his fault.

More than that, he was the one *making* her miserable.

Surely there was no circle of hell dark enough for that.

He sat alone in his darkened study, no candle, no fire, draperies drawn as much as they could while still letting in light enough to see and work by. He ran a hand over his face, wincing at the stubble and sensitivity of his skin. He had sequestered himself in this room for days, sleeping in his chair, taking his meals within… He was becoming more of a recluse than he had ever been in his life, and he couldn't see a reason to change that.

He only caused more damage when he attempted to be human.

Gemma had stopped looking for him. Had stopped sending for him. Had stopped caring, for all he could tell. And it was only right that she should. He was destroying what was most precious to him.

His reasons were sound, honorable even. But what good were reasons when he was slowly dying every day? Soon his wife would despise him, just as Celia had. Would she also seek for entertainment and comfort elsewhere? Would she turn cold and hard? How could she stand remaining with him?

Celia had stayed, but only to torment him. He had never abandoned her as he was doing with Gemma. She had taken matters into her own hands, not finding him to be enough for her. He had never been enough for her.

For anyone.

And now he was not enough for Gemma.

And there was no one to blame but himself.

He groaned and leaned back in his chair. He could catch snippets of her voice every now and then, faint echoes of laughter, complaints of a missing handkerchief, compliments of a meal, the soft strains of her violin echoing down the hall…

He was desperate for anything of her, but he could not bring himself to face her. To see the light in her eyes dim with his presence. To long to touch her while knowing it would abhor her.

Celia had been hell for him.

But Gemma…

He was hell for her.

Lady Raeburn's musicale was in three days. He had sworn not to attend to give himself further distance from his wife. But the more he thought on it, the more he decided that was pure folly. His wife was a talented musician and he had admired her gifts for years, long before he loved her. He had to make an appearance at some point; avoiding the world was irrational.

And he could see Gemma without having to speak to her, or explain himself, anything to ruin his plan to protect her by distance.

In fact, avoiding Lady Raeburn's musicale would do more harm than good. He had always gone, and he could not afford the affront to Lady Raeburn now when she had always been so generous where he was concerned.

And she adored Gemma. Anything he did to deliberately wound his wife would come back upon his head a hundredfold.

No, he would clean himself up and go. But discreetly. And separate from his wife.

For her sake.

A knock at the door roused him and he called for entrance, his voice sounding harsh and raspy from lack of use.

"This just arrived for you, sir," a lanky footman with an expressionless face said, handing out a tray.

Lucas frowned and grabbed the thick letter. "From whom?"

"Did not say, sir," the footman reported. "Courier said he had no information on that score."

Lucas nodded, his stomach curling. "Thank you. You may go."

The footman bowed and exited without a word.

He wasn't ready for another mystery. He could barely handle the ones currently plaguing him, more would be truly excessive.

Nothing this large had ever come without address, and yet it was not heavy enough to be strictly correspondence within.

He broke the seal with an increasing sense of uneasiness.

A bit of fabric fell into his lap, and he reached for it, glancing at the paper surrounding it.

There were only two words, written in a clean, perfect hand he knew all too well, far different from any of his other missives.

So close.

He dropped the paper as if he had been scorched by it, and his hands shook as if he had been.

The penmanship was Celia's

He'd know it anywhere.

But Celia was dead. He'd seen her broken body, he'd carried her back himself, he'd seen to every detail of her burial, for heaven's sake.

Yet her handwriting was before him, staring him in the face.

He looked at the fabric that had fallen out, and jolted to his feet, tossing it onto the desk.

Gemma's handkerchief, her apparently missing one, bearing her initials on the corner. She'd embroidered it at Thornacre with her new monogram, proudly showing him the work when it was done. She'd stated it was the only thing she'd ever embroidered worth beans, and he'd praised her for it.

Now it was sent to him with his late wife's handwritten threat.

She couldn't have written it.

She couldn't be alive.

She *wasn't.*

So close…

Whoever this was, they were close to Gemma. They knew Celia. And they knew exactly how to twist the knife in Lucas's stomach with maximum damage.

He began to shake uncontrollably, pacing the room like a madman. What could he do? It was beyond imagination, horrors upon horrors now facing him and his wife, and he'd been doing the only thing he knew how to protect her. Nothing was working. He couldn't protect her, not even from himself.

She had no idea what could happen if…

His knees buckled and he collapsed into his chair again, breathing frantic, vision spotting before him.

There were no options left.

Beverton could do nothing about this, he had limited power in London as compared to Hampshire. Kit would want to involve his brother, and Lucas did not know enough of Colin Gerrard to know if that would be sensible or worthwhile. He had run the course of what he could manage on his own, and he dared not attempt to hire Bow Street or anyone else, for there were details in his past that even he wished to forget.

His eyes snapped open as another name flitted through his mind, and he seized upon it like mad. He'd never employed him thus, feeling awkward about doing so with a friend, but there were literally no other options.

And after all, it was what he did.

But how could he communicate properly with him?

What was the name he went by?

It came to him and he scribbled out a few inconsequential lines on a spare bit of parchment. Then he went to the door and called for the same footman from before. James, he thought. And he was quite certain the lad hailed from London and would know what to do.

"Here, sir," he replied, coming to him.

"Have you a set of common clothes at the ready, James?" Lucas asked him without any preamble.

"Aye, sir."

"And do you know your way around London?"

The lad grinned. "Born and raised here, sir. Know it like the back of my hand."

Lucas nodded firmly, and handed the note. "You will please deliver this note and wait for instructions."

He took it, then frowned at the blank address. "Where am I to deliver it, sir?"

Lucas exhaled slowly, forcing back the last of the pride and restraint he had left. "I need you to take it to the Gent."

Recognition, understanding, and awe dawned on the young man's face, and he nodded, his jaw firming. "Yes, sir. I shall be discreet."

"Thank you." He indicated with his head for the lad to proceed now, and he did so.

Then, still shaking with slight tremors, Lucas went to the gallery, the only other place he dared venture anymore. Perhaps answers would lie within.

Or perhaps only more questions.

"And I've asked, but the servants tell me he only sits in there and stares at her portrait. He'll be in there for hours, and he is not to be disturbed unless it is of utmost importance. I thought one of the maids would cry out of terror from having to disturb him."

"Was he cruel to her?"

Gemma shook her head quickly, sighing as Marianne set her glass aside. "No, he never is. But his behavior is scaring them. It's scaring me." Tears swirled in her eyes and she blinked them back hastily. "I cannot reach him, Marianne, and I don't know why."

Marianne took her hand and squeezed it gently. "I wish I knew what to tell you, Gemma. You know I did not have an easy time with Kit when we first came back to London, but then it passed. You do know your husband cares about you, yes?"

Gemma nodded glumly. "Of course. I can see it in the rare moments he still sees me, and I cannot deny what has passed between us. But I wonder if he cares enough. Mr. Stanford says…"

"Mr. Stanford?" Marianne interrupted bluntly, raising a brow. "Bennett Stanford? Lord Oliver's brother?"

She nodded in response, unable to keep from smiling. "We have become more acquainted of late, and he has become a dear friend of sorts. He knows how worried I am about Lucas, and he knows and cares about him, so offers some advice."

Marianne frowned. "Kit knows Blackmoor and cares about him. I cannot see how Mr. Stanford can be of more help than him."

"Yes, well, I can hardly converse easily with Kit in the park about Lucas, now can I?" Gemma snapped, disgruntled by Marianne's lack of enthusiasm. "Your husband talks only a little more than mine does."

Marianne snorted softly, her delicate lips curving as her eyes sought out her husband on the far side of the room. "I know, but what he does say is really quite marvelous." She looked back at Gemma and her smile faded. "I will only say this: be wary of being too friendly with a gentleman, particularly an unattached one. I know little enough of Mr. Stanford to his credit or discredit, but you are not in a position where you can be who you once were where he is concerned. People will talk, Gemma."

"I know that," she muttered, looking away. "He is constantly reminding me of propriety."

"Mr. Stanford?"

She nodded.

"Well, at least one of you is sensible." Marianne squeezed her hand again, forcing Gemma to look up at her friend and catch the teasing glint in her eye. Instantly she relaxed, at ease once more. "Now, you were saying something about what he told you?"

"Yes." She straightened up, trying to remember. "He said that he can tell that my husband cares about me a great deal, and is very protective, but for some men it will always be the first wife who reigns supreme in their minds." Her heart had broken a little as he'd said that, but it felt truer every day. "Obviously, he does not know with Lucas, and he would not presume to guess, but it would make sense."

Marianne frowned, her eyes suddenly troubled. "I admit I know little of his first wife. Her final Season was my first, and I was hardly the creature I became at that point, but I envied her so. She was everything I wanted to be." She shook her head, chewing her lip slightly. "From outward appearances, at least. Kit doesn't say much on the subject, but I don't think it was a happy marriage."

"So I've heard," Gemma murmured. Indeed, it was all she thought about these days. How did she measure up to Celia? How did Lucas compare the two?

Did he regret taking a second wife so very different from his first?

Marianne suddenly snapped out of her reverie. "But you mustn't think on it overly much, Gemma. You are his wife now. You are here."

"But he isn't." She shook her head, feeling the weight in her chest. "What if I am always relegated to second best behind his first wife, Marianne? I don't think I could bear it, being married to a man who was measuring me against another all the time. I don't want to be his second rate wife."

"Oh, I doubt Blackmoor would do or think any such thing," Marianne scoffed, sipping her drink again. "He knows how different you are, and he wanted you just the same. And quite badly, if you recall."

She could barely remember those times, and it seemed a lifetime ago. Or that it had happened to someone else entirely.

"I don't know what my husband would do or would not do anymore," Gemma admitted with a bitter sigh. "I wonder if I know him at all."

"You know him," Marianne insisted, sounding quite fierce. "You do."

Gemma only shrugged, looking away, pretending to glance around Lady Raeburn's exquisitely decorated music room, far grander and larger than any else she had been in. She suspected it was meant to be a ballroom, but as Tibby had no use for such a place, she had converted it to a room for musical entertainment. It allowed her to host the most enviable musical events every year, and one was nearly as eager for those invitations as they were for any at the Rivertons'.

The performances had gone well, and Gemma had been lauded and praised for her excellent violin pieces, though she felt a little lacking in energy. The Rivertons had attended, to the delight of all, and it had pleased her to see at least some part of her new family treating her as such. They were all very careful in their attentions, being public and in company, but she had felt their sincere praises and it had warmed her.

If only her husband could be more like them.

She frowned at the thought. She could not very well wish her husband to be someone else. She had fallen in love with him, after all, as he was and for who he was.

The man he was now was *not* her husband.

And that was the problem.

"He couldn't take his eyes off of you, you know."

She shook her head and looked at Marianne. "Who?"

"Blackmoor." At Gemma's blank look, Marianne smirked. "Your husband?"

"He wasn't here," Gemma reminded her poor, deluded friend. "He isn't."

"Well, not anymore he's not," Marianne said with a light laugh. "The man escaped just after your final performance with Lily. Which means he missed Charlotte Truman, wise man."

"He… he came?" Gemma breathed, her heart pounding furiously.

Marianne's eyes widened perceptibly. "You didn't see him?"

She shook her head slowly, her mouth gaping a little.

That brought a small, sad smile to her friend's beautiful face. "Oh, my dear girl. If you could have seen him… The way he looked at you was breathtaking. I doubt anyone noticed, but I was so surprised at seeing him, given that he was not to attend, that I couldn't help but stare. And then I couldn't look away." Her throat worked slightly and her smile grew. "There are some very deep emotions there, Gemma. While you were playing, he would look nowhere else. Nothing else existed."

"Why would he not come to me?" she whispered, unable to swallow, breathing suddenly difficult.

Marianne chewed her lip, her brow furrowing. "I don't know, but believe me when I say that nothing about you is second rate for him. I could see it. And you know I never speak kindly of anyone if I can help it."

Gemma laughed against her will and squeezed her friend's hand in gratitude.

Did it change anything, him being here for her? Though she had not seen him, did it matter that he had been apparently transfixed by her, unable to stay away despite his declarations?

Her heart swelled within her and she had to smile.

Yes. Yes, it did matter.

It very much did.

Chapter Nineteen

Knowing his most trusted and capable friend was fully invested in his cause did little to comfort Lucas in the days following. Patience had never been his strong suit, and despite what he knew Rafe could accomplish, being the Gent and having the resources he did, offered only a brief satisfaction.

He'd met with him only hours after the missive he had sent off under cover of darkness and with Rafe almost unrecognizable in his disguise. This was the man he had come to know in his younger years, who did everything with intensity and listened with more exactness than any person on the planet. He missed absolutely nothing, from the inflection of tone to the barest hesitation, and the questions were pointed and direct.

It was a complicated matter, reconciling Rafe as the Gent with Rafe as the public knew him, or thought they knew him. It was no wonder no one in the world but a handful of people made the connection.

Lucas knew, and had been informed, that in order to properly investigate the matters surrounding Gemma and himself, his past would have to be delved into, particularly with regards to Celia.

"I have nothing to hide," Lucas had informed his friend boldly.

Rafe had met his eyes with a surprising amount of derision. "That does not mean I will not find things you'd rather I did not."

He'd grown instantly defensive, despite their friendship. "I didn't kill her."

That had earned him a snort. "That, at least, I already knew, thank you very much."

The conversation had lasted almost an hour, and afterwards he'd felt drained, but he knew that someone else would be helping him now. There would be an extra set of eyes on Gemma at all times, and he could be assured of protection and help always.

Although the idea of someone helping him now was a curious thought.

The morning after the musicale hosted by Lady Raeburn, wherein Gemma had performed with all of the brilliance, majesty, and perfection he had known she would, he had received a note from her, asking if they might have Bennett Stanford to dine with them.

A note requesting it.

She had not come in person.

His plan was working, then. Distance and separation would save her.

But he, who craved anything and everything to do with her, would not be safe from it.

He was powerless to refuse her anything, no matter how he might wish the puppy to be gone, and so he had agreed to it. And now he was to be on display for a young man who, though from a decent stock, had no more sense or intellect than a canary for no other reason than because his wife had somehow found something valuable in him.

That irked him.

Gemma was a kind heart, a sweet soul, but she was hardly naïve or insipid. What on earth could she find in Stanford to make him so worthy of her attention?

As he watched the fop present himself at the entrance, Lucas hid a small groan. He was dressed for a night at the Rivertons, it seemed, and his effusive greeting was grating.

But he was a decent enough lad, and a capable fencing partner. And apparently, he was devoted to both him and Gemma.

Surely that could not be so bad.

"Blackmoor!" Stanford called cheerily as he made his way down to him, grinning as though it had been years since they had seen each other as opposed to their fencing appointment the day before. "It is such an honor to be a guest in your home."

Lucas raised a brow at the man's downturned head as he bowed, then remembered to respectfully bow himself. "Of course, Stanford," Lucas said quietly. "It should have been done earlier, I expect."

The lad's dark features brightened. "No matter, no matter, I am delighted to be here at last."

He saw the dark eyes look around almost eagerly, and something in the pit of his stomach started to twinge. "My wife will be down presently," Lucas muttered, knowing he was correct by the faint color that appeared on Stanford's face. Really, the boy was like a young miss fresh out of finishing school.

"I have greatly enjoyed becoming acquainted with her, sir," Stanford said with another respectful incline of his head. "She is a credit to you, in every way."

"She is a credit to herself and nothing else," Lucas replied firmly, his cravat feeling too tight.

Stanford leaned in a bit. "I say, old friend, are you quite well?"

Old friend? Lucas nearly snorted at the presumption. They'd never been friends for their own sake, and the only thing he could honestly say about Stanford was that he lived up to every stereotype of younger brothers that Oliver had ever spoken of.

"I do not mean to pry," Stanford continued, misreading Lucas's expression entirely, "only of late you seem… preoccupied. Fixated, if you will. Your fencing yesterday, for example."

Lucas barely avoided wincing. He had been very aggressive yesterday, losing control in his form and wounding three men in the process. Not seriously, but enough to draw comment. Stanford had stepped in to be his fourth, and he had nearly wounded him as well.

"I apologize for that," Lucas said in a low voice. "I don't know what came over me."

Stanford's mouth curved into a half grin. "Something else on your mind, eh? Are you having… woman troubles?"

Lucas looked at him in disbelief. "Woman troubles?"

Stanford nodded in a very smug manner that did not suit his puppy image. "Indeed. I find whenever a woman is on the mind, a man is more wild and uncontrolled. So tell me, now, who is it? What sort of a woman can have a man like you so unhinged that he forgets himself in such a way?"

It took all of his strength to avoid punching the smirk off of the younger man's face. Did he really think that Lucas was the sort of man who would have such a low opinion and concern for his wife that he would take another woman for his own amusement?

Other men would, and did, but not Lucas.

Considering his family's past, however, it was not that illogical an assumption.

"I can assure you, sir," Lucas said stiffly, raising his chin, though he was already a good six inches taller than the man, "I have *never* forgotten my wife."

He saw the surprise in the sudden widening of Stanford's eyes and mentally smirked himself as the lad skittered back just a touch. "Of course not, Blackmoor. Forgive the implications, I meant no offense."

No, he probably did not. He doubted there was mental capacity enough to conjure up something designed to offend.

"I trust you know best, of course," Stanford continued, somehow still talking, "you are impeccable in your judgment. But if you should have need of anything, I hope you will think of me for support. I am at your service always." He bowed deeply, no doubt thinking his vow an astonishing one.

Lucas would most certainly *not* be calling upon him for anything, but a harmless lapdog was not the worst thing in the world. So long as he did not dote or become fawning, he could be as loyal as he thought himself. Lucas, however, would enjoy his solitude forevermore and forget Bennett Stanford existed as swiftly as he could.

"Bennett!"

Both men turned in surprise, and Lucas glowered as his wife descended, looking radiant and joyous. But not for him, her smiles were all for Stanford as he moved swiftly to kiss the air above her hand. And she had called him by his given name.

Echoes of the past grated on his nerves and he clenched his hands tightly inside his gloves.

"Darling Lady Blackmoor, I have told you before," Stanford scolded with a teasing smile, "you must not address me so informally. Propriety, my dear peach, propriety!"

Gemma laughed merrily and slapped his shoulder. "Oh, please, we are hardly in public. You are a guest in my home. I may address you however I please."

Stanford kissed the air above her hand again, and lingered too long.

Lucas cleared his throat slightly, and both pairs of eyes turned to him at last.

Ah, to be remembered.

Gemma's eyes dimmed a little, but somehow were still brilliant as they gazed upon him. Her smile softened, turned tender, and she came over to him, hand extended.

"My lord Blackmoor," she murmured, her voice somehow teasing despite her solemnity, turning his heart over in his chest.

He drew her hand to his mouth, unable to resist running his lips over her knuckles, drawing the barest gasp from her. "My lady."

Her quick smile lit his insides. "You are looking rather well," she told him, her voice softer than before. "Quite handsome. I forget that when I'm away from you."

He tried to find his voice, but he could only manage a weak clearing of his throat again, which made her smile knowingly.

He tucked her hand into his arm and averted his gaze. "Shall we go in?"

"Of course," she replied. She glanced over her shoulder. "Come along, Bennett. You will love what our cook can do, she's a wonder!"

Gemma's attention on him, however intense it had been, had softened his irritation briefly, but it soon flared up once more. That was the only time he had been involved in any sort of conversation beyond the bare politeness and the pretended consideration of his tastes and opinions. Everything else was between Gemma and Stanford, or Bennett, as she insisted on calling him.

It was the absolute worst dinner of his life, and he had suffered through several with his father and brother, let alone those he had spent with Celia.

Seeing Gemma smile and laugh for another man's attentions, watching him draw out emotions and delight that Lucas had not accomplished in some time, and being an outsider to this flirtatious interlude… He couldn't bear it. He could not leave, but how could he remain? His wife was infatuated with this young and handsome fop, and he was just as taken with her. His interest could hardly be blamed… Gemma was nothing short of perfection.

And Gemma… Well, he had hardly been a husband worth her concern, given his distance and reserve. An attractive man paid her some attention and treated her with the flattery and praise she deserved, and it was only natural for her to respond so.

All of this was true. It galled him to the core to admit it, but perhaps his precious Gemma ought to have been with someone like Stanford.

Perhaps he should have left her alone, let her fall victim to the charms of a man who could make her giggle and smile and charm an entire room with a glance. She could have been the wife of a man who wouldn't have so dark a past to haunt her steps. She could have been the toast of Society rather than a part of its derision.

She could have had anything.

And he had taken her.

Knowing the sham of a life he could offer and the secrets contained therein, he had taken her for himself anyway.

He glared at the pair of them, knowing neither would see it.

Gemma was *his* wife, like it or not, and he was not about to give her up. He was not going to endure this again, not with her. She was not Celia, and he refused to be played for a fool again.

He loved his wife, however little it might be apparent. Everything was different with her.

And yet he sat here, watching them, silent in his misery.

What could he do? Take away a source of what made Gemma happy? Bar Stanford from his home, her presence, and his club, and risk insulting a family that had always treated him fairly?

He was powerless here. Gemma needed to be happy for him to be happy, and if Stanford made her happy…

The thought made him cringe.

Surely she would never truly stray.

Surely she valued their marriage, perhaps even him, too much for that.

Surely…

Another lilt of her laughter rang through the room and his heart lurched.

Suddenly he could not be sure of anything anymore.

"I thought that might work, Bennett," Gemma sighed heavily, tempted to lean back against the bench in the park. "I truly thought that having you over for company might draw him out. You are friends, after all."

"Darling girl, I wouldn't go that far," Bennett laughed, giving her a scolding look. "We are friendly, and that is all I can say for us."

She glared at him. "Don't call me 'darling girl', I am older than you by four months."

"Yes, but you seem so very young right now," he shot back.

She nearly stuck her tongue out at him, but that would only prove his point. "He barely said a single word," she groaned, starting to fidget with her bonnet ribbons. "He spoke more to you in private than he did in my presence the whole evening."

Bennett chuckled and stretched out his legs, crossing his ankles. "Gemma, your husband is not a particularly loquacious man. I trust this is not news to you."

She snorted once. "No, indeed, but for a man he respects as highly as you…"

"Don't make the mistake of thinking that my respect for him is returned," he interrupted, suddenly stern. "I have yet to do anything to earn his respect at all, but he has mine eternally. He owes me no attentions or confidence, and I expect none."

She threw her hands up. "Then why did you encourage me to invite you for dinner?"

He grinned raffishly, the effect long lost on her. "Because dinner with the Blackmoors puts me in high society indeed."

She rapped his knuckles sharply. "Wretch."

"But also," he said more seriously, rubbing his bruised hand, "it allows me to spend time with people I care about. Your husband is troubled, Gemma."

"I know," she murmured, looking away. "I don't think he can stand me anymore, and I wish I could fix that."

Bennett tutted softly. "You know that is not true. He went to Lady Raeburn's musicale for you, despite his declaration not to."

"And did not speak to me," she reminded him pointedly. "I did not see him at all."

"More to be recommended for your good opinion, then," he went on smoothly. "He wishes to observe you without being observed himself, as he did last evening."

She glanced back at him, suddenly curious. "What do you mean?"

Bennett shook his head slowly, as if she were not thinking. "Darling, if you had been paying any attention at all, you would have seen how he looked at you. Tormented, I tell you."

Gemma shook her head. "I know he's tormented. I can see it. I just wish I knew what it was; how I can help." She lowered her eyes and swallowed with difficulty. "If it is because of me…"

Bennett sighed a bit dramatically next to her. "Oh, to be in love with one's spouse and in doubt of a return."

She threw a sideways glare at him. "Don't mock me, Bennett. You have no idea what this feels like. Or how it hurts."

"Just because I smile doesn't mean I don't hurt," Bennett muttered from beside her, his brow furrowing suddenly.

Gemma leaned her head back, groaning again. "He's taken to walking in the mornings. Did I tell you that?"

"You did not."

She nodded once. "I noticed it the other day, and this morning I followed."

"Intriguing," he mused with a teasing hint. "And where did the viscount lead his intrepid wife?"

She swallowed hard, her mind going back to the chilly morning she had spent following him. "A cemetery."

Bennett stilled beside her, but she hardly noticed.

"I didn't think of it," she murmured, finding herself shaking her head slowly, "but she must be buried here. Celia. She isn't buried at Thornacre, though I suppose her family could have her on their estate. But why else would he come to a cemetery early in the morning? His family are at Thornacre, I have seen their graves myself. But this was different. He was barely dressed, it was just dawn, and it was as if nothing else existed."

"That is unlike him. Blackmoor always has a plan." Bennett shifted, turning towards her more. "What happened?"

She shrugged her shoulders. "Nothing. He knew exactly where to go, and he stood there. Staring down at the headstone. Just staring. I don't know how long he was like that, but my legs began to ache before he moved. And then he only exhaled heavily, as if the weight of the world were on him, then he turned and walked among the others, but he didn't stop again." She blinked away a stray tear and frowned at her increased emotion where he was concerned. "I left after that."

Bennett seemed as struck by the information as she was. "And he has not done this before?"

She shook her head quickly. "I've asked the servants, and it is only lately that he has taken to morning excursions. And you know he would not dare go there during the day when someone might see him."

"Yes, it would draw comment," he mused softly. He shook his head again and sighed. "Well, I suppose this explains his comment the other night."

Something cold hit Gemma's midsection. "What comment?" she whispered, afraid of the answer.

He lifted a shoulder. "I made the mistake of suggesting, in a teasing manner, that his troubles might be because of a woman, and he gave me a very stern look, even for him, and he said…" He hesitated, giving Gemma a long look.

"Tell me," she pleaded.

"He said 'I *never* forget my wife'." He frowned, his perfect complexion marring. "I thought it odd at the time, but now I think I see it."

"He still loves her," Gemma breathed, her heart sinking. "I knew it."

"I can't say that," Bennett said swiftly, his eyes widening, "and it certainly does not take away regard from you."

"But I will always be second to her," she replied. "She will always hang over his head, always have his heart, and I will get whatever is left of him."

Bennett did not answer that, which told her all she needed to know.

"I need to know for certain," she whispered, wondering if it were possible to feel any smaller or less significant than she did now. "I cannot live like this, wanting him and not having him."

Bennett took her hand and kissed it gently, squeezing a little. "Well, my dear, then I think you had better pluck up the courage and ask him."

That was certainly easier said than done, but he was right.

How could she ask Lucas such a thing?

And when?

Chapter Twenty

The very last thing that Lucas wished to endure at the present was a ball, but he could hardly refuse to attend Colin Gerrard's elegant evening. It was an annual event and one he had long made a priority, given his proximity to the family and his respect for them. Now with having a wife, he absolutely could not refuse to attend.

He would be expected to show her off, at least a little.

He would even have to dance with her.

That might be a touch tricky. He and Gemma had spent no time at all together since the dinner with Stanford last week, and the separation was killing him. He was drowning in his own misery and craved the light and radiance she had once brought him. But her wishes and desires had been clear and he would take no pains to prevent her, if that was what she wanted.

He prayed it wasn't.

He couldn't bear losing another wife to the charms of others, especially one that he loved so fiercely.

He should never have gotten married again, and he certainly should not have married her.

Damn his selfish pride and foolish naiveté.

But there was nothing to be done about it now. He would move forward as best as he could, go on however he must.

It would be a right sight easier to do so if he wasn't so terrified all the time. Missives arrived almost every other day, having returned to the scrawled hand of before, and not the horrifying reminder of Celia. The notion that something was coming, to be aware, to watch, to prepare… The messages were varied, but thematically the same, and each chipped away at his already crumbling resolve.

He was as firm as ever on the barrier between him and his wife, but how long he could actually maintain the strength to endure it was coming into question.

He wanted to cling to her and never let her from his sight. He wanted to carry her off into the night and stay at Thornacre forever. He wanted to tell her everything, he wanted to hide all the evidence, he wanted…

He wanted more than he had ever wanted in his entire life, and such wanting was as painful as it was unfamiliar.

But nothing, not even the missive that arrived just before his departure, saying only the words "Prepare yourself," would sway him.

Not the repeated letters from Beverton offering help, not the scattered notes from Gent that contained nothing, not the curious looks at his club when he was too vigorous; his own mind was the only haven he would find.

He addressed nothing and no one. Silence had saved him before, been penance enough for the crimes of his family and his past, and such an atonement had served him well. While he suffered unseen, the rest of the world could speculate at will. Gemma would be free to do as she pleased, the distance now starting to be remarked upon. They would forget about him, as they had before, and she could enjoy her life however she chose.

While he only watched her from afar.

As he did now.

She was perfection embodied this evening, and he was not the only one to notice. She was dancing nearly every dance, whether for the spectacle of dancing with Lady Blackmoor or for her charms, he did not know, but he prayed for the latter. She deserved the attention she had never received before their marriage, but none of the censure from after. If her smile at present was anything to go by, she was enjoying every moment.

At one time, not too far gone, he had made her smile in such a way.

His cravat seemed to tighten more against his throat as he heard Gemma's rich laughter over the sound of the musicians, so real and genuine, cutting to his core. He ought to escape to the card room, as he had done so many times before.

Yet here he stood, watching his wife like a lovesick fool.

Which, of course, he was.

"Staring won't make her come over."

Lucas slowly turned his head to glance down at Marianne Gerrard, resplendent in her brilliance, as always, her fair eyes fixed on Gemma as well.

"I know that," he murmured, keeping his face as impassive as ever. No one in the world would believe the two of them thought well of each other, and they liked it that way.

"So why do it?" she asked, snapping open her fan.

"What else can I do?" he replied, his voice carrying far more emotion than he'd ever meant to expose.

Marianne sighed, and he heard the sad note in it.

"Don't go soft now, Mrs. Gerrard," he scolded in a very low tone, trying to remain gruff despite the situation.

"In my condition, I am as soft as a pillow," she muttered, fanning herself rapidly to distract from her quickly fluttering lashes. "If I were myself, I would tell you that you are an idiot, and you should do something about it."

He restrained the sudden urge to snort. "Yes, I am sure you would."

"You agree with me?"

"With your hypothetical scold? Absolutely." He shrugged a shoulder. "I am an idiot, and growing more so every day, and I should do something about it, but as I am neither all-wise nor all-knowing, I do not know what that something should be."

Marianne turned then, looking for all appearances as though she were about to walk away from him, but in reality bringing herself closer and allowing her fan to shield their conversation. "The pair of you are miserable. Everyone is talking about it. I know you, Blackmoor, you are protecting her and sacrificing yourself, but enough is enough. I can't bear this, and I am not even in it. I know very well I am well out of line to say anything… even Kit told me so… but there is no hope for it."

Lucas did snort now, wondering how his friend managed with a woman so independent. She was brash, interfering, and did not understand the meaning of the word discretion. Despite all of that, he admired her spirit and her heart, and his estimation of her was only growing as their association furthered.

His friend was a fortunate man, despite evidence to the contrary.

"I am telling you, Blackmoor," she murmured, dropping her voice further still. "Let her share the load, whatever it happens to be. She does not need your protection as much as she needs you. And surely you could get used to living in sunshine, could you not?"

His throat suddenly tight and having nothing at all to do with his cravat, he swallowed with difficulty. "The trouble with sunshine," he eventually managed, "is that the clouds always seem darker by comparison."

"But when there are two of you facing them together, they will not be so daunting." Marianne gave him a bit of a smile, but her eyes showed understanding beyond his comprehension. "Believe me, my friend, you need her for this, and she desperately needs you. Don't put distance between you when you ought to clinging to each other."

In the face of his suddenly overwhelming emotion, he turned to gruffness. "And you are an expert on my marriage because…?"

Her smile deepened and her eyes twinkled. "My dear viscount, haven't you learned yet? I am an expert on everything." She briefly set her hand on his arm, and then wandered away as if they had never spoken at all.

Lucas watched Gemma again, now chatting animatedly with Lily Granger, who looked a little paler than normal, and somehow less inclined to smile. That was concerning, but Gemma seemed to be easing her friend well enough.

She was gifted that way.

His cousin was approaching her, the charming viscount smile on his face attracting every female eye despite his recent marriage, and Lucas bit back the desire to grin. He could intercept them, appear to cut the much-adored man and claim his own wife for a dance. The room would positively explode with gossip and titters, with Lucas being further solidified as a ruthless villain with no manners or respect for decency, whereas Henry would see it all as the best sort of joke and laugh about it for days.

No one would know this was as close to familial interaction that he would ever get.

Or what a rare flash of pleasure it gave him.

He started in that direction, various patrons moving out of his path as if he bore a plague. He paid them no mind. He never did.

He was going to emphatically claim his wife once and for all, and before most of London.

Let them speculate on his relationship after that.

Gemma's smile turned to his cousin, growing surprised but brilliant, then she caught sight of him. Something in his face must have given her a hint of his intentions, for her smile suddenly tucked in and became a rather devious smirk that spurned him on.

This could be the start of something rather intriguing for them.

It was a pity he had to skirt the entire dance floor to get to her. He would rather march across the floor, through the dancers, to do so, but that was extreme, even for him.

A soft murmuring and a few gasps of surprise slowed him, and he found his attention turned towards the distraction along with everyone else.

Heads turned, the crowd parted, and he caught sight of the guest that had drawn so much attention.

He stopped dead in his tracks, his entire body going cold.

He had not seen that man in six years.

They'd vowed to have as little to do with each other as possible.

He never came to London, yet here he was.

It was the worst possible luck.

Gemma saw the change in Lucas at once and felt her breath catch. She had no idea who the new guest was or why it should shock everyone so, let alone leave Lucas so altered, but she was suddenly on edge.

The man, foreign looking but impeccably dressed, met Lucas's gaze and he stopped as well, his expression aghast.

Gasps went up all around as people stared between the two, and it seemed the entire room fell silent.

No one moved. No one breathed.

Then Lucas swallowed and nodded once. The other man's jaw tightened, then he returned the nod and continued on, expression taut and higher in color.

Lucas's hands were fists at his sides, and everyone in the room watched him in horror. He barely glanced towards Gemma, his eyes never quite making it to hers, and then he turned and exited the room, guests milling in and closing the gap after him, making it impossible to follow.

The room exhaled, then the soft chattering began, several sets of eyes glancing over at Gemma with wariness and disapproval. The music began to strike up, and dancing resumed.

Gemma felt unaccountably on the verge of tears and looked over at Lord Sheffield with watery eyes. "What happened?" she managed to ask.

He looked as troubled as she felt and it took him a moment to respond. "That was Mr. Antonio Lattimer. Brother to the late Lady Blackmoor."

"As in…"

"The first wife. Celia."

Gemma swayed a little and was grateful Sheffield secured her elbow before she could falter completely. "Why?" she whispered, the word ripped from her.

"I don't know," he replied, not needing any sort of clarification as to what she was asking. She glanced up into his face and found a surprising degree of understanding, and the shared torment between them settled her somewhat.

"I need a moment," Gemma begged, attempting to straighten up but finding herself weak.

He nodded and looped her arm through his, wandering the room as if they were simply conversing lightly, nodding very politely at the inquiring eyes. "I'll probably set the room aflame with gossip for doing this," he muttered to her, "but hang me if I care."

"It's fine," she replied, her head spinning still. "Sophie will come and you can spend the rest of the evening with her, forget all about me."

"If you think for one minute I am going to leave your side…"

"Please, Henry," she gasped, feeling the pressure of every eye upon her, the whispers of her husband's name and distress, the pangs of anguish for his suffering that she could not comprehend. "Make them talk about something else. Make them *look* at something else"

He exhaled in irritation. "I am not a shocking person, my lady. I leave that for other relations."

She raised a brow in a shadow of her usual attitude. "Then get Will to do something."

That brought him up short, and he suddenly smiled. "I have just the thing. Let me see you to a quiet place first, and give you the proper vantage point. You will wish to see this."

"Oh, lord," she muttered, shaking her head.

He nudged her gently. "Smile, Lady Blackmoor. Pretend it was nothing."

"Pretending is all I ever do anymore," she whispered.

He squeezed her hand tightly, then made a quick gesture with his head, and suddenly Sophie was with them, as was Lily. "Mind her," he murmured quietly to them both. "Make her smile, make her laugh, behave as usual. I'll be back in a moment."

The ladies nodded, taking her arms, and began chatting animatedly about the latest musical discoveries from Italy, of which both were informed, and Gemma attempted to join in the conversation. Or at least to look interested in it.

Sheffield made his way through the crowds, some looking curious, others simply impressed. He commanded that sort of respect and attention wherever he went, no matter how modest and unaffected he might be in private. He might not be shocking, but he would draw his own sort of attention no matter what he did.

Sophie and Lily found them some chairs and they sat for a few minutes, each keeping contact with Gemma whether by hand or sitting close enough for their bodies to brush. She was grateful for the reminder of their presence, the connection to her reality and keeping her grounded. Her thoughts were filled with Lucas, wondering at his pain and distress.

Was the reminder of Celia too much? Did seeing her brother bring back more of the horrible memories he could not seem to escape? Was his guilt and pain too much?

Did he love Celia too much to ever really love Gemma?

She clamped her hands together in her lap. Why did Mr. Lattimer have to come now? Lucas had been about to come to her, and the hope that sight had ignited within her had been a furious one. Now she was more crushed than she had ever been, feeling as though they were truly at an end.

"Oh, good lord, Will," Sophie suddenly muttered, her polite mask vanishing at once.

"Is that my sister?" Lily asked in surprise, coughing a little.

Gemma glanced up to watch, along with the rest of the room, Captain Riverton waltzing with Rosalind Arden, and thus scandalizing the eligible females in the room, for Captain Riverton by all accounts never waltzed. And no one in their right mind and reputation would waltz so close together.

Yet they were, and they did, and it was an oddly stirring sight, for they were quite good at it.

"I daresay that is nigh unto an engagement," Sophie scoffed, shaking her head. "Mrs. Granger, welcome to the family."

Lily laughed and shook her head. "Don't put so much stock into it. My sister is as stubborn as they come, and if this is truly more than a show, it will take a great deal to persuade her into anything serious."

"I think you underestimate Will's charms." Sophie chuckled, and then sighed. "I think this will do the trick. They will talk about this for weeks."

Gemma nodded, sensing the question was directed at her. She glanced around, and sure enough, the room had completely forgotten about her, and her husband's behavior. It would come back later, as it always did, but for now she was safe.

"Are you all right?" Lily asked gently from her side.

She shook her head, unwilling to pretend for even a moment.

"If you want to sneak away," Sophie said, keeping her eyes on the waltz, "now would be the time."

Gemma swallowed and offered a shaky nod.

At that precise moment, Colin Gerrard appeared before her and bowed. "My lady Blackmoor, might I persuade you to accompany me for a moment? My wife wishes to consult with you on a musical selection."

Gemma frowned, knowing that Susannah Gerrard was not musical by her own talents, but she trusted Colin, and allowed him to help her from her seat. He smiled broadly and somehow managed to get her out of the ballroom with only a handful of people noticing them.

"What does Susannah need?" Gemma asked, curious and weary and desperately longing for home.

Colin snorted. "At the moment? I daresay some cake and comfortable bed. She's quite done for."

She frowned up at him. "She doesn't have need of me?"

"We all have need of you, sweet," Colin assured her with his wild grin. "Right now we all need you to go home to your husband and not come out until something is mended. I don't know how Lattimer got an invitation, I know we did not send it."

"Is it a problem that he was here?" she asked.

He shook his head. "No, as far as I know. No, the Lattimers have never said a word about the situation, not even after… Well, their silence, coupled with Blackmoor's, made for all kinds of speculation. They never made any accusations, never said a harsh word against him, not a thing to indicate their feelings one way or the other. But things tend to be awkward when both parties are in the same place. It happens so very rarely, however, that no one ever expects them. Lattimers never come up for the Season; they stay in Brighton and Italy all year, I thought."

Gemma exhaled and found more tears at her disposal. "I wish we had never come to London," she whispered.

Colin encircled her shoulders protectively as he led her to her coach. "I know. Go to him, Gemma. I think he needs you."

"I think he needs his wife," she muttered. "His *real* wife."

Colin gave her such a dark, scolding look that she actually reared back. "And that would be you, pet. Don't forget it."

He nodded at the footman, who opened the door, and Colin helped her in, then signaled to the coachman, waving at her as she barreled off.

She barely avoided biting her lip, anxious and terribly apprehensive. He was right, of course. She *was* Lucas's wife, and it was time she reminded him of that.

He could love his first wife, she would never ask him to forget her. But he could not forget Gemma in the process, and she refused to be second to a memory.

She was going to claim her husband whether he liked it or not.

That was who she was.

Lady Blackmoor.

For better or worse.

Chapter Twenty-One

The house was dark and silent when she arrived, not even a servant to greet her or collect her things. No doubt Lucas had sent them away, and she was grateful for it. No one would need to see or hear this, and she could not promise that she would be able to contain herself. There was a great deal to be said, and it would be said at very great volumes, if it came down to it. Lucas was not a man of temper, but there was no accounting for what provocation could draw forth.

She knew exactly where to go, and needed no candle as she mounted the stairs, untying her cloak and letting it fall to the ground behind her, sending her long, white, pristine gloves after it. She may be Lady Blackmoor by title, and by determination, but she was also simply Gemma.

She was a woman of all heart and little finery.

The gallery door was slightly ajar, which was a sure indication of the trouble within. Lucas was always careful to keep his brooding to himself, and needed no audience for his displays.

She opened the door further, slipped in, and shut it firmly behind her. The only light in the room came from a candelabra on a table, all three tiers lit, and illuminating a man who sat in a straight-back chair, facing the grandest and most imposing portrait in the gallery.

Celia.

Her cold, yet laughing eyes stared at her audience, no matter their identity, and drew forth questions, uneasiness, and envy. Her figure was perfection in every way, and one could not help but admire the sight of her, no matter the personal opinions.

Gemma hated her, and felt no shame about doing so.

And Lucas was captivated and tormented, his gaze unwavering upon her.

He had to have heard Gemma enter, but he did not move.

How then to begin?

Gemma exhaled silently and pushed off of the door, her slippers making no sound on the carpet beneath her feet. He did not stir at her approach, and she halted mere feet from him, watching him. He had removed his coat and waistcoat, his cravat lay on the back of the chair, and his hair was mussed as if he had run his hands through it. Though it had been barely an hour since she had seen him, he was so altered she might not have known him.

Her heart swelled with emotion, and it took a moment before she could collect herself

"I am sorry," she said quietly to the empty room and empty man.

"What do you have to be sorry for?" he asked, his voice hollow and scratching against his dry lips.

"You have suffered an upset and I am sorry for it."

He nodded in response, but still he did not look at her.

She sighed softly. "You should not have left me again," she told him, scolding a little. "I could have…"

"You seemed to be doing well enough without me," he interrupted, the words cutting though his voice was flat. "I thought removing myself would be best for your efforts."

"My efforts at what?" she snapped. "All I am trying to do is be a good wife to you, to honor your name, everything that a viscountess should be. It might help if my *husband* would do something to aid in the efforts."

"I am. The less of me, the better it is."

"Better for whom?" she demanded. "I don't know what this is, Lucas, what is going on, what torments you, why you suddenly cannot bear me… But I am your wife, and so help me, that is not something you can just toss aside."

He winced and turned his face more away from her, still staring at the portrait.

"What?" she asked, seizing upon that expression. "What have I said to affect you? Do you wish to toss me aside? Are you unable to condone what you have done?"

He shook his head slightly, and she knew instinctively that was not in answer to her, but a reaction of himself.

She glanced up at Celia's portrait, and snarled at it. "Is it because of her?" she asked sharply.

Impossibly, Lucas stilled even further.

That was all the answer she wanted.

She folded her hands before her and stiffened. "I can't take it anymore, Lucas. If you still have feelings for her, tell me so at once."

His head came around swiftly and he looked up at her. "What?" he half whispered, half growled.

Gemma met his eyes steadily and shook her head. "I cannot continue on in this way knowing that you still pine for her like this. I won't play second to any woman, let alone a dead one. You can love her as you must, but you will not abandon me for it."

He surged to his feet, startling her. "Her? You think I love her?"

He whirled and grabbed the portrait, wrenching it from the wall and sending it crashing to the ground. "She could not be loved by anyone," he spat with more venom than she would ever have expected from him. "I hated her, and she hated me! She was nearly the ruin of all I held dear!"

Lucas shoved at the frame with his boot, sending it forward several inches, despite the weight of it. "She was cold, heartless, and cruel. I rejoiced in the accident that took her life." He shook his head, his hands clenching and unclenching at his sides as his uneven breathing slowed. "But still she haunts me, mocks me, torments me… I cannot scratch her out, no matter how I try."

His voice broke a little and he raised his head, glancing back towards Gemma but not facing her. "I love only one woman, one sweet, innocent fairy who was born out of sunshine, and I married her, knowing I was dooming her to a life bound to a monstrous wreck that was once a man."

Stunned by his behavior, she had not moved from her place. Now, with those words, she felt her knees begin to buckle and she clutched at the chair before her. "What?"

Slowly he turned to face her, his expression raw, his eyes dark and luminous in the candlelight. "Oh, darling love. My sweet Gemma, can't you see it? I love you more than I dare to comprehend. More than life, more than air, more than I hate myself, I love you."

He shook his head, and she felt all the longing and torment in it. "I ought to apologize for marrying you, for loving you this much, but I can't. Celia ruined me, Gemma. She broke me more than I thought a man could break. You are my only hope of restoration, and so I took you for my own, never considering what you would suffer by it. I've ruined your life, but you have saved mine. Am I to be damned for loving and taking so selfishly?"

Tears began to roll down her cheeks and her heart pounded furiously within her chest, threatening to explode entirely. "Lucas…"

"I tried distancing myself from you," he said hoarsely. "I thought it might turn the tide of rumors away from you. I couldn't bear to hear what they were saying, knowing I had brought you to this. It would be nothing for them to speak ill of me, to grow even worse than before, if it came to it." He slowly shook his head, his shoulders drooping. "But not you. I couldn't let it touch you. So I foolishly thought distance would save you, and save me, but I can't bear the distance from you any longer. I am so sorry, my love. I never meant for you to suffer for my conduct and my past, to tie your fate forever with so dark and horrifying a creation." He swallowed harshly and shrugged. "Perhaps distance could protect you, but I am not strong enough to endure it. I should be, but I'm not. You may do as you please, of course, I'll not bind you in any way. I wouldn't blame you after what I've done."

Gemma's heart burst and she rushed at him, throwing her arms around him and clinging as her tears streamed without mercy. "Oh, Lucas."

He stiffened slightly. "Don't pity me, Gemma," he choked out, his arms twitching as if longing to hold her. "I cannot bear it."

"This isn't pity," she told him through her tears, her breath catching on the words. "My heart is breaking for you."

"Don't. It's not worth it."

She continued to hold him, undeterred by his lack of response, his arms hanging by his sides still. "Nay, it is! Nothing could be more worth it. When will you see, Lucas, that no part of your past, however dark, could taint you in my sight?"

His frame shuddered, and she felt his face rub against her hair.

"Don't be kind to me, Gemma," he rasped, his words tickling her skin.

Gemma shook her head. "You know me too well for that, Lucas. I never say anything I don't mean."

With a low groan, he wrapped his arms around her at last and pulled her close, tucking his face into her neck. "Gemma, you have no idea what you do to me. I'm only alive because of you."

She ran her fingers into his hair and stroked the back of his neck. "You are alive because of yourself, Lucas. Your own heart is to thank."

"My heart is yours, failing and poor excuse for one that it is," he murmured, pressing his lips to her shoulder.

Gemma's breath hitched on more tears, and she tightened her arms around him. "If your heart should fail you, I pray you take mine."

A rough exhale escaped him, the air rushing across her hair and skin. "A heart so pure and good would never do for this frame."

"Yet it is yours for the taking."

He pulled back and looked at her, eyes wary. "What are you saying?"

She smiled and touched his chin. "I give my heart to you, Lucas, fully and freely." Going up on tiptoe, she brushed a feather soft kiss against his unmoving lips, whispering, "I love you."

He took in a shuddering gasp. "You can't…"

"I love you," she said again, kissing him more firmly.

His whole body began to quake slightly. "Gemma…"

Gemma took his face in her hands, forcing him to look at her. She stared into his disbelieving yet hopeful eyes, and then kissed him gently, tenderly, and smiled. "I love you, Lucas Sinclair," she whispered.

Releasing something between a sob and a groan, he hauled her against him, and buried his face into her shoulder. Then, with frantically showered kisses along her neck, he made his way back up to capture her lips in a searing kiss.

There was nothing gentle or tender in his ministrations, everything passionate and wild and poignant, wringing exquisite pleasure and delight from every fiber of her being. She clung to him and returned it measure for measure, spiraling desperately out of control as lips and arms and hearts and desire melded in a frenzy of heady rapture that threatened to consume them both. She could not get close enough, yet his hands were everywhere, scorching her and driving her and soothing her at once. There was no kiss deep enough, no embrace tight enough, no restraint strong enough to withstand the onslaught and fire bombarding them, and they were entirely lost to it, and each other.

Hours later, exhausted and sated and exhilarated, Lucas lay awake in his bed, his arms still running up and down Gemma's back in light caresses. He could not let go of her, could not stop touching her, and had begged her again and again to say the words that he could not yet comprehend.

She loved him.

She'd said it over and over, as many times as he'd asked and then some, the shock of hearing them never lessening, nor diminishing the depth with which they were said. He'd been unrelenting in his attentions, desperate to show her how he felt, what she meant, how much he needed her on every level that could possibly exist in human form. And then he ventured for more, feeling more alive and free than he ever had in his life.

He was the most fortunate of men, it seemed, and he was well aware that he would never deserve such goodness, but he was not about to refuse it.

Something rare and exquisite had happened between them, something so deep and profound that poets and playwrights could have only imagined it. Yet he had it, had experienced it for himself, and felt the lingering euphoria of it still.

And the shocking thing was, for all the involvement of body, it was entirely a matter of heart.

He'd never thought he had much of a heart, yet it ached and pounded and yearned with a fierceness now that was entirely centered and focused on the woman in his arms.

As impossible as it was to believe, she matched his fervor and passion, his need and his love. She was his match in every way.

How did any man bear such a thing?

The darkness of the night before crept into his thoughts and he leaned his head back against his pillow, groaning to himself. Would he ever be rid of them?

He slipped his arms from Gemma and sat up, moving to the edge of the bed. He swung his feet over, and rested them on the rug below.

"Where do you think you are going?" Gemma murmured sleepily from behind him.

He smiled softly, but did not look. He could see her in his mind's eye well enough. "Nowhere in particular."

He felt her rustle in the bed, then sit up. She scooted closer and pressed her lips to his back gently. "I think you need to talk, Lucas."

Her hair brushed against his skin and he restrained a sigh, loving the slight nuzzle of her. "I don't know if I can," he admitted, afraid of exposing himself in such a way. Not to her, he knew he was safe in her keeping, but to himself… Had he ever been that raw and vulnerable?

Gemma wrapped her arms around his back and pressed herself close. "Try. I'll hold you and let you say everything without interruption. Just try."

"It is dark," he whispered.

She kissed his neck and laid her head along his. "I love you."

The words rippled through him and he sighed, clutching her hands as they encircled him.

It was time.

Slowly, softly, he spoke of the years with his family before his marriage, the embarrassment of their association, the shame of his name, the determination to salvage something, anything of value. He spoke of his eagerness to marry Celia, a rare half-Italian beauty with a fortune and a reputation for liveliness and warmth that could save the family name.

He made no attempts to hide anything from Gemma, admitting his attraction and his hopes and desires for a real marriage, rather than the sham he had seen in his own parents' marriage, the pain of unrequited affection and neglect. Yet the veil had fallen from his eyes within the first two weeks of marriage, finding Celia with a lover in their home, and the identity was that of a man who had once been a friend to Lucas.

There had been a series of lovers that followed, no pattern or structure associated with any of them, no true affection to be found. He'd learned to accept it, and to do so with his now token stoicism and silence, which had infuriated Celia. She had thrived upon contention and emotions, and his indifference provoked her.

Thus had begun her torment of him. Parading about London and encouraging everyone with eyes to see, laughing and mocking him at every turn. Reminding him of how he had failed her, failed his family, how he was worth nothing without her… And the bitterest part was that it was true, and she knew it. She knew his insecurities and could twist them against him with such skilled manipulation that he could not deflect it.

They had lived apart, sharing a house for the public, but keeping their lives distinct and separate. He lost track of her numerous lovers, and had stopped caring. She, however, did everything in her power to provoke him, to stir any sort of response. Toying with his friends, severing relationships that he'd held for years, keeping him from trusting anyone but a very select few, and even those he kept at a distance. He had reconciled with his Riverton relations during that time, but he had never let Celia become aware of the relationship, knowing what damage she could inflict upon them all if she knew.

Knowing he was doomed to a life out of his control, knowing he had failed his family, knowing he would never be the credit to his heritage that he'd once hoped, he had settled into a routine of detachment, in heart and behavior and expression. Where his wife had been vibrant and vivacious and the envy of all, he had been spiritless and reclusive and unaffected. He was the one people scorned in their marriage, not she.

He never minded, so long as no one knew the truth of the matter.

He was powerless against his wife.

He could say nothing against her, for she was his wife and he needed her association to remain beneficial. And part of him vainly hoped that one day they might reconcile, not to be in love and happy and blissful, but to be companionable, at the very least. Perhaps one day to have a family. But Celia wanted nothing but money and attention, and as she had that of her own merit and only needed marriage to free her from comment, she was perfectly satisfied.

Then things had changed. She had become more cutting, more cruel, and more spiteful. She had been more bitter in her vitriol against him, painting him to be a villain instead of a laughingstock. And such was her sway that she began to be believed. She was rarely at home, leading him to assume that she was carrying on with less discretion to further her claims of his brutality and to embarrass him further.

The day had followed that she had left in a carriage, destination unknown, and only made it ten miles outside of London before a wheel axle had snapped, sending the carriage crashing off course and into trees. She had been tossed about, and had been killed instantly in the crash, her body broken and half exposed in the wreckage.

Lucas had carried her home himself in the dead of night, sending word for her family, who had known exactly who and what their daughter was, and they had come for her, begging him to let her memory remain as it had been rather than exposing her and ruining them all. He had agreed, of course. It would have done no good to try to discredit her.

They'd buried her in London rather than on family estates, as London was all that she had ever cared about. It was the last request they could fulfill for her. He owed her nothing at all, but that was something he could concede to. She would not be honored with his family plot, and her family wanted no painful reminders of her. It was for the best.

Lucas spoke until his voice ran out, and Gemma remained steadfast in her hold on him. He felt a tear or two splash onto his skin, but other than that, there had been no response.

"I wish I'd had the strength of character to refute her estimation of me," he murmured hoarsely with the last of his energy, "but she was a skilled architect in manipulation. Just enough truth to make it cut, and just enough fabrication to make one wonder."

"And you've wondered all this time," Gemma finally whispered, her lips at his shoulder.

He nodded slowly. "The years have only given them further root, and with the family life I'd enjoyed in my youth, I was used to believing the worst of myself. And then the rumors of Society started after the funeral, as we had all behaved so quietly. I think the outcry started from a lack of opportunity to mourn and a lack of investigation, though one had been done, of course. Discreetly. It made no difference. The Lattimers left London and did not return, and I remained longer than I should have, silent and going on as I had before."

"But you went into mourning," she reminded him.

He snorted. "I went to Thornacre. For two years, I rarely left. I never mourned a day in my life, but I let the world think so. Celia may have died in the crash, but her effects remained. Still do."

Gemma's arms tightened around him and he let himself feel her embrace more fully, leaning against her. "You listen to me, Lucas Sinclair," Gemma hissed, her voice a bit choked, but strong. "You are not a failure. To your family or to anyone else. You are the best man that I have ever known, and have far more strength of character and honor than I believed possible in anyone. I will tell you a hundred times a day that I love you, but until you believe me and not her, it will do you no good. Let her go, Lucas. She is dead, and so should her hold on you be."

"Help me, Gemma," he pleaded softly. "Help me let her go. I can't do it alone."

"Let me love you, darling," she soothed, tugging him back and moving to lie down. "Hold onto me, and let me love you."

"Yes," he rasped, turning and crawling on the bed over to her. "Don't give up on me, Gemma."

She shook her head as she cupped his face. "Never. Do you hear me? Never!"

He leaned down and kissed her tenderly, feeling as though his heart could break and fly all at once. "I love you," he managed to say somehow, fast losing control on his emotions.

She smiled and pulled him down to her. "I love you."

The words lit up his heart, and he kissed his wife again.

Chapter Twenty-Two

$\mathscr{L}$ife went on, regardless of the reprieve they would wish for. Gemma could have spent days in Lucas's arms, secluded in their house, forgetting the entire world, but it was not possible.

Lucas, for one, had business that had to be tended to out of the city, and he could not be put off, especially as he was determined to be back for Miranda Ascott's musical evening and give Gemma the proper attention and due as befits the man who desperately loved her.

She had rolled her eyes a little, trying to assure him it was no matter if he attended Miranda's or not, particularly as Miranda had approached Gemma and asked if it would be possible for her husband to *not* attend her event, as the attention would distract from everyone else. She suspected Miranda meant that it would distract from her desire to impress as hostess, but she could hardly say such things.

Gemma did say, however, that she was not about to prevent her husband from attending anything in Society, particularly when Gemma would be performing, and if Miranda found that disagreeable, she could find another person to play the violin in her stead.

Miranda knew full well that there was no other woman in London at this time who could do as well as Gemma, and she would be foolish to try.

Lucas found that as delightful as Gemma had, and vowed even more fervently to attend, just to give Miranda something to set her nerves askew.

He would only be gone two days, but it felt as though he was leaving for longer as he lingered, kissing her again and again and murmuring his love.

"You'll never get anywhere if you don't leave," Gemma murmured with a laugh.

He chuckled and kissed her again. "Trying to be rid of me, are you?"

She gripped the back of his neck tightly and touched her nose to his. "I am trying to get you to come back to me, you dolt."

He nuzzled her tenderly, nipped at her chin, then kissed her. "Right, as my lady commands. Two days. Then never again."

She grinned. "You cannot promise to never leave me again."

"Yes, I can."

He would brook no argument, and left without proper resolution of his ridiculous claims.

Gemma had amused herself for several hours with various tasks, unable to keep the silly smile from her face. She knew that there was more to her husband's past and emotions than one night of confessions. It would take time and considerable patience, but at least he was sharing with her. At least he had told her the truth, and told her of his love and fidelity. She could stand by his side and wait as long as he needed her to, so long as she had that.

Amidst all of that came the realization, with some certain calculations and unusual symptoms, that life would most certainly be changing for them in a few months' time. If she had known this only yesterday, it might have brought worry and fear, but after the events and confessions of the night before, she was only filled with joy and anticipation, wondering what Lucas would say, how he would look, when she told him there would be a child.

With giddiness in her step, she sent a quick note to Bennett, asking for a meeting in their usual park location. She must let him know the truth about Lucas's reticence and the joy they had found! How delighted he would be! He had been so concerned for them, and for Lucas especially, that she could not wait to inform him that all was changed.

His response was swift and affirmative, and she rushed out with Hattie as chaperone, per usual, and they arrived first. Gemma tapped her foot impatiently as she waited, wanting to laugh and dance and sing loudly so everyone might know her join and delight. Hattie knew nothing of the situation, but Gemma's antics amused her, and she repeatedly shook her head, laughing softly.

She supposed servants were not to laugh at their employers, but this was a special circumstance, and she was not about to tell her to stop when she was laughing at herself.

"You, my dear Lady Blackmoor, are making the sun envious with all of your glowing," crowed the now familiar voice.

She turned, already grinning, and watched Bennett approach, impeccably dressed and looking like the very picture of one might imagine a handsome young man to be. He drew gasps and stares from several ladies, but his eyes were on her, and his smile a bit more of a smirk.

"You may tease all you like, sir, but I will not apologize for my joy," she said, smiling up at him.

He looped her arm through his and began to stroll, nodding politely at Hattie, who followed them. "Well, tell me so at once, dear woman, so I may join you in your felicity."

Gemma clamped down on her lip with a silent giggle. "Lucas loves me."

Bennett gave her a surprised look, smiling. "Does he now? I am glad to hear it. What of his odd behavior? Of his first wife?"

She shook her head. "He was tormented by her, she was not at all what people thought. But you must keep that a secret, Bennett, and it makes no difference now. He loves me and only me! I'm not second to Celia or anyone else!"

A musical laugh erupted from her and she threw her head back, beaming in delight. "We were so worried for nothing. My husband might be a man of mystery and reserve, but still waters run deep. I should have known, I feel so silly for ever thinking otherwise."

Bennett was silent beside her, and his tread remained steady, but she sensed a change in him and glanced up at his suddenly stoic features.

"Bennett?"

He glanced behind them, then gripped her arm in a vice-like hold. "Keep smiling, my dear. You are about to elope with your lover."

Gemma reared back in surprise. "I beg your pardon?"

Something sharp was suddenly jabbed in her side and she glanced down to see a sterling pistol, no doubt rarely used, tucked against her, completely obscured from anyone else's view.

"Make any move to escape or give the smallest sign of distress," he hissed, his voice positively venomous, "and I will shoot you here and now. And wouldn't that be something for your husband to come home to?"

"H-how do you know my husband is not at home?" she stammered, her mind whirling. "He *is* at home, he is waiting for me."

He gave her a sardonic look. "If your reunion was as histrionic as your expression says, there is no possible way he would let you come out and meet me, servant or no. And your servant in question is worthless. She is distracted by ducks at the moment, making this far too easy. I thought I was going to have to strike her or bribe her at least, but this is perfect. She is simply not mindful, and that is so much better."

The pistol nudged against her more tightly and she clamped down on her lip hard. "What are you doing? Why are you doing this?"

He snorted, somehow still smiling jovially. "I am making your husband's life hell, as he has made mine. Have you not wondered why he has been so strange since your wedding? That was me. I could not have him be happy, not after what he did to Celia, and what that did to me. I have been seeking revenge for years, and you were the perfect opportunity. To drive him mad and drive his wife away at the same time would be the sweetest vindication. Your insecurities and his fears were too easy to play upon. And now you would ruin months of work with your ridiculous resolution?" He shook his head fiercely. "No, that I cannot allow. We will drive a stake into the coffin of your husband's happiness in this final blow."

"And that is?" she asked in a very small voice, her heart quivering within her as her feet mindlessly moved by his command.

He grinned too easily, looking adoring but for the coldness in his eyes. "We are eloping, my dear, and your maid will verify that we were seen rushing off together in a waiting carriage, and she knows of our regular meetings, how familiar we have become… Even your idiot husband has seen our closeness. His envy and suspicion reek on his very person. He doesn't trust you, how can he? He's never been able to sustain a woman's affections, and I… Well, I had the greatest love of the century because of his ineptitude. She is forever lost to me because of him, and you shall now be forever lost to him."

"He'll come after me," Gemma snapped, even as her breath hitched on her words. "He loves me. He will not stand for this."

Bennett sneered a little and dragged her along. "You think that, Gemma. You go right ahead and think your husband will not wonder if he has been mistaken in you, that he has failed yet another marriage, and that he is not worth the effort of a woman's affections."

A whimper rose in the back of her throat and her eyes burned with unshed tears. She couldn't say that she could refute his claims, for she knew of Lucas's doubts and fears, his own insecurities. Their love was so new, for all its depth and passion, and it would be too easy to think himself mistaken in her, if he chose.

Did he believe her enough to know the truth? Did he trust her enough to know she would never leave him?

The evidence would be against them, and it would be too believable, given his past.

She had been so cruelly deceived, but he had been shockingly abused. Bennett had been tormenting him somehow over these months, intentionally dividing them for sport and vengeance. He could not know Bennett's true nature, nor his past, any more than she had, or he would never have permitted her to meet him. They had both failed to see the danger before them.

Would he see it now?

"I told you to smile, woman," he growled, somehow still looking handsome. "Don't make me wound you."

"I don't care," she shot back, struggling as much as she dared and preparing a quite startling volume of scream.

"You will very much care when your misbehavior will force me to injure your husband."

That silenced her forthcoming scream and removed all energy in her limbs. Resistance fled and she looked up at him with wide eyes. "You wouldn't…"

He raised a brow. "After all this, you think I make idle threats? I would love nothing more than to run your husband through repeatedly. It has been hell to not take advantage of fencing with him all these years."

The venom in his voice left no question, and Gemma let herself go with him willingly, fear for her husband and their newfound happiness reigning supreme.

What would happen to her?

And more importantly, what would happen to Lucas when it did?

Early the following morning, Lucas arrived back to his home, exhausted from riding hard and working a back-breaking amount of hours the day before, but he was determined to return to Gemma's side as soon as possible, and his drive had been inhuman. Yet now he was home, and relieved to be so.

He tugged at his cravat and coat as he made his way up to the bedchamber, smiling to himself as he imagined the delight of waking her, knowing it would take an age of time, but more than willing to do so, and quite creatively. The distance between them had been too much, and he was determined to make up for lost time.

And when he had regained some sense of himself, he would tell her of Gent's discovery of Celia. The information had come to him shortly before his departure back to London, and it changed much for him.

Celia had taken a lover, but more than that, she had sustained one for quite some time. Her heart had been apparently decided to behave as such, and she considered herself to be in love. Her fleeing in the carriage the night she died had been an attempt to elope with her lover and leave Lucas for good.

It explained her increased resentment of him, the coldness that had been without reason, the sudden cruel streak that had been harsh even for her… Celia had been in love and her marriage had gotten in the way of that.

For some reason, that seemed to satisfy him. He felt no relief in her finding love, no pity for the state in which she had found herself, no guilt for the way things had turned out. He only felt tension ebb away now that understanding had been found.

It certainly shed some light on matters, and there was a sense of relief there. Perhaps this might help them to figure out details of the notes, which he would certainly tell Gemma about now. Gent would help, he had already gone beyond what Lucas had thought possible. And with someone else to worry about the details, Lucas could focus on rebuilding his life with Gemma.

He looked forward to it.

He opened the door to her bedchamber quietly, and frowned at the empty bed. Not only empty, but untouched.

No one had slept in here last night.

He moved over to his bedchamber, wondering if she might have felt sentimental enough to spend the night in his dark and rather unaccommodating chambers, but that, too, was empty.

Panic, that rare and unwelcome companion, swirled within the pit of his stomach and he checked each of the bedrooms, family and guest, even the ones that had not been completely refurbished yet. No sign of Gemma anywhere at all.

He began tearing through the house, bellowing her name at the top of his lungs.

There was no response.

Servants began emerging from various quarters of the house, and each was interrogated on the spot. No one had seen Gemma since yesterday, and no one could quite seem to meet his eye. No answers, no information, no help at all.

He nearly fired them all right then and there.

At last, Hattie came forward, and he could tell from her expression that she knew something.

"Where is Lady Blackmoor?" he demanded without any sort of preamble.

She immediately began wringing her hands together. "Where, I do not know, sir…"

He folded his arms tightly, grinding his teeth. "Well, what *do* you know?"

She shifted anxiously. "We went to the park yesterday, and met up with Mr. Stanford, as we often do."

Something in Lucas started to crack and it was all he could do to keep his composure. Impossibly, his arms seemed to tighten further against himself.

"I…" Hattie flinched and looked away.

"You what?" Lucas asked, his voice deadly calm.

The maid clamped her lips together on a soft cry. "I became distracted and was not minding them, I saw them both getting into a carriage some distance from me, and at great speed. I tried to reach them, but they were off before I could…"

"They ran off," he said flatly.

She nodded once, swallowing. "I know how fond she was of him, my lord, but I never… I would not have…"

"That is all, Hattie."

She hiccupped and rushed from the room.

Lucas sank against his desk, his sense of loss complete and absolute.

Gemma was gone.

It was only an hour or so in his study, reflecting and wallowing, before Lucas realized he was being a fool and the worst sort of coward.

Gemma was not Celia.

He was not going to give her up so easily, and he doubted very much that things were as simple as Hattie seemed to think.

For one, Gemma was not a flighty or impulsive person. She was as steadfast and sure as any creature on earth. She would never have run away with another man, it was not in her nature.

For another, she loved him. She'd told him, and he'd told her, but he had also seen it. Felt it. And Gemma could not hide anything, could not be anything but what she was.

She just was.

He was not the same man he was before, and Gemma's hold on him was far greater and more enduring than anything Celia's could ever have been.

For all his doubts, he could not deny what he knew in his heart, and that was a certainty of Gemma's character and fidelity. More than that, he would choose to trust her, in her word, in the feelings she had so sweetly declared to him. His life had been one of darkness and deception, but he trusted that her light could give him faith and hope for the future. He could cling to her and find his way. He would let go of what kept him in the shadows and step more fully into the haven she gave him.

He might not understand what drew her to him, but he knew what ties held his heart to her, and those refused to stand idly by and let anyone or anything prevent his being with her.

He would have no idea where they might have gone, but a quick visit to Stanford's house would surely enlighten him. The man was too much of an idiot to think of proper ways to cover his tracks. Yet he was an idiot who had apparently run off with another man's wife, which seemed to show a streak of deviousness, or stupidity, that he'd never thought possible.

He rose from his desk and moved to the door when it opened and his young footman James appeared. "Letter for you, sir."

Lucas shook his head, shrugging into his coat. "No time."

James stepped directly into his path and held it out more firmly. "Sir. A letter for you."

Lucas glanced into the lad's face and saw the set of his jaw.

He snatched the letter and opened it quickly, scanning the lines.

Source witnessed Gemma being forced into a carriage at gunpoint by a man yesterday. Carriage followed as far as Richmond, then lost. Scouring for details. If you have need, a lad named Jem has been posted at your house and on your person. Whistle and he will appear.

Lucas swallowed a lump and nodded, shoving the note into his pocket. "Thank you, James. Tell Adams to have a horse saddled for me."

James bowed and did so, no doubt sensing the urgency in his tone.

Minutes later, Lucas was galloping madly away from his home, heading for Stanford's town residence in a very fashionable part of London. People stared at him in stunned disapproval, but he could not bring himself to care.

He was shown into the house at once, and frowned when the

aged butler said he would let the master know he was here.

"Your master is at home?" he asked, his mind turning over in bewilderment.

The butler did not respond as he shuffled out of sight, but only moments later, Stanford himself appeared, seemingly surprised to see him and looking far too pristine. "Blackmoor, you look quite done for. What is it?"

"I…" He shook his head, an unsettling confusion pervading his senses. "Gemma is gone. Taken, apparently."

Stanford gaped and waved him over, leading him to a near study. "Taken? My dear fellow, how dreadful! What can I do? I am at your service, of course."

The concern and sympathy in his tone turned him more around. "I don't know," he admitted, running his hands through his hair and pacing the unfamiliar room. "I don't know what to think or what to believe. I've already heard different stories, different events… She wouldn't leave me of her own accord, I know this."

"Of course not," Stanford said as he sank into a chair, his voice dripping with consolation. "What a horrid mess. And the two of you were just beginning to mend things."

Lucas looked at him swiftly. "How do you know that?"

Stanford looked surprised. "No doubt you heard that we met yesterday. I hope you do not mind, she was so keen to tell me about the promising start, to assure me that your marriage had hope."

"How was she?" he asked, painfully aware of the crack in his tone.

"Delightfully happy, and a little preoccupied." Stanford tilted his head with a sad smile. "I told her to go home to you, my dear chap, and not waste her time thinking of me. You may wish to rethink her maid, though, the poor thing was so distracted by the park, I do not think she minded us or anything but her own imaginations. Someone could easily have carried off dear Gemma without her noticing."

"Don't say that," Lucas snapped, clenching his fists.

"Of course, you are distressed." Stanford nodded sagely. "It is understandable."

Lucas pressed his fists to his head, exhaling roughly.

"And after all the trouble with your first wife. Running away with a lover, crashing in the very carriage she escaped in, the scandal was horrendous. When word breaks of Gemma racing off in a carriage, it will only come back on you once more, a hundredfold worse."

Lucas stilled and slowly lowered his arms, glaring at the simpering, pitiful man sitting before him. "How do you know that Celia was meeting a lover?"

Stanford's eyes widened at the dangerous tone. "That… is common knowledge."

Slowly, the very motion paining him, Lucas shook his head. "No, it isn't. No one knew that. I didn't even know that until recently. The details of her death were never released. The only one who could possibly know that is…"

He let the unspoken hang in the air and saw the change in the young man at once. Where once there had been a stupid, inane fool there was now a cold and calculating man whose eyes were filled with hatred.

"You," Lucas breathed, going suddenly cold. "You were Celia's lover."

"I was so much more than that," came the sneering reply.

The wheels began to turn in Lucas's mind. "You have been sending me the threats."

"Prove that."

"You restarted the rumors of my family."

"What rumors? From what I heard, that was all true."

"You invited Lattimer to the Gerrards."

"I was not invited there myself, how could I do that?"

The coldness within Lucas suddenly turned colder still. "You have Gemma."

A derisive look and impatient sound met his accusation. "Do I look like I have your stupid trollop of a wife?"

Lucas slammed his hands on the desk. "Tell me where she is!"

Stanford scoffed and propped his legs up on the wooden surface. "That would be a fair parlor trick, knowing the location of one missing viscountess. Why in the world would I know? She probably did run away from you, considering your complete and utter worthlessness. Celia knew that all too well. Shall I tell you how many nights we lay awake, entangled with each other, while she regaled me with your many failings? How you ruined her life? How you were incapable of sustaining any relationship of value, let alone one of romance? She found you lacking in every possible respect. I, on the other hand, fulfilled her. In every way." He smiled, his mouth curving on one side. "And given less than half a chance, I could do exactly the same with your current wife, Blackmoor. Provided you have not lost her forever."

Lucas snarled and rounded the desk in an instant, shoving Stanford's legs down and seizing him by the jacket and the throat. He whirled and slammed him against the thick window, squeezing and pressing with such force his hands ached.

"Where is my wife?" he roared into the rapidly paling face.

Fear flashed across Stanford's features and he scrambled to try to release himself. "Not here," he gasped. "Not here!"

"Where?" he bellowed, squeezing and slamming him harder against the glass.

"Feltham!" came the weak and almost keening response. "Feltham, for God's sake! Abandoned warehouse on the edge of the village!"

"Did you hurt her?" Lucas asked, leaning close and lowering his voice dangerously.

Frantically, Stanford shook his head. "No!"

Lucas exhaled slowly, tempted beyond reason to squeeze the remaining life out of this rat who had caused him so much grief. But he was no murderer, despite the opinions of Society and the temptation before him. "Never come near me or my wife again," he hissed. "Ever. One word about either of us, any of this, or Celia, and I will end you."

He tightened his grip perceptively and Stanford nodded with shaking, panicking motions.

Lucas dropped him as he whirled away, not caring what happened or in what state he left him.

He raced out of the house, whistled once, and grunted in satisfaction when a lad appeared from the shadows.

"Jem?" he asked as he mounted his horse.

The lad nodded firmly, a perfect soldier.

Lucas met his eyes seriously, despite his racing heart. "I need him. The road to Richmond. I'll not wait."

"Aye, sir," Jem replied, dashing off at once, a shrill whistle lighting the morning air.

Lucas turned his horse towards the road and galloped away, heart in his throat.

An abandoned warehouse in Feltham. Anything could happen there. She could be in any state, despite Stanford's words. She would be alone, probably restrained, and certainly frightened.

Did she know he would come for her? Did she believe he would see the truth in the matter? Did she know that he trusted her, completely and without reservation?

Was she even alive?

He forced his fears and worries back and focused on the hard ride before him.

He was fetching his wife and bringing her home, no matter what happened.

Then neither of them would ever be alone again.

Chapter Twenty-Three

$\mathcal{G}$emma buried her head into her arms as they rested on her knees, the tremors coursing through her body growing more and more wild. She couldn't help herself, considering the circumstances.

She had been in this cold, dark, dank cell for hours, had been forced to huddle in a corner the entire night in an attempt to sleep, which had proven worthless. She was filthy and freezing, and her only food since the day before had been some very hard, dry bread that her captors had tossed into her cell as if she were a dog.

The two burly men, Arthur and Brutus, if she had heard right, stayed at the furthest end of the room, apparently forced to remain with her. They chose to ignore her, for the most part, and she could only say she was grateful for that. She could easily be beaten and worse, severely mistreated for no other reason than sport.

But no, they quite simply did as they had been bid, and would continue to do so until payment was received. They were entirely immune to her tears, unmoved by her attempt at hysterics, and unimpressed by her rage. They had no idea of niceties or propriety, did not care that she was a fine woman, and had absolutely no manners at all that she could see, particularly after witnessing their evening meal.

All told, they seemed to be a bit dim-witted and chosen for their size and strength rather than capability and intellect.

If she knew what to do with that, she might find a way out of here.

She wrapped her arms more tightly around her, feeling abandoned and alone, despite their presence in the room. They had the only sources of light and warmth and no amount of pleading had swayed them to share it with her. Too many echoes of her past haunted her in these circumstances, crying where no one could hear, dark where no light would come, alone with no hope of salvation…

Bennett had tormented her the entire ride from London, sharing far too many details of his past with Celia, their joined amusement at Lucas's distress, the many stories Celia had shared of how she strove to wound him… Then he turned even more cruel, telling her every horrible and depraved way in which he would see her and her husband ruined, both through her and through his machinations against her husband.

It seemed he had been sending anonymous threats and warnings to Lucas all this time, playing on fears and taunting him with hints, all designed to wound Gemma and ruin their lives, and Lucas, used to scorn and so careful with everything he did, had become nearly obsessed with them, fixated and driven to spare her from the effects that may unfold.

It was agony to imagine what Lucas had suffered, and knowing what he would suffer still with her being gone.

She'd been terrified that Bennett would actually follow through on some of the horrors he had described for her, but in reality, he had simply deposited her with her captors and instructed them on her neglect and incarceration, then left without a second thought.

She could not tell if he were a cruel man or a cowardly one.

It made no difference, it would all play out the same way for her husband, who had been broken down too many times to endure more.

She wondered if he would even know she was missing yet. And when he did inevitably find her missing, would he think the worst?

Why shouldn't he? What had she ever been for him but a source of torment and strife? None of this misery would have begun if she hadn't started that blasted wager with her friends. If she had simply let the requested dance pass as anyone else might have rather than encouraging him, they might have remained as polite acquaintances.

She shook her head at herself, irritated with her self-pity. She refused to regret what had passed between them, for she had discovered far more than she had ever expected in him, and had come to love him with a fierceness that startled her. Their life might have been more difficult than either of them had expected, but it was hardly enough to make her wish it away.

And with the child she now carried within her, she had more reason than ever to wish for it all to remain.

She rubbed at her tired, weeping eyes and leaned back against the wall, tremors fading. She needed to have faith in her husband, in his feelings for her. He loved her, and with a depth that still took her breath away. They needed years together to fully explore and understand their connection and each other, and he would not give up on that, not after what they had shared.

And neither would she.

Lucas deserved a wife that was as determined and strong as he, one that would not shirk in the face of uncertainty or doubt. He had faced enough horrors in his life on his own; he would not have to do so now.

He had spent the entirety of their marriage trying to protect her, thinking all of the weight should rest on his shoulders.

No more.

She was going to fight tooth and nail for her marriage, and he was going to have to bear with her fierceness, for he was worth such a defense. She loved him and he loved her, and no pride or rumors or former lover of a late wife was going to get in the way.

She would choose to believe the best in her husband, and pray he would do the same with her. Despite Bennett's claim that her husband could not love her and would not miss her and all the other lies he had spouted, she would choose faith. She would make the best of all situations, even this one, and hold on for dear life.

Even if he did not come, even if she had to save herself, she would hold on.

Lucas had given her that strength and confidence.

He had never left her alone in truth.

She had simply been too blind to see him there.

She sniffed back the last of her tears and glanced over at her captors, chewing on her lip as she strained to catch what she could of their conversation. She may not have all of the skills of a refined woman of Society, might have no idea of the current fashions or styles of hats, and certainly had not garnered the attention and respect a viscountess ought to have done.

But none of those skills would help her here.

There was one skill, however, that Gemma had always possessed, her greatest strength and most unconventional attribute.

And that just might save her now.

Lucas rode wildly along the miles to Feltham, and the man beside him rode just as madly.

He'd been joined shortly after reaching the outskirts of London, and there had been no conversation between them at all. It had been unnecessary and unwanted. He could feel the drive and fire of his friend, dressed almost unrecognizably as the Gent, and it was a comfort to have such a man beside him.

His mind conjured several scenarios of how they might find Gemma, what she might have suffered, and he somehow found the strength of will to force them aside. It made no difference to him, except for the agony slashing his heart at each. He would take her in whatever form she was in, however ruined she might be. She could not be ruined in his eyes, could never be less than his perfect match and ideal, would never be anything but the woman he loved.

This horrifying, cruel plan would not succeed.

"Stanford is your man," Rafe suddenly announced from his saddle.

"I know," he grunted in response.

"I've taken the liberty of informing his brother of that. Hope you don't mind."

He almost smiled in satisfaction. "Not a bit."

"Thought not."

"Bow Street?"

"Them too."

"Good."

Feltham was approaching and his throat was suddenly on fire, every breath and swallow agony. His horse sensed his change and jolted forward awkwardly against him.

"Steady on," Rafe ordered, ever the controlled man. "You don't know what we're facing."

"Gemma's in there," he replied roughly. "That's all I need to know."

Rafe had no response, and as the warehouse loomed before them, he veered off to scan the perimeter. Lucas let him, his eyes focused on the barely lit building.

His wife was inside.

Was there any way to prepare for the sight he was about to see?

Rafe reached his side as he dismounted before the building. "No additional guards, no other exits. We should… Wait! Don't do anything stupid!"

Lucas ignored him as he marched forward, not waiting for him to dismount and enter with him. He barged through the door and scanned the darkened room anxiously.

In the furthest corner, next to a poor makeshift cell, sat three figures around scattered candles, a lone female with tattered dress and scattered golden hair chatting animatedly.

"You cannot simply tell her what to do," she was saying, giving the largest man a scolding look. "It sounds to me that Agnes is a woman of strong opinions…" She paused as both men laughed heartily. "…which you sorely need, and if you would try for a bit of understanding, you might find her more agreeable to *your* opinions."

Lucas's heart jumped into his throat, and he barely heard Rafe enter behind him, nor the cocking of his pistol.

The three figures turned at the sounds they made and all froze.

Gemma's eyes widened and a hand went to her mouth.

"Gemma?" he managed, hardly able to believe that she was not only well and whole, but charming the very men holding her captive.

That was, in effect, the brilliance of his wife.

"Lucas," she replied, the whisper carrying across the room.

Then they were moving, and she was flying into his arms. He clutched her head to him in one large hand, shaking and barely able to breathe as he enveloped her against him.

"Thank God," he breathed. "Thank God."

Gemma said nothing as she clung to him, the quaking of her

frame the only sign of her distress. She eventually pulled back and cupped his face as he stroked her hair and cheeks. "You didn't believe him, did you? You knew I would never leave you, right?"

He opened his mouth, but he could not say anything. The truth was too painful. He had doubted, for a moment, and he would not deny that he had.

Her eyes welled up and she pulled his head down to hers, touching her forehead to his. "Oh, Lucas. Can't you see that I love you? Can't you see that you are everything to me?"

"I want to," he vowed, holding her tightly, his fingers clutching at her hair. "I want to so badly."

Gemma sniffled and kissed him gently. "Then open your eyes. I am right here in your arms where I will always be."

He shook his head against her, running a hand along her hair. "I love you," he whispered in a low, growling, passionate voice that seemed to be ripped from his chest.

One of her delicate hands gripped the back of his neck tightly. "I know you do," she replied as she kissed him, her lips effectively shredding the last of his resolve.

He clung to her, letting his kisses confess everything he had felt and feared, and all the promises he would make later.

A scattered sniffling broke the moment and Gemma gave a small laugh against him, breaking off. "Would you two stop?" she scolded, turning towards the captors. "I told you he would come for me, did you think I was lying?"

"I'm jus' happy to see you so happy, my lady," one of the thugs said as he mopped his eyes.

Lucas raised a brow and looked down at his grinning wife. "You made friends with your captors?"

She shrugged, sliding her hands to his chest. "It seemed a better option than cowering in my cell and waiting for you. I can be quite charming when I put my mind to it."

He shook his head in wonder. "Weren't you scared at all?"

She reared back and snorted. "Of course I was! I was hauled into a carriage at gunpoint and bound and gagged and sat in that horrid cell for hours before I wore Brutus and Arthur down. It took all of my best efforts, I have never had to work so hard."

He shuddered and held her closer. "I believe it, love." He kissed her quickly. "You are so brave, so brilliant."

"And I was worried for you."

He jerked in surprise. "For me? You'd been abducted and could have been killed, and you worried for me?"

Gemma shook her head with a small smile. "Silly man, when will you realize that my life is bound up in yours?"

It took him several attempts to properly breathe or swallow. "I don't deserve you," he admitted roughly.

Her smile grew and she tugged on his greatcoat. "And that, my dear viscount, is precisely why you do."

She glanced behind him at Rafe and her brow furrowed. "I know him, don't I?"

He cleared his throat awkwardly. "Do you?"

She nodded. "I do, and yet I don't."

He assumed rather than heard Rafe shrug. "That happens a lot," Rafe admitted in a fake Cockney accent that was really quite good. "I'll jus' be waitin' outside, milord."

Lucas closed his eyes, suddenly wanting to laugh hysterically at the one secret he may actually have to keep from his witty and captivating wife.

"I do know him," Gemma muttered to herself. "I'll figure it out, see if I don't."

"I am sure you will, love," he assured her, only half placating. Knowing Gemma, she just might do it.

She looked up at him, slipping her hands around his neck again. "How did you find me?"

His jaw tightened and he pulled her closer, suddenly more fiercely protective. "I went to Stanford. He was at home, all superior and preening, and then I figured it out, and… quite lost my temper. It did the job."

Gemma tilted her head, seeming torn between smiling and frowning. "You don't have a temper."

He smirked at her. "Oh yes, I do. When someone interferes with my wife, I very much do have a temper. When someone threatens her and abuses her and takes her from me, I have quite the temper indeed."

Her eyes widened and her throat worked on a swallow. "Oh dear. Did you kill him?"

Now it was he who cocked his head at her. "I thought you said I could never kill anyone."

"I am revising my opinion, just this once."

That oddly pleased him. "No, I didn't kill him."

Gemma exhaled in relief. "Thank God."

"But I was damn close."

And then, of all things, Gemma sighed, smiling a bit dreamily.

Confused and amused, he nudged her with his nose. "What on earth was that for, love?"

She shrugged, sighing again. "Every now and then, I must give in to some distinctly feminine impulses and sigh pathetically over my husband. If you give me a moment, I may work up a swoon and be quite overcome."

He barked a short laugh. "From my temper?"

She gave him a devious look that started a fire in his bones. "From *you*, my love. I could become quite accustomed to swooning over you."

Lucas smiled a slow, heated smile that made his wife's eyes darken. "Swoon away, darling. I won't tell a soul."

Gemma's fingers began toying with his hair. "Oh, I wouldn't mind if you did. I should swoon publicly."

"Why ever for?" he asked, afraid to hear her answer.

"So that the world will know that Lady Blackmoor swoons and pines for her husband. Let them speculate on *that* for a time."

Lucas threw his head back and laughed, then kissed her quite thoroughly.

When he allowed it, she broke from his lips. "You owe me money for that laughter, my lord," she said in a breathy voice that curled his toes. "And even more for such a kiss."

He swung her up into his arms. "Bill me," he growled as he kissed her again.

Epilogue

$\mathcal{T}$he party was a truly glorious one, far exceeding any of the previous events, however incomparable they had been declared. It was extravagant, elaborate, and entirely overdone, yet with such taste and refinement that one did not even notice how excessive it truly was.

Such was the nature of the Rivertons.

But this, Gemma thought with a wry grin, was bordering on the ridiculous, even for them. Or perhaps it was excessive and ridiculous and overdone because all of the finery of the Riverton events was suddenly in place at the Blackmoor residence. And that was the most bewildering part for the majority of the guests.

It was a bit much even for the hostess.

She shook her head at Sophie, who had been watching her from across the room. Sophie shrugged and rolled her eyes in response, then returned her attention to the conversation at hand.

Gemma had no such needs, as she was currently unimpeded by conversations and could observe the fine gathering at her own leisure.

It was slightly untoward, having what was technically an engagement ball after the couple had already married, but Will had been asked to serve as a liaison for several months in Spain, and his bride-to-be refused to wait at home without him.

As the Rivertons had been quite delighted with Will's choice, and quite desperate to marry him off, they agreed and allowed the slight twist of protocol.

Given the splendor now, it seemed that no one else in Society truly minded either. It was as much a welcome home ball as it was an engagement ball, and all had been reassured that a true Riverton event would be set up in the coming weeks.

Just what they all needed, more excesses.

Gemma frowned as she looked around, catching sight of Henry mingling with several influential guests, Lord and Lady Riverton being fawned over by their enthusiastic admirers, and Will laughing jovially with some of his former Naval associates.

There was one person missing from this melee.

Her husband.

She smiled to herself and shook her head, knowing exactly where he would be at this moment. She slipped out of the ballroom, smiling at Lily and Marianne, talking with Lady Raeburn and her new husband, Lord Roger Tinsdale. That was an odd pairing, but Gemma was not about to question it.

Tibby did whatever she wanted, and always made it work for her.

Gemma moved up the back stairs to the family wing, the pattern easily one she could have done in her sleep. It was second nature to venture up the back stairs for one reason or another during events now, especially since they had become all the more infamous as a couple.

In the last three years, the announcement of the now public relationship between their family and the Rivertons had become accepted as the most unexpected turn of fate for them. No one could believe the good fortune that had fallen upon that horrid Lord Blackmoor and his peculiar bride.

They had difficulty believing it as well, but as they were now considered less horrid and less peculiar, and universally far less exciting than anyone had thought, they did not mind at all.

It had not changed Lucas's reclusive nature, but it had made him more inclined to warmth and laughter, which had changed everything.

He was so alive when with his family, and they delighted in being able to claim him as a relation. They attended every Riverton event, even the masquerades Lucas despised, and dined with them at least twice a week when in Town. More than that, they hosted several events in London now, including, apparently, the unofficial Riverton events, being unofficial Rivertons themselves.

During their time at Thornacre, Riverton relations visited often enough that they were no longer announced properly, and the children ran as wild through the house as if it were their own.

They loved it that way.

Gemma sighed a little to herself as she reached the door to the nursery, shaking her head. She knew the sight she would find, and she would need to steel herself for it. It always made her far too emotional, which made her husband more attentive, which made her cling more, which usually meant they would not be making whatever appearance or event they were expected to in the appropriate time.

She was impossibly weak to the charms of her husband, even now, and he had only improved his craft with the years of marriage.

It was a terribly distracting way to live.

She pushed open the door, securing her most scolding, disapproving face.

As she predicted, Lucas was sitting in the nursemaid's rocking chair, a tiny, brown-haired girl in his lap, her mouth gaping and her thumb just out of reach as she slept.

Lucas had the sleeping child tucked tightly against him, and one finger toyed with a curl, his eyes far away.

"My lord Blackmoor," Gemma murmured with disapproval. "There is a party downstairs, and you are missing it."

"I am missing nothing," he replied softly, his eyes shifting to her, running over her with quick heat and appreciation.

She folded her arms. "You know what I mean. You ought to be downstairs celebrating Will's marriage."

He snorted, rocking slowly. "Will has been married for nine months, and considering the fact that it took almost two years for him to convince Rosalind that marrying him was a good idea, I don't think we should be celebrating him at all. Pitying her, perhaps, but not celebrating Will."

Gemma chuckled and shook her head. "Then come and celebrate Rosalind being the best thing that ever happened to Will and try to convey your proper sympathies to her. You can't stay up here forever."

He sniffed and glanced down at the girl in his lap. "I can if Violet cried for me."

"She's not crying now."

"She might start again."

Gemma smiled softly and came closer. "You know she only does that so you will come to her. When you are away, she never cries in the night at all."

He returned her smile and stroked his daughter's hair. "I know. I know it all too well, and I can't make myself tell her to stop. She'll stop wanting me to come on her own eventually, and I'm not sure I can bear that."

"She will never stop wanting her father," Gemma assured him, stroking his cheek with the back of her fingers. "You will always be her favorite, Lucas."

"Not always."

Gemma looked up at the ceiling with a half-smile. "She is not even three, Lucas. Can we not worry about her falling in love at the moment?"

"You cried about Jack going off to school last week, and he's not even walking yet."

She glared down at her husband and tugged sharply on part of his hair, drawing a laugh from him. "A mother can cry over her son if she wants to."

"And a father cannot dote on his daughter?"

She sighed and stroked his cheek again. "I did not come here to debate on how we love our children. I came to fetch you. I don't want to be down there alone anymore, so come and give your wife some attention."

He looked up at her, raising a brow. "I can give you plenty of attention without going to that blasted festival downstairs."

She shook her head in warning. "No, my lord, we have responsibilities. You are respectable now, and getting to be a popular sight. Come and do your duty."

He frowned, but rose, cradling his daughter and moving towards her bed. "Spoilsport."

"If you are good, we may calculate your bill later."

That brought his head around, his eyes sparkling with interest. "Indeed?"

Gemma smiled in the way she knew would drive him mad. "If you are good."

He laid Violet down in her bed and tucked her in, then glanced over at the bassinet where their sleeping son lay. He looked back up at Gemma and slowly made his way to her. "Then I shall be the most perfectly behaved gentleman that ever behaved at all."

She laughed softly. "You've never behaved a day in your life."

He kissed her nose, then the corner of her mouth. "Care to wager on that?"

She shook her head, despite her breathing growing uneven. "You've gotten yourself into enough trouble with wagering."

"It's not my fault that Henry and Sophie's twins are devious little rascals," he protested as she led him from the room. "How was I to know that three-year-old boys know how to cheat with toy soldiers?"

She grinned back at him, intertwining her fingers with his. "Do you know who taught them how to do that?"

"I suspect Will. He's too mischievous."

"It was Rosalind."

That drew a loud laugh from him as they closed the door and started down the hall. "I thought she was doting on baby Emma."

"She did for a moment, but then she was racing with the boys and teaching them all sorts of tricks." She grinned up at her husband and nudged him. "She is a fine match for Will."

"Lily Granger's sister is a rapscallion," he mused thoughtfully. "How perfectly bizarre."

Gemma sobered at the mention of her friend. "I heard that Granger's fortunes have changed. Perhaps he will be kinder to Lily now."

"He's never been unkind to her. Merely neglectful."

"When a woman loved a man as Lily loved Granger," Gemma muttered, "neglect is the most hurtful thing of all."

Lucas squeezed her hand tightly. "If you would watch him instead of Lily for once, you would see the love there. He's not so horrible, you know. He adores her. There is still hope for them."

"Unless it is too late," she said with a shrug. "Lily has hurt for too long."

Lucas pulled her to a stop and cupped her cheek. "You and I both know," he murmured softly, "that love is not that simple. And I would rather not debate the state of the Grangers' marriage with you. We won't see eye to eye there."

She leaned more fully into his hand. "We certainly won't." She smiled a little and gripped his coat. "You know, the wager with the boys was not the wager I was talking about."

He smiled in response. "Oh no? What wager was that?"

"Me."

His thumb stroked her cheek gently. "You were the easiest wager I ever made. Undoubtedly the best one."

"I certainly have proved a challenge, haven't I?" she sighed dramatically.

"Absolutely," he murmured, kissing her tenderly. "But what about your wager? You've become quite the gambler, madam."

"Oh, I know," she informed him with a nod. "It is amazing the lengths I go to in order to draw you out. And your methods of payment are most unorthodox."

"Creative."

"Glad *you* think so."

He looked almost outraged. "You object to how I repay my debts?"

She grinned mischievously. "I should have a fortune by this time, my lord, and yet I do not. All I've received from this wager is a fine house, two beautiful children, and an adoring husband who never lets my heart rest or my breath settle, and I've become the most ridiculous sort of craving, lovesick woman with absolutely no self-control where he is concerned." She shook her head sadly. "How the mighty are fallen. And I held such promise."

Lucas stared at her for a long moment, his throat working. Then he slowly pushed her against the wall and bracketed her with his arms. "You mercenary wench," he murmured, his lips dusting faintly over her skin. "To think I devote my life to paying your exorbitant debts, and this is how you thank me? By feeling short-changed and underpaid?"

"It seemed cruel to deceive you longer," she managed, arching her neck and fisting her hands in his coat. "I may be mercenary, but I am no villain."

He grinned against her cheek and pressed against her a bit more. "Ah, but you are married to the mysterious and dark Viscount

Blackmoor, madam. And he is quite the villain."

"He *thinks* he is," she replied stubbornly. "All I find is a perfect gentleman with rather captivating eyes."

He chuckled and captured her lips in a searing kiss that curled her toes in her beaded slippers. "Oh, the wicked things he could do to prove you wrong," he whispered, sending shivers down her spine. Then suddenly he lifted away from her, cool as the morning air. "But, alas, his wife has insisted he attend a party for his family. So if you are quite finished with delaying…?"

Gemma laughed merrily at his composure and his outstretched hand, and she took it tightly in her own. "You are a devious man, my lord."

"Who loves you. More than yesterday."

"Yesterday was a good day… are you sure?"

"Positive."

She drew his hand to her lips and kissed it softly. "I love you more."

"Care to wager on that?"

Gemma grinned at her darling, handsome, warm, slightly mysterious viscount, with whom her future seemed brighter by the passing day.

"Later, my lord. Raise the stakes."

Coming Soon

A

Gerrard
Family
Christmas

"Deck the halls with
boughs of folly."

by

Rebecca Connolly